"Skillfully grounded in time and place, full of colorful characters and pearls of wisdom, Ollie's story shows how it's possible to save ourselves when the people around us can't."
—Wendy Mass, *New York Times* bestselling author of *The Candymakers*

"A truly wonderful book about art and mystery, friendships and family. You are bound to fall in love with Ollie, and you'll long remember her story."     —Patricia Reilly Giff, Newbery Honor author of *Lily's Crossing* and *Pictures of Hollis Woods*

"Though *All the Greys on Greene Street* is a mystery, its real intrigue is in the secrets we keep from ourselves and others, and the promises we must sometimes break out of love."
—Jack Cheng, award-winning author of *See You in the Cosmos*

"This is a beautiful book—a love letter to art, friendship, and family. I devoured it."     —Tae Keller, author of *The Science of Breakable Things*

"[An] exquisitely written novel . . . Tucker portrays the struggle of depression and how it affects the family . . . All ages will appreciate the beauty and allure of Ollie's world."
—*VOYA*

"Tucker channels E. L. Konigsburg with her characters, plot, and style, and Lynne Rae Perkins with her keen observation."
—*BCCB*

# ACCOLADES for
# ALL *the* GREYS *on* GREENE STREET

A *Wall Street Journal* Best Book of the Year

A *New York Times* Best Book of the Year

A Chicago Public Library Best Book of the Year

A *Publishers Weekly* Best Book of the Year

A *Kirkus Reviews* Best Book of the Year

A Junior Library Guild Selection

An Edgar Award Nominee

An ALA Notable Book

# ALL
## *the*
# GREYS
## *on*
# GREENE
# STREET

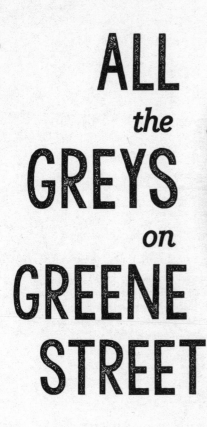

**LAURA TUCKER**

*Illustrations by*
**KELLY MURPHY**

PUFFIN BOOKS

PUFFIN BOOKS
An imprint of Penguin Random House LLC, New York

First published in the United States of America by Viking,
an imprint of Penguin Random House LLC, 2019
Published by Puffin Books, an imprint of Penguin Random House LLC, 2020

Visit us online at penguinrandomhouse.com

LIBRARY OF CONGRESS CATALOGING-IN-PUBLICATION DATA IS AVAILABLE

ISBN 9780451479556

Printed in the United States of America

Set in Jenson Pro       Book design by Mariam Quraishi

10 9 8 7 6 5 4 3 2 1

For Doug
this and everything

# MAYDAY

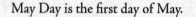

May Day is the first day of May.

"Mayday" is a radio signal used by ships and aircraft in distress.

This spring, May Day was the first day that my mom didn't get out of bed.

Unfortunately but maybe not coincidentally, it was also one week to the day of my dad's disappearance.

# MOM HABITAT

My mom woke up when I kissed her forehead hello. "How was school?"

It was almost four in the afternoon.

"Okay." I scratched the back of my leg with my sneaker. "Did you work late? Is that why you're still in bed?"

My mom makes sculptures. Sometimes I'd surprise her still at her worktable when I came out of my room to go to school in the morning.

She shook her head, silvery grey strands moving against the pillow in the red darkness of her hair. Then she closed her eyes again.

"I guess I just didn't feel like getting up today."

My stomach tilted. It set itself right again when she patted the spot next to her on the bed.

"Thanks for getting my stuff, babe."

That morning, when I'd gone in to kiss her goodbye, she'd asked me to bring her two packs of cigarettes, a can of peanuts, and a six-pack of Tab from Mr. G who owns the Optimo on Broadway. Mr. G told me scientists think that Tab causes cancer, which makes sense to me. If cancer tastes like something, it's probably room-temperature Tab.

I sat down, and my mom scratched my back, hard, the way I like it. I pushed back against her hand like a cat.

"You want to watch something?" I asked her. Sometimes when she gets like this, she likes to watch TV, but this time she only shook her head.

"Are you going to get up now?"

"I don't think so. Not yet. Take money off my dresser later, if you want to order in. This isn't going to be forever, honey. It's just that right now I'm . . ."

She didn't tell me what she was right now, but pulled the comforter back so I could get in. "Vouley Voo?"

That was her making a joke. Our nickname for the woman my dad ran off with is Vouley Voo. Her real name is Clothilde, and she's French-from-France, which was one of the reasons he'd gone there. My dad's an art restorer. He used to fix damaged artwork in his studio on the floor above us. But in the seven days since he'd been gone, his partner, Apollo, had taken over most of the work.

Apollo has a Greek name like me, even though he's Polish. My name, Olympia, comes from a painting by Manet, who was French like Vouley Voo. The painting caused a tremendous scandal in 1865, the first time it was shown—not because Olympia is nude, but because of the way she's looking straight out at the viewer. I guess nudes weren't supposed to look back.

My mom opened her arms and I lay down so she could spoon me, leaving my feet sticking out from under the covers because I was still wearing my sneakers. My mom doesn't care about things like that, but I do.

We lay there together in the half-dark for a while, and I let myself be comforted by the warmth of her body and the mom-habitat smell of the bed.

When I could feel that she was asleep again, I rolled out from under her arm and went back out into the big room where it was still light.

# TWENTY-SEVEN KISSES

Our loft is in a building that used to be a factory. My parents' bedroom has a door. The bathroom does, too. My bedroom just has a curtain.

The rest of the apartment is the big room. I learned to ride a bike in there.

I used to wish we lived in a normal house, with a living room and a dining room and a backyard and a doorbell, except there's no way my parents would ever live in a house like that. Artists need lots of space and light.

Lofts have both, and they're cheap for New York, but to live in one, you have to prove that there's an artist-in-residence. Our artist-in-residence is my mom.

I wandered over to her workbench, an enormous stained wooden slab propped up on sawhorses between the windows on the Greene Street side of the loft. As I leaned in to see if she'd made anything new, I kept my hands by my sides—an old habit, to remind me not to touch.

The pieces were all connected, balancing at impossible angles. I knew that when she was done, the way they were positioned would tell a story. I'd already seen the button marked PUSH, strong black letters painted onto the old-fashioned green glass, wires trailing from the back of the panel like hair. I'd seen the used tea bag, stained an antique yellow, that she'd cut open and embroidered with wandering stitches so minuscule you couldn't imagine the needle small enough to make them. And I'd seen the tiny fan, woven like cloth out of ordinary dressmaker's pins, waiting on a tattered piece of red flannel. I still couldn't figure out how she'd made it.

Not everything was small. There was an enameled sign from a store that used to sell ladies' dresses, hammered almost beyond recognition into a rough crumple and slashed with paint. But she hadn't added anything new in a while.

I wouldn't say I was worried. Still, the fact that she wasn't working wasn't great.

I pushed the button on the answering machine on the windowsill, mostly to hear my dad's recorded voice boom out through the loft, telling people to leave a message like the past week had never happened.

There were two new messages. The first one was from my mom's new gallerist: "Hello, darling. Checking in." The second person hung up, but not before the machine recorded them breathing for a while. In the movies, a heavy breather is usually a creeper, but this sounded more to me like someone thinking about what they wanted to say before deciding they didn't want to say it.

Restless, I looked around the big room for something to draw. The late afternoon sunlight slanted through the enormous windows, cutting across the worn wood floorboards on a diagonal. Drawing light through glass is difficult, but my dad says you won't get better if you don't push yourself. I opened up my notebook and squinted like he taught me, reducing the shadows to a puzzle of light and dark shapes.

Apollo gave me this notebook, the kind that real artists use; he also buys me Blackwing 602 pencils, which are the best. He's always trying to get me to use color, but I've got enough on my plate with grey for now.

I sharpened my Blackwing and began roughing out the shaky outline of the sunlight on the floor, the smudged shadow where the window was dirty. Then I built on the network of loose lines I'd sketched, making them stronger and darker as the composition took shape under my fingers.

My dad had left a week ago. In the middle of the night. Without saying anything to anyone.

My pencil moved faster as I marked out the shape of a muscular tabby cat with thick black stripes, lounging like a tiger in the center of the page. I want a kitten, but my dad says that people are barely allowed in our building, let alone animals, so I draw a lot of cats.

Everyone had been surprised by how well I'd taken my dad's sudden disappearance. But the morning after he left, I'd gone to pour myself a glass of orange juice, just like I did every day. Stuck to the bottom of the container, I had found a piece of paper, precisely folded to fit underneath.

It was a note from my dad.

*Ollie,* his note read. *There's something I've got to do.*

*Not everyone agrees that it's the right thing, which is why it might be a little while before I can call.*

*In the meantime, you're going to have to give yourself twenty-seven kisses every morning and tell yourself that I love you. (That part won't be hard because you know it's true.)*

*P.S. Don't tell ANYONE about this note and get rid of it ASAP.*

After adding a little shade to the triangle of the tabby's white chin, I made myself stop before I ruined the whole drawing. I looked critically at it. It was good—good enough to give to Mr. G, who trades me a Goldenberg's Peanut Chew every couple of weeks for a piece of original art, which he hangs next to the Spectacular Landscapes of Iran calendar that his cousin sends him from Tehran.

I had destroyed my dad's note by tearing it into confetti, like Lily Holbrook in *Eve's Vengeance*. Except that I flushed the pieces

down the toilet, and they would never have shown a toilet flush-
ing onscreen in the fifties.

I missed him, but I was trying to be patient; I knew he'd call
when he could.

Except now that my mom had stopped getting out of bed, I
found myself wishing he'd call sooner rather than later.

# FEW, SEVERAL, MANY

"Bobby Sands is going to die," Alex told me.

The garbage on my block is usually pretty interesting. For example, there are always these long cardboard tubes outside the United Thread factory that make good lightsabers. Alex and Richard were dueling with two of them on Monday morning outside my building when I came out to walk to school. They stopped when they saw me come out because they think playing Star Wars is babyish now.

I was impressed. Usually they forget that I'm someone to be embarrassed in front of.

I've known Alex forever. He lives a block away, and we walk to school together most days. There aren't that many kids in SoHo, so the public school closest to us is in the West Village. Richard lives closer to school, but he'd spent the night at Alex's house.

It had looked warmer out the window than it actually was,

and I shivered. Alex pulled off the blue sweatshirt I knew his mom, Linda, had made him tie around his waist before he left. When I put it on, the sleeves came down over my hands.

"Sweater weather," Richard said happily.

Spring comes all at once in New York. One day, the sun comes out and the birds start chirping and the trees in Washington Square Park get flowers. A month later, the pavement melts and everything starts smelling like the greasy stain below the dumpster outside C-Town. But there are about two days every fall and every spring when it's warm but still cool and breezy and clean-smelling, and this was one of them. Sweater weather.

"Sixty-five days without food, Ollie," Alex said. "Sixty-five days." He was talking about the Irish hunger striker, Bobby Sands. But I had woken up thinking about my mom and everything that had happened the last time she went to bed, and I didn't want to talk about Bobby Sands.

I kept walking. Alex was doing what Alex does when he has to get someplace, which is a combination of vaulting over trash cans, balancing on ledges, and walking on his hands. It's difficult to have a conversation with a person doing that.

He tried again. "He has to be on a waterbed now, his bones are so fragile."

"Let's not be macabre," I said, in my trademark perfect imitation of his mom. In fact, it was exactly what Linda had said when she'd first found out that Alex and I were interested in the hunger strikers. The secret to sounding exactly like Linda is to keep your teeth shut even when you are talking. Open your mouth, but not your teeth, and you'll sound exactly like her, too.

The trademark imitation worked. First Alex looked surprised, then he shot me a furious look and sped up so he was walking way in front of me. I watched him disappear around the corner onto West Broadway, his lightsaber in front of him, and I fell back to walk with Richard.

Richard was using his tube as a staff. He is the slowest walker of anyone I've ever met. Richard does everything slowly. His mother says it's because he is deeply thoughtful, but even she gets annoyed if they're in a hurry.

"Who was that big guy on your block?" he asked me.

I shook my head; I had no idea what he was talking about.

"He was stopping people, to ask questions. He tried to show us something, but we ran."

That was weird. "Creeper?"

"Probably not. We just didn't feel like getting into it." That meant Alex hadn't felt like getting into it. He doesn't like to stop.

"How come you slept at Alex's house?" Linda wasn't usually a fan of the school-night sleepover.

"My mom had to go to a meeting." Richard's mother is a professor. She is very politically active.

"Was his dad there?" Richard shook his head no; Alex's dad travels for business all the time. "What'd you have for dinner?"

This was an important question because Linda is always on a diet. I don't see why she bothers because she always looks the same, but that is the number-one reason why it is terrible to sleep at Alex's house. At least when Linda was doing Atkins they had steak and hamburgers all the time, even if you didn't get a bun. It had been pretty hard on Alex since she'd started Pritikin, though.

I privately thought Alex was interested in Bobby Sands because he was always hungry. I wasn't sure why I was interested in Bobby Sands.

"We had vegetable soup, and Linda counted out eight crackers." Richard talks slowly, too. "Afterwards"—he grimaced— "there was cottage cheese. With sugar-free jam."

Cottage cheese is punishment, not food. It is certainly not dessert.

Richard and I crossed onto Bedford. It's so narrow you have to go single file, which makes it hard to talk, but Richard never minds a long silence. I have to say, he is a very comfortable person.

I was distracted, too wrapped up in my own thoughts even to ask to pet people's dogs. That morning, I'd gone into my mom's room to say goodbye. I'd hoped that she'd tell me her plans for the day, or some news about my dad, but she'd barely opened her eyes. Even her hair looked tired.

Friday night, the reading lamp had made all the clutter in her room look cozy and nestlike. In the morning, though, the sunlight leaking in through the sheets over the window washed everything out, making the room look grey and dirty. On my way home from the park on Saturday, I'd stopped to get her favorite pasta from Luizzi's, but she hadn't eaten more than a bite, and the sight of the cold, hard spaghetti sitting in a puddle of congealed clam sauce had made my stomach flip. Afterward, I went back into my own room and made my bed.

Alex was ahead of us, dragging his lightsaber across a brownstone's wrought-iron front gate. Winter pale and extra-skinny, he was wearing the red Kool-Aid T-shirt he usually lent me when I slept over at his house. It was getting to be a little too small for him, even though it was still a little too big for me.

The guy from the deli on Houston and Sixth was whistling as he hosed off the sidewalk outside, and the smell of the cool spray hitting the pavement made it feel like it was already summer. Except that I didn't want to think about summer just yet. Alex would spend the summer at the beach with his Auntie Em, on a little island with no cars on it. Richard would go to his grandparents on his mom's side, on another little island off North Carolina. My parents are both orphans, and my mom doesn't really like to go away, so I'd planned on hanging out with my dad and Apollo in the studio like I did last summer, drawing and mixing paints and doing odd jobs for them. But what was going to happen now was another thing I didn't know.

I stepped carefully over the trash bags crowding the narrow sidewalk. Before she went to bed, my mom was always moving—sorting, stacking, foraging for her sculptures. She'd give me a boost into a dumpster: "Poke around and see if there's anything interesting in there." If I found something I thought she'd like, I'd pass it out so she could take a look, turning it slowly in her strong hands. I'd love that.

Richard didn't say anything more until we were a block away from school. Then: "Also, I got up in the middle of the night and ate some ham."

As if we'd been talking about dinner at Alex's house the whole time! That's just what he's like.

Maybe that's why I told him. Or maybe it was the restless feeling of spring in the air, or the noisy cluster of kids on the corner enjoying their last minutes of freedom before the first bell. All I know is that the words had slipped out of my mouth before I'd decided I wanted to say them.

"My mom," I said, and stopped to wait for my voice to get less shaky.

A turning cab driver honked, and I grabbed at Richard's elbow to hurry him along, glad Alex had gone ahead. Even though Richard doesn't like to keep things from his parents, he can if you need him to. Alex likes to think of himself as a tough guy, but he'd crumple like a Coke can if Linda so much as looked at him twice, and I needed this to stay secret.

I cleared my throat and started again. "She's not getting up right now." As soon as the words were out, I wished I could call them back.

Alex would have made a joke; Richard didn't. "How long?"

"A few days," I said. Not strictly true. According to our third grade teacher Mrs. Prewitt, a few meant three, so I changed my answer: "Several." Several means four or more, although I couldn't be sure Richard would remember that.

The last time my mom had gone to bed, of course, the answer had been many. Many, Mrs. Prewitt said, was an uncountable noun.

Richard's eyes widened. Patient for once, I waited as he marched in his mind through everything that meant, hoping he'd see an angle I'd missed. But he only scratched at his forearm, fingernails carving silvery trails into the dark brown of his skin.

"You'll bleed," I warned him, from experience. We're all allergic to the herbal stress-reduction potion that Linda sprays on her sheets, even Alex. Not to mention that it smells like a tissue you'd find at the bottom of somebody's grandma's purse.

Richard frowned but switched to rubbing his arm with the flat of his fingers. "What if it's like it was last time?"

I looked at the lines on his forearm and didn't say anything. There wasn't anything to say that wasn't too terrible to say out loud.

"Ollie. If she doesn't get up and your dad isn't around, then what's going to happen . . ."

I cut him off with a fast shake of my head, and he closed his mouth, which was good because I really didn't want him to finish that sentence.

We'd caught up with the kids at the corner, their backpacks in a messy pile at the center of the circle. As the first bell rang, I peeled off the blue sweatshirt and tossed it back to Alex, then sped up to walk into the building with my art friend Lady Day.

"It's going to be fine," I called back to Richard over my shoulder. But I didn't turn all the way around so I wouldn't have to see the look on his face.

# SMUDGE

Lady Day Rodriguez is the other really good artist in my class. We always sit together in art; Mrs. Ejiofor usually lets us start working while she gets the boys settled down.

That day, we were finishing our self-portraits in charcoal. I *hate* charcoal. You'd think I'd like it because there's no color involved, but I hate the horrible scratching sound it makes against the paper and the smudgy mess of it. Every time Mrs. Ejiofor gives us an assignment to use it, I tell myself that I'm going to keep my filthy fingers away from the white spaces on my paper, that I'm going to use one hand for blending while keeping the other one clean, that I will neatly shade and hatch and highlight instead of making a furious little Pigpen cloud.

Every time, though, I end up with a blob of grey on dirty paper, and I walk out of the classroom looking like one of the kids in the book of Dust Bowl photographs my dad used to suggest I look through when I was complaining about something. Give me a properly sharpened Blackwing any day.

"I have a good fact for you," Lady Day said. Her grandma sent her a book of cat facts for her birthday. "Okay. What's the biggest difference between dogs and cats?"

I knew the answer to that one. "If you die in your apartment, your dog won't eat you. Your cat will."

Apollo told me that. He also told me that the difference between a cat person and a dog person is that a cat person generally doesn't mind the idea of being eaten.

Lady Day looked a little deflated, but also impressed. She has a calico named Sammie who steals the celery out of the Kung Pao chicken when Lady Day's dad brings home Chinese. I wouldn't care because I never eat the celery anyway, but Lady Day's dad lets her do it because he thinks it's funny. (Sammie is a girl. Calico cats almost always are, according to the book.)

Anyway, Sammie doesn't eat the celery, either. She licks it.

"I was going to say that a cat will explore a new room or situation without looking back for her owner," Lady Day said, adding a few scattered freckles to the bridge of her self-portrait's nose. "Dogs need more support. Cats are more independent."

That seemed right. You didn't see cats looking tragic outside of the Eagle coffee shop on Broadway, sure that they'd been heartlessly abandoned even though they could see their owners through the window, reading the *Post* and eating scrambled eggs on toast like they did every morning.

Maybe cat people were like cats and dog people were like

dogs. Lady Day was definitely a cat person, curious and independent.

"You think Sammie would eat you if you died?" I asked Lady Day, accidentally making my self-portrait more accurate by smearing a black thumb across my cheek.

"I'm pretty sure she would." Lady Day wiped her long, graceful fingers methodically on a damp paper towel, then dabbed them dry on another.

"Harsh," I said, experimentally blowing on the surface of my drawing like Mrs. Ejiofor had showed us, to clear some of the dust and expose the white surface below. Nothing happened, except maybe the paper looked a little damp.

Lady Day blew expertly at hers. An obedient puff of dust rose, exposing pristine white detail beneath. "What do I care, if I'm dead? Why should she go hungry when I'm lying there like a big stupid roast beef?" She picked up her charcoal again. "Something's going to eat me eventually. It might as well be Sammie."

Apollo had been right.

I hoped Lady Day would tell me another cat fact, but her long, lean body was bent nearly double over her drawing, and the tip of her tongue stuck out one corner of her mouth, meaning she was done with talking. Charcoal, it turned out, was the perfect medium to capture the spun texture of her hair when it's brushed out and pulled up into two clouds on top of her head.

I smudged halfheartedly at my own self-portrait a little while longer, but it was hopeless. I spent the rest of the period at the big sink, scrubbing at my hands and face with the waxy grey paper towels from the metal dispenser and thinking about what a mess everything was.

I hadn't been keeping the thing with my mom a secret—or maybe I had been, a little. But having it out in the open had changed it, the way an apple turns brown after it's cut. I didn't like the way I felt now that Richard knew the truth. Anything could happen, and I couldn't stop it.

There was something else, too: I felt ashamed.

All the stinky pink soap in the world wouldn't get rid of the black half-moons the charcoal had left under my nails, but I clawed at my palms anyway; it was better than thinking.

Even if I *could* find my dad, what if he didn't want to come back? What if he couldn't?

I ran a paper towel around the edge of the wide, trough-style sink to pick up the grey droplets I'd scattered, then dried the stainless taps to a shine.

I was a cat person, too. At least, I thought I was. But I couldn't help wondering if it was possible for an independent, curious cat person to be having a please-love-me, don't-leave-me, desperate, doggy kind of day.

# PURR

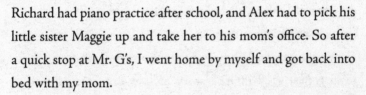

Richard had piano practice after school, and Alex had to pick his little sister Maggie up and take her to his mom's office. So after a quick stop at Mr. G's, I went home by myself and got back into bed with my mom.

I almost told her about the math test, but that wasn't the kind of thing she cared about even before she went to bed. "Bobby Sands is dead," I said instead. I'd seen the headline at Mr. G's.

My mom put her arms around me.

"He believed in something more than his own life," she whispered, and I couldn't tell if I thought that was the craziest thing I'd ever heard, or the bravest.

We lay there quiet together for a while and then my mom said, "I'm sorry about all this, baby girl." Her voice sounded weak, watered-down.

*I don't want you to feel bad. I want you to get up.*

Instead I said, "It's not your fault." Then I added, "It's Dad's fault. And Vouley Voo's."

She shook her head. "No, babe. This isn't him; it's me," she said. "The work I'm making—it's not right." She paused. "And yes, him leaving, a little. But mostly me."

That would have been the right time to tell her about the note, but my dad had asked me not to tell anyone. And I knew it would worry her, especially the part about not everyone agreeing that what he was doing was the right thing.

I did ask her if she'd talked to him, though. Even with my head on her chest, I could feel her slowly shake her head. "Can you?" Another shake, and I believed her. If my mom knew how to get in touch with my dad, she would have told me then.

We were quiet for a minute, and I could feel her going away again, so I asked her to tell me a story I'd heard a thousand times. "Tell me the story of how you started making your sculptures?"

She shifted next to me. "Olympia, please—you know this story."

I did, but I'd never gotten tired of hearing it.

My mom used to make gigantic paintings. When I was born, she stopped. Then she started to make sculptures out of little things she found lying around our house. She uses garbage, mostly—except that things stop being garbage when my mom puts them into one of her sculptures.

For a long time, she didn't show anyone what she was making, until last year when she got picked up by an important gallery uptown. They'd given her space in a big show coming up in the fall, but she only had part of one new piece. This was another reason that she really needed to get out of bed.

"Please?"

She bunched the pillow under her head and left her arm there. I felt her chest rise as she took one deep breath and then another.

"Before you were born, I made paintings, like the one in the living room." The canvas in the living room covered an entire wall between the windows, all soft blues and greens and yellows melting into one another. Looking at it made you want to hold your breath and go quietly, as if you were deep in a forest and trying not to disturb any of the creatures living there. Alex said it made him think of swimming underwater.

"It was hard for me to paint after you were born. Your dad would take care of you so I could work, but I'd just stand in front of the canvas. I didn't have the same things to say anymore.

"Then, when you were a toddler, Apollo gave you a set of blocks, made of beautifully sanded and polished wood. There were columns and triangles and long planks, graceful arches, chunky half-moons. And there were a *lot* of them."

My mom and I had always agreed that was one of the best things about those blocks: there were enough of them to really make something.

"You played with the blocks. *I* wasn't allowed to touch them." Even though the room was dark, I could hear a smile creep into my mom's voice.

"But I wasn't allowed to get up, either; I had to stay and watch while you squatted there like a bossy little sumo wrestler with your 'Pollo blocks,' your brow furrowed with the concentration it took to pinch and stack." Her voice turned dreamy and sad then. "We have to work hard to learn the things we know."

The tone in her voice ran chills down my spine, and I was relieved when she started talking again.

"If you'd let me build with you, I probably never would have made anything." That part wasn't true. The thing about people like Lady Day and my mother and Apollo is that they *have* to make things. "Sitting there on the floor with you, I'd sweep the floor with my hand. A house like ours, one that used to be an industrial space? You could sweep every day for a thousand years, and it never gets clean, not really. I started to see things in the garbage I was sweeping up, things I'd never seen before. You taught me to notice, Olympia."

That was usually where the story ended. As if on cue, a heavy truck backed up against one of the loading docks downstairs, and two men shouted at each other in Spanish.

This time, though, my mom kept going.

"The tenants before us here made blouses. I spent hours on my hands and knees when I was pregnant, pulling straight pins out of the spaces between the boards."

I'd never heard this part before.

"Apollo saved the day by renting an industrial magnet. It looked like a lawnmower, but I was so frightened I had to leave— those spiteful pins flying through the air, thousands of them, the terrifying noise they made when they hit. Even after the magnet, though, even after I'd swept the floor hundreds of times, a twisted corkscrew of metal worked its way up through the floorboards and bit into my palm one morning as I was sitting with you, taking a pass with my hand over the planks."

She raised her hand, and even in the half-light, I could see it: a white half-moon at the base of her thumb. I rubbed it under my fingertip, felt the slight ridge of scar tissue under her skin. I'd seen that scar a million times, but I'd never thought to ask how she'd gotten it.

"We found out later that they made ship propellers here, before it was a textile factory. For massive ships, like the *Lusitania*." The hardness in her voice made me twist around to look at her. "The cut was a message. That nasty little piece of metal had missed its grand voyage to drive home what everyone had told us: that this was no place to raise a child."

My mouth opened to protest, but when I saw the look on her face, I closed it again. It didn't seem like she was talking to me anymore.

"That was the day I made my first sculpture. Sitting there on the floor with you, I found the stuff of a thousand nightmares. Vicious little wire twist ties; deadly, candy-colored pushpins; an aspirin, escaped. I used my own pincer grip to sweep a penny into the pocket of my jeans. A penny can kill a baby—so fast, so easily. The menace in these everyday objects overwhelmed me. Why couldn't everyone see the wicked, fanged mouth at the center of the plastic chip that held the bread bag closed?"

I knew the sculpture she was talking about. It had sat on her table in the big room before it sold for a lot of money. There was a picture of it in a book about women's art that had come out in the fall. It had always scared me a little, but she'd never told me the story behind it.

I waited, but she didn't say anything more, so I lay there and listened to her breathe. Eventually, I closed my eyes, too—just for a minute. But when I woke up, it was dark.

My mom was still curled up next to me, motionless, and suddenly I could see how you could stay in bed forever, if that was where your mom was.

I lay next to her, breathing in the warmth of her, and remembered another one of Lady Day's cat facts. We had been doing string art that day in Art Club, winding colored embroidery floss in patterns around nails we'd driven into painted plywood.

"People think a cat's purr means 'I'm happy,' but it doesn't always," Lady Day had said, tying off a piece of fuchsia thread with a neat, close knot. She'd picked up a fat skein of turquoise then, pulling at the loose end to free it.

"A sick cat will purr, and a scared one, too," she told me. "Purring just means 'Don't leave.'"

My arm was asleep. I tried to wiggle my fingers without waking my mom, but she stirred, so I carefully inched myself out from underneath her and got up.

I crossed the room silently, holding my pins-and-needles arm in front of me like it was broken. But when I turned to shut the door behind me, I saw that my mom wasn't asleep after all.

Her eyes were open, looking blankly at the indentation in the covers where my body had been. There was no expression on her face at all.

My numb hand sat, alien and slick, on the cut glass door-knob.

"Mom," I said. "Are you going to get up soon?"

She didn't do or say anything for so long I worried she hadn't heard. When I was about to ask again, though, she shook her head and closed her eyes.

"I won't go back there, Ollie. I can't."

Then she rolled over onto her other side, away from me and the shape I'd left in her bed.

# WAKE UP!

Back in the big room, I watched TV for a while. Then I grabbed my notebook, rolled open the huge window, stepped up onto the splintering sill, and crawled out.

Most of the cast-iron buildings in SoHo have fire escapes running down the sides. I spend a lot of time on ours. You're invisible to people on the street when you're out there; nobody ever looks up.

It was cold out there, but it felt good, so I sat with my arms wrapped around my knees and watched the trucks leaving the button factory next door for the day. When they'd gone, Greene Street was empty and quiet, which might have been the only reason I noticed the movement in the empty lot across the street.

Someone was climbing the chain-link fence.

I leaned forward to see, pulling my sweatshirt around me against the chilly spring evening. A small guy, wearing a wide-shouldered brown suit and a brown fedora over longish dirty-blond hair, skillfully avoided the barbed wire at the top of the fence and jumped down to a crouch before heading over to the brick wall at the very back of the lot.

He was putting up a poster.

His suit surprised me. When my mom went through her poster phase, all of my jeans had scaly patches on them from the wheat paste, even though I was just the lookout. It isn't the kind of job you'd wear a suit to do, unless you were trying to look like someone in an old movie.

*Dapper*, my dad would have said.

The guy stepped back to look at his work, now drying on the wall. I could tell he was happy from the way he was standing. I picked up my notebook again, thinking I'd sketch him through the thickly painted iron bars of the fire escape.

But he turned around to face my building and looked right up to where I was sitting.

My heart sped up, even though I wasn't doing anything wrong. In fact, *he* was: paste-ups are illegal, although the cops don't usually arrest people for them the way they do for graffiti.

Then he tipped his hat to me.

Before I could do anything—in fact, before I could even think of what that could possibly be—he had clambered back over the heavy barbed wire fence. By the time I'd gotten myself together to respond, he was already halfway down the deserted block, moving fast, with small, tidy steps that made it look like he was dancing.

I watched him go, then grabbed two of the iron bars and pulled myself up to a squat so I could see the poster.

It was an egg, wearing black sunglasses and white gloves. Fat, flowing, bright yellow script ran along the top: WAKE UP! When you looked closely, you could see the egg's shell was covered in cracks.

I sat back against the bars. I knew it was stupid, but the poster felt like a message to my mom.

# SIR

It's twenty-two steps up to the studio from our fire escape. I don't have a fear of heights or anything, but I do it without looking down.

Once I had my face pressed up to the huge studio windows, I could see Apollo standing in front of one of the easels, cleaning a painting of triangles with a cotton ball. The big floor fans weren't on, so I guessed he was just using water. My dad says you can do most of what you need to do in this life with intelligence and water.

Even though the window was closed, I could hear Apollo's music, which is always jazz and very loud. If my dad needs a little quiet, Apollo listens through earphones connected to the bright yellow Walkman he clips to his belt. Every once in a while, he'll stop what he's doing to lead the band, or to shimmy.

My dad and Apollo usually work back-to-back, but there was

nothing on the easel where my dad usually works. There hadn't been, since he'd left.

Something else was missing, too, but I couldn't put my finger on it. Nothing had felt quite right since my dad had gone. Except for Apollo, who is my favorite and always the same.

The thing about Apollo is that he's the ugliest person I've ever seen. I'm not saying that to be mean; it's just a true fact. When I was really little, I did say it right to his face, and he laughed. Mostly, he looks like a lion. He's enormous, first of all, and when he was a teenager, he had the kind of acne that hurts and leaves scars, so his face looks like it's melted. But he has incredibly kind eyes, and once you get over being scared to look at him, you can't stop: His face never gets boring like regular people's faces do.

Apollo seems younger than my parents, even though he's the same age. Mostly, that's because of his clothes. He was wearing a pair of olive-green army pants, a yellow button-down shirt over a red T-shirt, a shiny black patent-leather belt, and an aquamarine bandana as a scarf. For him, this was fairly toned down. He says he loves color because they didn't have any in Poland when he was growing up, which is the kind of joke he makes. But my dad says Apollo knows more about color than anyone he's ever met.

I didn't want Apollo to think I was a creeper, so I tapped on the window. He turned around and smiled wide when he saw me, then rolled the gigantic window up to let me in. He held my hand to help me down from the windowsill like I was a fancy lady getting out of a carriage. On one foot, he was wearing a purple sneaker; the other one was white. Sometimes he does that, just to throw you off.

"You provide a delightful interruption, Olympia; I am about ready to stop. It is very stupid garbage, this painting. But money is money, am I right, little bird?"

I nodded. Money was something I'd been thinking about a lot since my dad went off to France. It's hard not to worry when you don't know how much money there is and how much everybody needs.

Apollo saw the look on my face.

"Sit for fifteen minutes and let me finish, and then we will have supper together? If you are up for it, perhaps we could take a walk over to The Spicy One?"

I nodded gratefully. The Spicy One is our favorite restaurant, but we usually only go on the weekends because it's all the way over on East Broadway. On school nights, we go to Wo Ping because they have the best pressed duck and the line is shorter there than at Bobo's on Mott. But the long walk over to The Spicy One would be a good time to ask Apollo if he knew how to get in touch with my dad.

The sign outside The Spicy One says Hwa Yuan Noodle Shop, even though the best thing there is the roasted pork, which they make with Szechuan peppercorns. Eating one Szechuan peppercorn makes your mouth go numb; Richard says they make your tongue feel like it's a zombie. My dad and Richard share an interest in movies about monsters, so my dad calls The Spicy One "Zombie Chinese."

While he was finishing up, I asked Apollo what color he thought his T-shirt was.

"Vermilion," he said immediately. Then he looked down and changed his mind. "Cinnabar." Those are basically the same thing, except that cinnabar is the unground mineral and vermilion is the color. But if there's a difference between the way it looks ground and unground, Apollo can see it.

I love the studio. The walls are white and tall, like in our apartment downstairs, but in our apartment, the two couches and the trunk we use for a coffee table seem lost in the space. The studio, on the other hand, is filled with a wonderful mess—everything a person could possibly need to build or fix or make some art.

The planks of the wood floor are spotted with paint and pieces of masking tape, and there are fingerprints—paint and solvent— on every surface. But everything has a place. Brushes are kept under the long, low tables by the windows in big tin cans; rags are under there, too. Taking them to the Beautiful Vieques Laundry and folding them when they come out of the dryer is one of my jobs.

In the middle of the studio, there are four tables like my mom's workbench downstairs, big enough that you can really spread out. Between them, paint-spattered wooden carts on wheels hold spools of cotton batting, putty and film for patching, long-handled Q-tips for detail work, and little trowels for mixing paint.

Shelves between the windows hold chemicals in white plastic containers, as well as different types of paints. There's a pegboard covered with tools: screwdrivers, saws, pliers, hammers, planes.

Opposite, three long shelves sag with hundreds of hardcover art books, most of them found on the street or bought used. It's hard to have a conversation with my dad or Apollo without one of them running over to the bookshelf to show you a picture.

But my dad wasn't there, and I wasn't in the mood to look at a book, so I cleaned the brushes in the sink while I waited. The brushes that art restorers use are very expensive and need to be handled carefully, but I've known what to do since I was little. You have to get every smidge of paint out, which means rinsing long after the water has run clear, keeping all the hairs going the same way.

When he was done with the triangle painting, Apollo took out his own notebook to find the telephone number of the girl-friend he was supposed to have dinner with.

Apollo always has seventy-two different girlfriends going at once, and they're almost always crying or mad at him. This one was no different. She had a lot to say when she heard he'd made other plans, but Apollo held the phone away from his ear and winked at me.

"It is beyond my control. This thing that has come up is very important and must be attended to. I am very sorry, but it cannot be helped."

They went on like that for a while. I didn't listen to all of it, but wandered off to the corner of the loft where Apollo keeps his colors.

I love everything about the studio, but I love this corner the best. Narrow wooden shelves are stacked with jars, their labels

soaked off—another one of my jobs. Some of the jars have pow-
ders inside, or oils, or chunks of wood. Some have nothing in them
but one tiny rock. Every one of them has a paper tag, tied to a piece
of string around the neck of the jar and labeled in Apollo's bristly
European handwriting.

The jars hold our pigments. For hundreds of years, artists
made and mixed their paints themselves instead of buying them
from a store, and Apollo still does it that way. It's useful to know
how to mix colors from pigment when you restore canvases that
are very old. But Apollo mixes colors for his own paintings too,
which is why they're so beautiful they make your chest hurt.

Most of our pigments don't look like the colors they make. In
fact, most of them don't look like anything at all. But the names on
the labels are clues that there's magic inside: Orpiment. Azurite.
Rose madder. Ochre. Ancora. Cinnabar. Malachite. Antimony.

Our grinding table is a giant slab of bottle-green glass that
Apollo found on the street and set up on sawhorses. I ran my
finger over the wavy glass with the uneven spray of bubbles inside.
There was a fine layer of dust on it. With my dad gone, I guess
Apollo hadn't had much time to make colors.

The easel in the corner held a yellow study we'd been working on before my dad left. The best yellow comes from Cambo-
dia. To get it, you tap a tree like you're making maple syrup; it
takes a whole year to get a bucket. Dried gamboge doesn't look
like much—just another sticky, ugly brown rock. But put a drop
of water on it, and that rock will weep a tear so brightly yellow it
will hurt your eyes.

Last year, Apollo made me his apprentice and gave me the first color study we made together: a wash of blues, some so light they looked white, others almost black in their intensity. The blues in between were so deep and rich that looking at them made you feel like you were learning something. It hangs opposite my bed and is my most prized possession.

"Please accept my most sincere apologies. I will make it up to you, Beautiful. I promise." On the other side of the loft, Apollo's call seemed—finally—to be winding up. With a sigh of relief, he replaced the heavy black receiver on the wall, and I grabbed my sweatshirt and my notebook, my stomach growling in anticipation of dinner.

But as we were heading toward the door, the phone rang again.

Apollo backed away like the phone was a bomb about to explode, eyes wide with mock terror. Annoyed, I rolled my eyes at him and took the heavy black receiver from the cradle on the wall.

"Greene Restoration," I said. Whenever I answer the phone in the studio, I pretend to be a secretary in an old-fashioned movie. On the side Apollo couldn't see, I snuck up a hand to remove an invisible clip-on earring.

It wasn't the girlfriend again but some guy with an accent, who sounded like Alex when he's pretending to have an accent. The guy on the phone pronounced Apollo's last name correctly, which is practically a magic trick.

"Hold please," I said, sounding bored and professional like a real secretary, and held the phone out to Apollo. When he took it from me, I rolled my finger at him—*keep it moving*—so he wouldn't get stuck for twelve hours on one of his hot topics, like the pros and cons of painting on canvas with automotive enamel. (In case you care: The colors and finishes are beautiful, but the paints can make you sick, and they sometimes yellow as they age.)

Except that it wasn't another artist on the phone.

"As I have said many times now, I am not in possession of this piece of art," Apollo said, turning his big bear body away from where I'd planted myself in front of him. "I would be happy to help; unfortunately, my partner is not here. He is out of the country at this time."

The man on the other end interrupted; I could hear his agitation. The skin on the back of my neck prickled: Apollo was talking about my dad.

What piece of art?

Apollo sighed. "I am very sorry. As I told you the other day, I am not in touch with him."

That had the alarming ring of truth, and my stomach sank. I'd been counting on Apollo to help me to get in touch, dead sure that the trickiest part of getting the information would be hiding what was going on with my mom. But if Apollo was telling the truth—if he really didn't know how to get in touch with my dad—then nobody would.

Which meant I was back to square one. Worse, even, because I didn't have another plan.

"Yes, I have your number. If I hear anything at all about the

piece, I will not hesitate to call you. Thank you, sir. Good night."
With that, Apollo replaced the heavy black receiver onto the
cradle on the wall. Hearing him call someone "sir" felt like the
worst thing that had happened yet.

I was right in front of him when he turned around. "What
was that about?" I asked.

He shook his head, not looking at me, his big body moving
uncomfortably from side to side. "Forget about it. Please. It was
nothing, little bird."

At least he looked miserable lying to me.

I cut to the chase: "You don't know how to get in touch with
him? Was that part true?" We both knew which him I was talking about.

"We have not spoken since he left," he said, setting his jaw
and looking toward the windows. In that moment, I realized that
Apollo might be one of the people who didn't agree with what my
dad was doing. And I didn't like that at all.

I tried to think of something mean or smart to say, but I ended
up saying what I was thinking, which was, "Why won't anybody
tell me what's going on?"

We looked at each other for a long time and then Apollo
made a face and shook his head: *I can't.*

I bit my lip hard as the weight of the day crashed down
around me. I thought about the dumb fight I'd picked with Alex
on the way to school, and Richard's panicked eyes when I'd told
him about my mom. I thought about my blotchy, botched self-
portrait in charcoal, and about my mom's blank eyes.

When I could trust my voice, I raised my chin. "How do I know he's okay?"

Apollo came forward to reassure me. But there wasn't anything he could say, and I turned away from the comfort of his familiar face.

Even if my dad was okay, my mom wasn't. And if my dad didn't come home, I wasn't going to be okay, either.

# FIVE FOR A DOLLAR

Upset as I was, my stomach growled again as I followed Apollo out of the studio.

I waited as he bent down to pick up a ball of newspaper and some other scraps of trash that had blown into the little tiled vestibule at the bottom of the stairs. He passed them to me to hold while he pressed down the ratty silver duct tape securing the ARTIST-IN-RESIDENCE sign to the front door of the building.

The A.I.R. sign is there to let firemen know that our building isn't abandoned, or a factory—empty at night. Some of the A.I.R. signs you see around SoHo are official look- ing, white letters embossed onto plastic plaques like the name plate outside the principal's office at my school. But the sign on our door is a piece of cardboard box wrapped in plastic and duct-taped to the window, A.I.R. 2 written in thick black marker on the front. The two is because we live on the second floor.

Maintenance complete, the two of us walked down Greene Street toward Canal. Even though it was almost dark, there were very few lights on in the buildings we passed. The lofts near us that don't have factories or artists in them are mostly used for storage. Bundles of old rags and paper, and not very many people around to call 911 when they smell smoke? There's a reason that firefighters call my neighborhood Hell's Hundred Acres.

We turned left at the corner of Canal, and the subliminal mind control I used on Apollo must have worked, because he looked across the street at the art supply store, but he didn't cross to go in. I love Pearl Paint, too, but I was way too worn out and hungry for an hour of small talk about solvents.

We did stop to look at the boxes outside the hardware stores on Canal. Apollo was standing over a tray filled with skinny spatulas when a cardboard box filled with tiny brass objects caught my eye. They were little faucets, like the red ones you use to turn off the water supply under a sink, except brass and miniature—only a little bigger than my thumbnail. Too big for a dollhouse, too small to be used under a sink for real.

"I bet my mom would like these," I said, breaking the silence and dropping one of the brass faucets into Apollo's palm. "Five for a dollar." He looked at it closely and then nodded and pulled two bills out of his wallet. The woman who had come out of the store handed me a small brown paper bag, and I counted ten of the tiny faucets into it.

My mom and my dad and Apollo and Alex's mom all met at art school in Brooklyn, even though my mom and Apollo are the only ones still making art. My dad can draw anything; he's the one who taught me. But now he only works on other people's art.

My mom, on the other hand, can't help but make things. Over breakfast at a coffee shop, she'll knot napkins and the wrappers from our straws, using a drop of water or coffee or juice to mold the paper. By the time we've finished our bacon and eggs, she'll have turned the whole table into a sculpture garden. One time, she didn't like a book I brought home from school about the first Thanksgiving, so she cut it up to make a collage about the Pilgrims stealing land from the Wampanoag and the diseases they brought that practically wiped out the tribe. Another time, my dad asked her to sew a button back onto his favorite shirt, and she stitched geometric patterns, wild like vines, up the sleeves instead. The next time he wore it, a lady on the street offered to buy it off him for a hundred bucks.

Apollo and I turned off Canal Street onto Mott. Little kids chased one another up and down the narrow block while moms squeezed melons and grandpas smoked between the parked cars. We stopped at a fruit and vegetable stand where Apollo bought a bag of the tiniest mangos I'd ever seen, the size of walnuts. The green beans right next to them were as long as my forearm. Honestly, the size of them is the only special thing about them. We get them at Wo Ping with garlic and ground pork, and they taste exactly like the short kind.

My dad says observation is a muscle that artists have to build. You have to choose the details you include in a drawing, and to choose them, you have to *see* them. "Don't draw a cartoon of what you think a strawberry looks like," he'd always tell me. "Look at a strawberry, then draw what you see—not what you *think* you see."

So I practiced my observing. Most of the stores on Mott had big metal garage doors that rolled up in front instead of windows, making it hard to tell where the sidewalk ended and the stores began. At one place, whole fish stared back at me from beds of melting ice, sparkling purple-brown and blue and silver underneath metal hanging scales. Pink shrimp, cooked and cleaned, lay next to grey ones with their heads still on. At the back of another store, I saw an aquarium crowded with silvery brown carp, and another one, the water dark with eels.

I looked into a woven wooden basket almost as tall as I was, standing by the curb. Inside were hundreds of live crabs. The slow chitter of their claws moving over the hard bodies of the others made me shiver. They had greenish-greyish-brown bodies, and beautiful blue claws.

"Lapis," I said out loud, and Apollo smiled.

Lapis lazuli is the stone you grind to get ultramarine, the most beautiful and the most expensive of the blue pigments. It used to cost so much that Michelangelo had to leave a corner of one of his most famous paintings unfinished because he couldn't afford the paint. Lapis is expensive now because it comes from Afghanistan, which is in a war with Russia, so it's hard to get. Apollo has some, though. And before you grind it into ultramarine, lapis has streaks of grey and brown and white in it, the same colors as the crabs.

Apollo said, "They tell me that in Old San Juan, the streets are cobbled with bricks cast from the waste that comes from making iron, brought to Puerto Rico three hundred years ago as ballast in the bottom of Spanish ships."

The stones they used to make New York's cobblestones came as ballast on ships from Belgium. My dad told me that.

"The iron made these bricks blue—all different shades. Imagine! Ordinary streets, paved in cobalt, azure, indigo." Apollo smiled down at me. "Perhaps you and I will go to Old San Juan one day, and dance on bricks the color of a blue crab's claws."

I looked at the crabs crawling on top of one another, going nowhere, and wished I could tell Apollo about my mom. But the emptiness on her face when she said she couldn't go back scared me into silence.

Maybe—if things didn't get better, and my dad wasn't back yet—I could tell Apollo. Maybe he'd let me stay with him for a while.

The two of us stood there for a minute more, watching the crabs.

"I didn't know they had cobblestones anywhere but here," I said finally.

Apollo nodded. "Paris is famous for them, actually."

Paris. In France, where my dad was.

We were quiet the rest of the way to Hwa Yuan.

# STILL IN LOVE

As soon as we saw Hwa Yuan's neon sign, my stomach started to grumble again. It only got worse when we went inside.

Apollo and I took two seats at one of the big round tables. A big family was already seated at the other half, everybody happily talking at the same time. Not for the first time, I wished I understood Chinese.

A waiter came over right away with a metal teapot, filling the short amber glasses in front of us with steaming hot tea. I put a lot of sugar in mine; Apollo doesn't put any.

We didn't even bother to look at the menu, because we always get the same things: Szechuan pork, cold sesame noodles, and water vegetable, which is sort of like spinach but crunchier and less disgusting.

We drank some tea, and I said, "It sounded like your girl-friend was pretty mad about dinner." I was pretty sure this one's name was Sari, but not sure enough to say it. I did know that she was a sound artist, whatever that was. The last one was an art critic. The one before that was a mime.

"Eh, that one," Apollo said with a dismissive flick. He took a swig of his beer, then pushed the bottle over to me so that I could remove the label.

"You're always friends with them after you break up with them. It's the boyfriend part you're not good at."

Apollo shrugged and took his beer bottle back, rubbing with his thumb at the sticky glue I'd left behind.

I pressed the damp label I'd peeled off the bottle onto the circle of green glass covering the Pepto-Bismol–pink tablecloth, meticulously smoothing out the wrinkles. "Are you in love with her?" I asked. It was a rude question, but Apollo would rather answer a rude question than do what he calls "chitchat."

Apollo thought for a moment. "I am not in love with her, no," he said. "But we have a good time together, when she is not so mad."

"How come?" I asked. "How come you're not in love with her? Is she pretty?"

"She is very pretty, Olympia," he said. "But many people are pretty. Pretty, thank God, is not everything." He waggled his eyebrows, then struck a pose with his hand behind his head like a model in a magazine. The family across from us found this very amusing.

"Is she nice?"

"Yes, she is very nice. She is a good person. And smart. But those things aren't everything, either."

Then the waiter came with the food, and the two of us dug in. We made a lot of noise. It's not rude to slurp noodles; what you're not supposed to do is bite them.

When I was little, the waiters used to rubber band a wad of paper between the tops of my chopsticks to make them easier to use, but last year Apollo showed me how to use them the regular way. It's not hard, but your hands have to be big enough.

Pretty soon Szechuan peppercorn firecrackers were going off in my mouth, and my lips were burning in a way that made them feel like they were twice their normal size. After a few more bites, my whole face had gone numb, all the way up to the bottom of my eyes.

Zombie Chinese.

When we started to slow down, something occurred to me: Apollo always had a girlfriend, but he never seemed to be in love with any of the women he went on dates with.

"Hey, Apollo? Have you ever been in love?"

That surprised him, and he chewed away at the noodles in his mouth like he wished they weren't in there.

"I'm just curious," I told him. Curiosity goes a long way with Apollo, which is good because I can't do anything about mine. I never understand when grown-ups say, "Don't tell me; I don't want to know." I *always* want to know.

He chewed some more, swallowed, and then there wasn't anything to do but answer me.

"Yes, Olympia. I have been in love." He sighed and looked around for our waiter, holding his beer bottle up to ask for a new one.

"What happened?"

"Nothing happened. She married someone else."

That surprised me. "What? How could she marry someone else when you loved her? Was it because of the way you look?"

That made him laugh. "No, I don't think so. It was complicated. There were other factors."

The waiter came over with the new beer, but Apollo didn't drink from it right away. The family at our table laughed uproariously at something the mom said, and the dad slapped his knee in appreciation, something I'd never seen outside of a cartoon. I turned to see if Apollo had seen it, too, but he wasn't looking at me. He picked up a piece of pork, inspected it for a minute, and then put it down on his plate, squaring off his chopsticks.

Then it hit me.

*Holy cow*, I thought. *He's still in love with her.* That was why Apollo couldn't fall in love with someone new. He was already *in love* with someone.

I thought about the poor sound artist—Sari, or whatever her name was. She probably didn't know that getting stood up for dinner was the least of her problems.

At that very moment, the mom across the table started to tell a story. She waved her hands and talked so fast and loud that Apollo and I didn't even have to pretend that we weren't watching. If you can't help being a naturally curious person like me, eavesdropping is an excellent hobby. Apollo is also a champion eavesdropper; he says it's how his English got so good.

When the mom saw we were watching, her gestures and eyebrow waggles got even bigger. Then—with a gigantic wave that started out looking like she was welcoming a king and turned into a gesture that looked more like she was decapitating a chicken—the story was done.

The punchline made everyone at the table clap and laugh. Apollo and I were so caught up in her dramatics that we clapped, too. Shy suddenly, the mom dropped her chin to her chest and smiled while the rest of the family talked excitedly, repeating the final gesture to make the others laugh.

Apollo had gone back to messing around with the food on his plate. He looked sad, sadder than I'd ever seen him, so sad he looked almost handsome.

Whoever she was, it was serious.

"Hey," I said. "Tell me about a color?"

He knew I was trying to distract him, but still he looked relieved. He leaned back in his chair and took a long pull on his beer.

"Have I ever told you about Egyptian brown?"

I shook my head, a little disappointed. Brown is my least favorite color.

"Well, Egyptian brown was *the* color in the nineteenth century. Many artists swore it was the best brown paint they'd ever used: soft and velvety, with warm, sweet tones of yellow and green. It was transparent, too, which made it perfect for skin, or to depict the plaster walls of a room in the magic light of the late afternoon."

I imagined painting my mom's room as it had looked that afternoon, the sun leaking weakly into the dim room through the white cotton curtains covering the window, my mom lying without moving in the bed.

"But it was controversial. Some painters said that it was unpredictable—that the color was never the same twice, that you never knew what would come out of the tube. Others complained that it was hard to work with, that it cracked and changed the chemistry of other paints if you mixed them."

This is very common with the paints that we mix by hand. Not all of them play well together, Apollo says. It's the type of thing you have to know.

He continued. "They don't use it, this Egyptian brown, anymore. Do you know why?"

I shook my head, humoring him. Apollo is not usually boring when he talks about color, but so far, this had not been great.

Apollo sat back and crossed his arms over his chest. "Because they ran out of mummies."

"What?" I said this so loud the family at our table looked over at me in alarm.

"You heard me: They ran out of mummies. Egyptian brown, also known as mummy brown, was made of ground-up Egyptian mummies mixed with myrrh and white pitch."

I was so appalled, I could barely make words.

"They were painting with *people?* With ground-up dead people?"

"Well, people and animals. The ancient Egyptians mummified a great number of their pets as well so that people would have company in the afterlife. Mostly cats, but others, also—even an alligator! Digging up mummies was a booming trade for the Victorians. They made medicines from them, and fertilizer; they unwrapped them for fun at parties. And, of course, they used them to make Egyptian brown."

This was the most disgusting thing I had ever heard of. I didn't care how nice the brown was. I didn't even feel great about sepia, which comes from the ink cuttlefish make when they're scared. Plenty of things make nice browns, and most of them are just plain old dirt.

"Apollo! Would you paint with a ground-up dead person?"

"Of course not. But many artists didn't know how Egyptian brown was made until the paint companies had to explain why it was getting so hard to come by. The painter Edward Burne-Jones felt the way you did when he found out. The story is that he took his last remaining tube of Egyptian brown out to his yard and gave it a proper burial."

I pushed my plate away, disgusted now by the slimy brown sauce, thinking about all the hours those artists had spent pushing paint made of dead people around on a canvas. What it would feel like to look at the work you'd made with that paint, once you knew?

Apollo signaled for the check and laid the money to pay for it in the little plastic tray. We said goodbye to our friends at the table and to our waiter and to the lady who's always at the cash register up front, and then we were back out on East Broadway.

It was cooler, almost cold, and I hugged my sweatshirt tightly around me, the little faucets heavy in the kangaroo pocket at the front.

A few blocks later, Apollo broke the silence. "You are very quiet, little bird. What are you are thinking about?"

*I'm thinking about my mom, who did not get out of bed this morning, and I am wondering if she will get up tomorrow. I am trying to figure out how I can get my dad to come home if nobody—not even you—knows what he's doing or how to reach him. And I am worrying about what will happen to me if he doesn't.*

I didn't say any of that.

"I'm thinking about Egyptian brown," I said, which was also true. "I can't stop wondering if it's possible to make something beautiful out of something awful."

Apollo's face looked handsome-sad again.

"A lot of people would say that's exactly what art is," he said, taking my hand, and I let him.

We didn't talk much on the way home, either.

# A LONG WAY DOWN

"Hold up. I forgot my sweatshirt," I told Alex, who was sitting cross-legged on the loading dock outside my house.

It was Saturday morning, and we were going to Washington Square Park like always.

"Race you," Alex said, already halfway up the building wall.

One of the things that Alex likes to do best is climb. He can climb anything, including a lot of things that regular people can't, like the front of my building. "Alex the Cat," my mother calls him, or sometimes, "Alex the Cat Burglar."

To get up the front of my building, he jumps from the standpipe on the sidewalk onto the decorative brickwork running up the front, the grooves barely deep enough for the tips of his fingers, wedging the rubber soles of his sneakers into the cracks to climb. Then he reaches out to grab the metal ladder coming down from the fire escape, swings himself up and over—and more often than not, comes in through our window without knocking, which my mom does not enjoy.

Alex makes stuff like that look like it's no big deal. I once jumped off a wall that was taller than my dad because Alex had made it look so easy, and I practically broke every single bone in my body and bit my tongue in half. He's good at normal sports like baseball or basketball, too, but he doesn't like them as much as he likes messing around. You know that part in *Singin' in the Rain* when the other guy, not Gene Kelly, runs straight up the side of the wall and does a flip at the top and then lands on his feet at the bottom? We found an old mattress on the street one time, and Alex pulled it up to a wall and spent the entire day practicing that move, and by the time it was dark, he could do it. I wouldn't let him try it without the mattress because I am not in the business of scooping sidewalk brains, and also we are both scared of his mom. Still, it was pretty cool to watch him run straight up the side of the wall like that.

Even though I use the hallway stairs like a regular person and go as fast as I can, I never, *ever* beat Alex to my apartment when he's climbing up the front. That morning was no different: I whipped open the front door of our apartment, only to see Alex through the window, lying on his back on the fire escape. His arms made a comfortable pillow for his head, and his eyes were closed like he'd been out there for hours; he wasn't even out of breath.

With his eyes closed, he couldn't see the face I made at him, which didn't stop me from making it.

My sweatshirt was on the chair next to my bed, right where I'd left it. Everything, these days, was right where I had left it. I'd been buying an extra can of peanuts from Mr. G for myself, and a bag of apples from C-Town. There was a small pile of cores on the trunk in front of the couch.

Usually on Saturdays, I'd tell my dad that we were going to the park, and he'd ask me if I had any requests for dinner. He'd give me pizza money, and extra if he needed me to pick up something from C-Town on my way home: three pork chops, maybe, or a pound of green beans.

Of course, my dad wasn't there.

I looked at the closed doors leading into my mom's room. The little faucets were still in my sweatshirt pocket, but I liked their soft weight and decided to hold on to them for a bit. The night before, my mom hadn't even opened her eyes when I'd dropped off her stuff and the leftovers from Hwa Yuan. I could give her the faucets when I got home from the park.

Alex was still lying out there on the fire escape, one leg crossed over the other, eyes closed against the sun like he was taking a nap. I found this so annoying that I didn't knock on the glass or anything to tell him I was done; I just left. Still, by the time I got downstairs, he was sitting on the loading dock with one leg swinging like he'd been waiting down there the whole time. I honestly don't know how he gets down. I've never been fast enough to see him do it.

"What took you so long?" he asked, like he was curious. I balled my hands into fists and kept walking.

At the corner of Greene and Prince, though, I couldn't stop myself from looking back at the front of the building he'd climbed.

He'd Spider-Manned his way up the front, cramming his fingers and toes into cracks too small to see, and then leaned out to grab the metal ladder coming down from the fire escape like he was catching a trapeze—a trapeze with no net, twenty-five feet off the ground.

If she knew, his mom would kill him for sure.

To be honest, it made my stomach float, too. Alex acted like it was nothing, but it *was* something—and that something was a long way down.

# THE LAST OF THE HEROES

Alex caught up to me at the corner of Spring Street and held out half of the peanut butter on health bread that Linda puts in his pocket for lunch, even though we always get pizza.

I was hungry enough to forgive him.

"Protein," he said. That was his way of making fun of Linda, because protein is pretty much her favorite topic of conversation. Linda drives both of us nuts. Still, I sometimes wondered if I would mind having the kind of mom who worried about what you ate.

There's a playground closer to our house, but we always go to the one in Washington Square Park because of the Terrorpole. The Terrorpole is a tall platform in the playground, with rungs up the side so you can climb it. Richard and I call it the Terrorpole because it's surrounded by concrete, and if you fall off one of the little stands on the way up, you will become splatter. But Alex loves it so much he should marry it.

I finished the sandwich and wiped my hands on my jeans.

"After Bobby Sands died," I said as we crossed Houston, "a hundred thousand people lined the streets for his funeral." The sentence came out sticky. There is not enough spit in the world for peanut butter on health bread.

"I thought you didn't want to talk about Bobby Sands," Alex said, also stickily, without looking at me. I guess he was still a little bit mad.

"I didn't."

"How come?"

"I don't know."

Of course, I did know: The bad feeling I got from knowing about Bobby Sands made the bad feeling I had about everything else a little worse.

I kept my head down as we passed through Richard's courtyard. There's a statue there, with a lady with both eyes on one side of her face like two sunny-side up eggs. I'm not crazy about it, even if it is a Picasso.

Outside of Richard's building, I sat down while Alex jumped up onto his pet ledge.

When Alex gets obsessed with a trick, he does it over and over and over again until he's mastered it, and then he finds something harder, and does *that* over and over again. He'd been practicing this one move for a while: jumping up onto a step from a standstill, keeping his legs together the whole time. He'd gotten so he could jump up a hundred times in a row on a regular stair, but a ledge was higher and hard even for Alex. (I couldn't do it at all.) This meant that we were spending a lot of time outside Richard's building, though, because there was a ledge there that was precisely the right height.

On the way over, he'd set himself a goal of thirty. It was hard to do, so he had to go slow. I took out my notebook; we were going to be there for a while.

I started to draw him silhouetted against the sun, the tight curve of his neck as he gathered himself to jump. But the pebbly sand-colored stone was warm and rough against my back, and the pencil felt fat in my fingers, so I leaned back on my elbows and basked instead, listening to Alex's breathing get heavier as he jumped up and jumped down.

I guess I dozed off. I hadn't slept that well the night before, what with worrying about my mom and my dad and poor dead Bobby Sands and all the rest of it. I woke up to the nap taste in my mouth, and something velvety and wet licking at my ankles.

I held very still and squinted one eye open.

Richard had come downstairs while I was asleep. He was sitting quietly next to me, looking through his own notebook, a huge scrapbook of monsters that he calls the Taxonomy. He did not seem to be alarmed. Alex was standing near his pet ledge, the sweat dripping off him to make dark spots on the concrete between his feet.

He was talking to Joyce Walker, who lives with her husband Peter above the gallery that she runs on Wooster Street. Mystery solved: Joyce's chunky yellow Labrador retriever, Saint Fall, was diligently using her tongue to cover every exposed inch between my rolled-up jeans and my sneakers, like someone had hired her to clean my ankles.

It wasn't a completely unpleasant feeling, to be honest.

Alex towered over Joyce, who looked like a plump little bird next to him. "Am I shrinking?" she asked with a funny old-lady hunch, then nudged Richard over on the ledge so she could sit down next to him.

My dad says that Joyce learned everything she needed to know about working with artists from having four boys who were all teenagers at the same time. Her kids are grown up now, so she likes to visit with us. That's what she calls it: visiting.

"I've done quite a lot of work on the Taxonomy since I last saw you," Richard volunteered, spinning it around on his lap so Joyce could see.

The Taxonomy is an enormous scrapbook with pictures and detailed descriptions of every monster Richard knows about, organized by their characteristics. Is the monster humanoid, mammalian, or reptilian? Does it walk on two feet, or four? Is it little or big? Is it slimy or scaly? Where does it live? What does it eat? (Mostly they eat people, as far as I can tell.) How does it kill what it eats? Then all the monsters are cross-referenced with one another across their categories.

Joyce thinks the Taxonomy has the makings of a really interesting art project, but Richard thinks of it as a science project, even if monsters aren't real. Richard is probably going to be a scientist when he grows up. My dad says he was put on earth to make monster movies, but his mom wants him to get a real job.

Alex is going to be a stunt man, so he can get thrown out of windows and dangle from helicopters and balance on top of speeding cars like he's surfing. I'm going to be an artist. I don't know what I'm going to do for money.

Joyce turned the page, and Richard pointed to one of the drawings: "Ollie drew that for me."

There are a lot of my drawings in the Taxonomy. When Richard started it, most of the monsters were ones that he'd seen at the movies, cut out from the monster magazines he buys. More recently, though, he'd started researching monsters from other countries at the library, and making some other ones up. He'd gotten pretty good at telling me what he saw in his head.

Joyce leaned in close to look and nodded, and I flushed with pleasure. I'd seen her look at art with my dad enough to know that nod was a compliment.

I didn't mention that I'd based the grainy texture of the monster's yellowing fangs on Saint Fall's teeth. But seeing the way I'd made the monster's spit hang down in thick ropy strings like snot made me pull my soggy ankles up out of the old dog's reach. Insulted, she sniffed at the rubber bottoms of my shoes for a bit, then lay down with a satisfied grunt and closed her eyes. She knew she'd done a good job.

Joyce was still looking at the drawing I'd done. On the opposite page was a picture of the monster from *Alien* that Richard had cut out from *People* magazine. He must have opened the Taxonomy up to the Mucus section.

"You're getting good, Olympia," was all she said, and my chest hummed.

Richard turned the huge book around and started flipping through the pages excitedly.

"I need a whole new section now, on Transformations. People and other animals turning into monsters, monsters turning into other monsters, bizarre mutations. Werewolves, selkies, the fox people that the Japanese call *kitsune*. It will require a substantial amount of work." He looked about as happy as I've ever seen him.

Joyce leaned over to pick up Saint Fall's worn leather leash. "Transformation is a subject worthy of you, Richard."

She turned to me then, the leash dangling down slack to the slumbering dog.

"Speaking of change, Ollie, how you holding up?"

She was looking at me the way I'd seen her look at an artist who'd delivered a pathetic excuse for being late to turn in work for a show. I thought she might somehow know about my mom, so I stood there, not saying anything, as the question changed on her face with every second I didn't speak.

Then I realized she was asking about my dad.

"It's okay, I guess," I said. "I miss his cooking, for sure." And then, like it was no big deal: "Are you in touch with him at all?"

"No, ma'am; I am not," she said, the South in her voice chewier than usual, and I believed her.

"I left a couple of messages for your mama, but she hasn't rung me back," Joyce said.

I looked down at Saint Fall stretched out on her side, the occasional snore escaping her loose black lips. "I think she's working pretty hard. You know she's got that show in the fall?"

Joyce nodded, her lips pursed. This was a sore subject: Joyce had represented my mom before she'd gone with the fancy gallery uptown.

She started to say something else, then stopped, angling her head to one side like a parakeet.

"Did your dad say anything to you, the night he left?"

That startled me. There had been a bunch of people at our house that night, coming down from the studio in a steady stream, even after I'd brushed my teeth and gone to bed. They'd come to see the Head, a small piece of painted wooden statuary my dad and Apollo had been hired to restore. Joyce had been there, too.

The Head was a big job for my dad and Apollo, and unusual— it was much, much older than the pieces they usually worked on, for one thing. The client was the Dortmunder Collection, a small museum in a mansion uptown that had once been some rich guy's private collection.

Apollo hadn't been happy about the Head, even though she should have been right up his alley. But my dad had been really excited. In fact, the first time he'd showed her to me, I'd had the feeling that he was a little bit in love with her.

Later, when I knew more, I thought it was probably his feelings about Vouley Voo spilling over. But the weirdest thing is that I wouldn't have blamed him if he *had* been in love with the Head. Because she was beautiful. Not pretty like a movie star, but the kind of beautiful that comes from never thinking anything mean, even if it's funny. I couldn't stop drawing her, trying to figure out what exactly the artist had done to make her radiate goodness the way she did—whether it was the gentle slope of her cheek or her melancholy smile, or the sweet way she was looking down.

Even though I filled whole pads with those sketches, I never got close to capturing her beauty, or that look. The Head was just perfect—right up until you got to the bottom of her, to the raw, ugly scar where she'd been ripped from her body.

Every time, it was a shock to follow the flowing lines of her face down to that violent stump of splintered wood. It changed the way you looked at her, as if the soft sadness in her face had come from suspecting that someone would eventually do something so horrible.

Restoring the Head should have been a good job for Apollo and my dad, but she'd caused a lot of problems. I'd heard my dad and my mom fighting about her, late at night when they thought I was asleep. My dad and Apollo had fought about her, too. Apollo was the one who had called Vouley Voo in the first place. She was an old friend of his, a visiting conservator at the Met, and he'd thought they'd needed her help. That had caused another fight, although I guess my dad and Vouley Voo had worked it out in the end.

Anyway, the night he left, right after I'd fallen asleep, my dad had come into my room to kiss me goodnight.

"Take care of your mama, Ollie," he'd whispered. "I've got to take the lady home."

I'd thought he was talking about Joyce. He always walked her back to her house after dinner if Peter didn't come, even though she always told him not to bother, that nobody in their right mind was going to bother with a tough old bag like her. But that night, he must have meant that he was taking Vouley Voo back to France, because that was where my mother, eyes tight and tired over her mug of tea the next morning, had told me he'd gone.

And I'd felt a clutch of sadness, because even though I'd swum up through my dreams to meet his kiss and the familiar leather and coffee smell of him, I hadn't made myself wake up all the way, the way I would have if I'd known we were saying goodbye.

"He said he was going to take somebody home," I told Joyce. "I thought he was talking about you."

Joyce shook her head quickly. When she looked back at me, she was chewing on the inside of her cheek, like she was trying to figure out how much to say. Then she looked back up at the sky between the buildings and said, "Never one to pass up a grand gesture, your dad. The last of the heroes."

Alex looked over, panting slightly; he's interested in heroes. I looked at Joyce, too, curious how she'd meant it, but she was looking down at Saint Fall, heroically chasing squirrels in her dreams.

Joyce jangled the leash a little to wake her and said, "It's time, old friend." In the same tone of voice, she said to me, "Listen, you don't hesitate to call me or Peter if you need anything, you hear?"

Peter is a great cook. He runs a framing business from their loft above Joyce's gallery, and Apollo and my dad always call him if they have a complicated engineering puzzle to solve. Everyone knows that Joyce has a great eye for new work and that she's good at helping young artists to stop acting like idiots. But if they didn't know how to get in touch with my dad, then I couldn't imagine anything I would call them for.

I nodded again anyway. "Thanks. I will."

"Now, Nana," she said to Saint Fall, and this time it was clearly a command.

The old dog got to her feet with a wheeze and one last regretful sniff in the general direction of my dampened ankles. She's a good sport, but she doesn't really enjoy the exercise part of a walk anymore.

I turned back to my friends. Alex had gone back to his ledge, and Richard was lost in the Taxonomy. I sat down next to him again, Joyce's words buzzing around my brain.

*The last of the heroes.*

I had no idea what she'd meant.

# REACH OUT AND
# TOUCH SOMEONE

Sweaty and triumphant, Alex finally finished his jumps, and the three of us walked over to Washington Square.

As we were coming up on the park, Richard stopped short.

"Guys, I almost forgot. My mother invited the two of you for dinner," he said. "Can you come? She asked me to tell her before noon so she can shop."

I nodded yes, with feeling. I love going to dinner at Richard's house.

Alex had to ask, so he went over to the payphones at the edge of the park to call Linda. I went, too, even though I didn't have anybody to call. Richard went in and found a bench near the playground so he could start planning out the Transformation section of the Taxonomy. Richard never minds being left behind, which is one of the comfortable things about him. Too many people take it personally when you want to do something different from what they want to do.

While Alex was digging through his pockets for change, I told him about dinner with Apollo. He was jealous we'd gone to Hwa Yuan. Linda doesn't like Chinatown. She lives and works down here, but she's not really a downtown kind of person. I told him about Egyptian brown, too, but he wasn't anywhere near as freaked out as I had been by it.

As he dialed, he asked me if I'd heard from my dad yet. That was rich, coming from Alex: His dad travelled so much for work, we had thought LaGuardia was some kind of magical city until we were most of the way through third grade. "My dad's flying out of LaGuardia tonight," Alex would tell us, reverent and hushed, so that we could practically see the jacketed doorman hailing a cab while his dad waited under a heated marquee, beautiful globe lights reflecting off rain-slicked roads.

Then someone figured out that LaGuardia was just an airport in Queens.

As he waited for Linda to answer, Alex bounced up onto his toes, held it for a second, then touched down quickly before lifting up onto his toes again. This is supposed to make his legs less scrawny.

I'm not sure it's working.

*Up, down. Up, down.* "What I don't get is why your dad had to, like, *disappear.*"

The snaky metal cord on the payphone next to him had been twisted until it kinked. I took the receiver off the hook and dropped it, letting it spin out, the silver cable uncoiling as it fell.

*Up, down. Up, down.* "There has to be a reason, right? I mean, besides Vouley Voo."

I knew what he meant. When Manny Weber's dad left his mom for our second grade teacher, he moved to an apartment about fifteen blocks away from where he used to live with Manny's mom. Manny spent a lot of time *wishing* that his dad and Miss Delario had vanished into thin air, like the time that they took him uptown to Serendipity for frozen hot chocolate and Miss Delario told him he was welcome to call her Phyllis. But his dad had only moved to an apartment in the East Village without any furniture in it, and Manny still saw him all the time.

"Maybe there was something he had to do," I said, watching the receiver slowly spinning at the end of its cord.

"Yeah. But what? What did he do that he had to sneak off like that, in the middle of the night?"

I reached down to grab the dangling receiver, not bothering to keep the edge out of my voice. "Who said he *snuck* anywhere?" I slammed the phone back into its grimy cradle. "He *went*. To France."

Alex quit bouncing and raised one hand—

half in surrender, half to shut me up. "Hey, Mom," he said into the receiver. "Sorry to bug you at work."

I kicked the metal base of the payphone he was using.

Linda said it was fine if Alex went to Richard's as long as he remembered his pleases and thank-yous. While she was telling him ten thousand things about manners, I picked up my own receiver again and punched in a random combination of numbers, thinking about my dad while I was doing it.

I knew it wouldn't work; I'm not stupid. I hadn't even put any money in. Even so, I felt a little jolt of hope in the half-second before the recording told me to hang up and try again.

I hung up and stuck my finger into the slot.

No dime. I found four once, though, so I always check.

# BIG IDEAS

As soon as we were back inside the park, Alex took off at a dead run toward his beloved Terrorpole.

Under no circumstances are you supposed to jump from the top of Terrorpole.

Of course, Alex jumps.

I wasn't sorry to see the back of him. I was only sorry that I couldn't tell him about the note so he'd know my dad hadn't snuck off into the night like some criminal.

Richard had gotten us a good bench, which was lucky because we weren't the only ones in the park enjoying the sweater weather. Barefoot college kids played guitars and drums against the spray paint–covered arch. Harried moms ran after toddlers. The old people on the benches shook their newspapers out against the sun. There was a lot I'd have liked to sketch, but Richard already had a brand-new monster in mind. We were going to use it to launch the Taxonomy's Transformation section.

I learned pretty fast that it's extremely difficult to draw one thing turning into something else. Luckily, Richard keeps a pad of paper for me in the worn brown-and-white PBS bag his mom gave him for the Taxonomy. The paper's thin enough that I can trace through it, so I don't have to worry about making mistakes. He tapes the finished drawing into the Taxonomy when we're both satisfied.

Still, even ten minutes in, I could tell that it was going to take me the better part of the pad to get this one monster right.

Richard was methodically working his way through the new issue of his favorite magazine, *Famous Monsters of Filmland*. He'd look over at the drawing every once in a while, to offer diplomatic critiques. "I like the way the scales look, all new and shiny and kind of wet underneath; it's cool the way you did that," he'd said, after I'd been working for about an hour. "But I was thinking the skin ripping would have a more ragged look to it. Not so much like a cut with scissors, but more like when you tear white bread?"

I blew my bangs off my forehead in frustration; the thin paper was already close to translucent from so much erasing. Somewhat annoyingly, I also thought he might be right.

"You know, I'd be happy to give you some drawing lessons," I told him, only half joking.

To my surprise, he looked tempted. Then he saw me noticing and shook his head in embarrassment. "That's okay. It's better when you do it," he said.

And then—probably to change the subject—he asked about my mom.

I shook my head to mean *no change* and detached a new piece of paper from the pad so I could trace the parts of the drawing he'd liked.

"Has your dad called?"

In his slow, quiet way, Richard can be quite persistent, which is one of the good and the bad things about him. Today, it was one of the bad things.

I shook my head again, keeping my eyes steady on the prominent bony ridges that would make up the monster's cheekbones and forehead. If I got this part right, the drawing was going to be terrifying. "There have been a bunch of hang-ups on the machine at home, but I don't know if it's him. And nobody knows how to reach him; I asked. Not Apollo, not my mom, not Joyce."

Richard bent down the corner of the page before closing *Famous Monsters*. There was an ordinary woman in a pink sweat suit and sneakers on the cover instead of the usual gruesome monster face. *The Incredible Shrinking Woman*, the yellow headline shrieked, although the woman looked regular size. Of course, I couldn't tell how big the robot was that she was standing next to.

Richard watched me sketch for a while, and I distracted myself by trying to remember what bread looks like when it rips. It worked, until it didn't.

After a little while and in a much smaller voice, he asked, "Ollie? Do you think we should tell a grown-up? About your mom?"

I dropped the pad and fixed him with a look so ferocious he had no choice but to drop his eyes. "No, I do not," I said, my tone so sharp and final that the dachshund on the bench next to us startled up from his nap with a short bark of alarm.

Richard slumped back against the bench. Heart hammering in my chest, I got to my feet and crossed the path to sharpen my pencil. I don't like to waste Blackwing, but I stood there longer than I needed to, watching the cedar curls fall onto the heavy black plastic lining the can.

If we got a grown-up involved, they'd have to *do* something, and whatever that was could be worse than what was already happening.

The last time my mom went to bed, she'd had to go to the hospital.

She'd told me she wouldn't go back there. But if we told a grown-up, they might make her. And if that happened while my dad was still gone, then what would happen to me?

I couldn't take that chance. I needed a little more time to fix it first.

I went back to sit down on the bench next to Richard and picked up the pad again. "It's all going to work out," I said casually. "Anyway, I was thinking I might stay with Apollo for a while."

Like it was settled already, like it was no big deal.

Richard nodded, his lips pressed tight together, and we both looked down at the monster in my hands.

My dad says that even a minute away from a drawing can be helpful when you need some perspective, and I could see right away that the nostril holes would be scarier if they were smaller. But Richard had been right: The skin did look better ripped.

"Apollo has a True Lost Love," I said, in a friendlier tone of voice. "He told me without telling me at dinner."

Richard let me change the subject. He likes Apollo. "You don't know who it is?"

"No idea," I said. Apollo had had a million girlfriends in my lifetime, but none of them had stood out. Plus, he was still friends with most of them. Could you stay friends with a Lost Love?

Richard's magazine was open again. Something in there had caught his attention. "Get Alex to ask Linda," he said absent-mindedly.

I always forget that Apollo knows Linda, mostly because it seems impossible that two people who are so completely different could know each other. But when my parents and Apollo and Linda were all at art school together, they were friends. Linda became a real estate broker around the same time that my dad and Apollo started the art restoration business. The story is that she came to see their studio and figured out how to buy a loft the next day. A month later, she was selling them.

If Apollo had met his True Lost Love while they were in art school, then Linda probably knew her, too. Plus, Linda liked nothing better than to talk about other people, especially if she could be disapproving about what she calls their life choices.

"I don't know. You know how he is about this stuff." It is Alex's opinion that love exists mostly to ruin perfectly good movies about car chases and bombs.

"I'll talk to him," Richard said, lifting the magazine close to his face so that he could scrutinize a picture. I could feel one of his Big Ideas coming on.

Richard's Big Ideas are exclusively about monsters, and they always mean more work for me.

I rolled my Blackwing back into the V of my thumb and scratched at the callus on my middle finger. Hoping to intercept the Big Idea, I asked, "Why do *you* think you're so into monsters?"

It didn't work. Richard's nose was about an inch from the magazine, and his eyes had narrowed in concentration. He wasn't interested in the question. "My mom thinks it has to do with race and puberty. But I think I just like them." He dropped the magazine to take another long, critical look at the drawing on the pad on my lap.

Then, just as I'd predicted: a Big Idea.

"Hey. Remember that lizard we saw that time at the Bronx Zoo?" Richard asked me, his voice rising at the end of the sentence the way it does when he gets excited. "What about, instead of fish-type gills that lie flat, ones that pop up? Like in a ruff?"

I blew at my bangs again before ripping a fresh page from the pad.

Later, to make myself feel better, I sketched the dachshund on the bench next to us. The guy he was with was very complimentary about the drawing, so I gave it to him.

I consider myself to be more of a cat person, but that dachshund had an extremely intelligent face.

# WILD TIMES

By five o'clock, the three of us were starving, even after a trip to Joe's for a slice of Sicilian around two.

On our way out of the park to Richard's house, we slowed down to watch the guys break dancing on flattened cardboard by the fountains, and sped up past the guys who mutter. Then, crossing the street toward the library, I saw that same goofy, bright yellow cursive running along the bottom of a poster pasted to the side of a building across from the park: WILD TIMES!

This painting was of a paper coffee cup, the kind you get at every deli in New York. It's the color of the cornflower crayon, and has a Greek temple on the side and the words "We Are Happy to Serve You."

There was a wave of coffee coming out of the top of the cup. My dad had showed me a famous Japanese woodblock once with a wave like that one. The wave was smiling.

The deli cup reminded me of my dad. He used to take me out on Saturday mornings when I was little so that my mom could sleep in, especially if she'd been up working late the night before. He'd get black coffee for himself and a corn muffin for me from the bodega on West Broadway.

I'd run up the ramp outside Joyce's gallery and then jump off the end as many times as I wanted to, while my dad leaned against the rusted metal door in his worn leather jacket, drinking his coffee. I always begged for a sip, and he always gave me one, even though we both knew I wouldn't like it any more than I did the weekend before. I still don't understand how something so bitter can smell so good.

If Joyce and Peter were inside, they'd come out to chat, or we'd all go inside so my dad could see what Joyce was hanging. The vast gallery space echoed when they talked. I'd head straight to Joyce's desk at the back, and the mug Peter kept filled with peppermints to help Joyce with her stomach. There was a swivel chair behind the desk that I could swing around in until I got dizzy, which made the white-painted pipes crossing the gallery ceiling look like they were moving. Sometimes I drew on the big rolls of brown paper they kept in the corner, or painted designs on my hands and arms with Joyce's Wite-Out.

Eventually, my dad would take the top off his deli cup so Peter could give him a warm-up from the Mr. Coffee on the windowsill. And his cup looked like the one in the poster.

"C'mon, Ollie." Cranky hungry, Alex poked me out of my daydream.

I was hungry, too, but I wanted him to see the poster. "Did you see that poster? The one that says WILD TIMES? There's one like that in the lot across the street from my house, except it says WAKE UP. I saw the guy putting it up." I looked at Alex, who had gotten the same hard patches on his jeans during my mother's poster phase. "He was wearing a *suit*. To do paste-ups."

Alex hadn't helped us wheat-paste for long. When his mom found out what he'd been doing with us, she'd called my mom.

"For God's sake, Linda, they are not going to arrest a child for putting up a poster," I'd heard my mother snap impatiently on her end of the call, but Alex didn't help us any more after that. Which was too bad, because he liked being vaulted over fences a whole lot more than I did.

"I didn't see any poster," Alex said, probably because of the fancy footwork he was doing alongside the curb.

"Too busy with your hopscotch?" I asked. Not super nicely, if I'm being honest.

Alex rose to the bait. "It's called an agility drill? Football players do them?"

Richard was walking more quickly than usual, probably because he was hungry, too. He's the kind of only child who doesn't like it when people fight, so he interrupted before I could point out some of the more obvious differences between Alex and a football player. "Those posters; it's got to be the same guy, right?"

Reluctantly, I left Alex alone. "Did *you* see it?"

Richard shook his head, and I snuck a look over my shoulder, serious for a minute about making them go back to look. But after a day on the Terrorpole, Alex is basically only one missed meal away from devouring human flesh, so I let it go.

Anyway, I didn't need to see the poster again to know how it made me feel. The cup reminded me of the coffee-leather smell of my dad on those Saturday mornings, but the out-of-control wave made me think of my mom.

### WILD TIMES!

Wild times are supposed to be fun. But they didn't feel that way to me.

# A BIG FAT NOTHING

We cut through Washington Square Village to get to Richard's house. It's not a real village; just a bunch of big buildings with a path running through them.

Alex was tightrope-walking on a thick black chain hanging between two posts with a sign on it that said PLEASE KEEP OFF THE GRASS.

Catching Richard's eye and pausing for dramatic effect, I made my announcement: "Apollo has a Long Lost True Love."

Alex scowled and fell off the chain, windmilling his arms like a clown for effect.

"How do you know?"

"I just do," I said, knowing that would annoy him even more.

"Who even cares," he muttered under his breath, scuffing his sneakers against the pavement.

"We're starting a club, to solve mysteries." Richard stepped in. "This is the first one."

This was smart, even if clubs weren't cool. The summer before, Alex had been obsessed with a series of books featuring a smart kid, an athletic kid, and a bossy kid triumphing over a bunch of criminals so dumb they'd made the ones in Scooby Doo look like physicists. (Richard thought the boys' clubhouse, a trailer hidden in a junkyard, was the best part.) When he was reading them, Alex had become obsessed with finding a mystery for us to solve, but it's hard to find a good one in real life.

We walked through the courtyard to Richard's building. Alex hadn't said no yet. "It's more of a squad," I offered.

"I'll join your squad, but I'm not going to look for some chump Lost Love," Alex said, holding his hand up for a high five from Isidro, Richard's Saturday doorman. Isidro is always yelling at us to stay in school, even during summer vacation, but he'd laid off it a little after finding out that Richard's mom was a professor.

Richard pressed the elevator button. Alex shifted from one foot to the other and pressed it again. The elevator in Richard's building takes forever. Most of the time, Alex can't stand waiting and runs the six flights instead.

Five seconds later, he pressed the button again.

"How are you going to find her?"

Richard looked around carefully before answering, in case of spies. "If you agree to participate, you'll have the crucial role of the mission, Alex: handling the most important agent we have in the field."

Alex looked excited for two seconds until Richard told him who the agent was.

"No way," he said flatly. "Forget about it."

Truthfully, I didn't blame him. You don't get involved with a mystery investigation so you can talk to your mom, especially if your mom is Linda. But Richard was right: Linda was our best bet, until I could get in touch with my dad.

Alex looked accusingly at Richard. "Why do *you* care who Apollo's in love with?"

"Oh, I don't," Richard said mildly, and I realized that was probably true. "You're missing the point. It's not about love; it's about solving the mystery."

Richard let me go into the elevator first, like his mom was there to see. Alex was already in there, shaking his head and kicking the metal wall just gently enough so that Isidro couldn't hear. I looked over as I got in, giving him one last chance to change his mind, but all he did was make a face even more hideous than his real one.

Richard sighed, and the elevator door lurched shut.

I looked up at the brass plate above the door with its dim row of numbers and thought about mysteries.

Last summer, when Alex was still obsessed with those books, he'd found a small circle of faded purple buttons behind some bushes in the park.

"It's a clue, guys," he'd whispered as he was dragging us into the brush to see the buttons, so excited I thought he was going to pee his pants.

Alex's sister Maggie had been with us that day, upset about

Rolando, this sick bird she'd found and taken to the pigeon lady. The bird had died anyway, and Maggie was pretty bummed out about it, so Linda had told her she could go to the park with us. (Maggie can be funny, but she drives Alex up the wall and asks too many questions, even when you aren't worried that she's dripping with some disgusting bird disease. So we only bring her to the park when Linda makes us.)

It seemed like he was right about the buttons, though. There were six of them, the kind you'd see on an old lady's blouse, laid out in a small, perfect circle, and even Richard and I couldn't help but be curious. Who had left them? What did they lead to? And what did it all mean?

Alex ran the investigation. He made me measure and draw the position of each button, so we'd be able to replace them exactly. We collected them, examining them for clues with a magnifying glass we'd borrowed without asking from the science lab at school, and we dug a deep hole to see if anything was buried underneath. (Maggie wasn't allowed to touch anything, so she held a funeral service for Rolando on the bench where we could keep an eye on her as we dug.) Then we filled in the hole, put the buttons back, and staked out the bushes from behind a *Daily News* left behind on a bench.

We did that for three weekends in a row. And you know what we found?

A big fat nothing.

There was no answer to The Mystery of the Mauve Buttons— or none we could find, anyway. Just six ugly buttons in a circle in the dirt behind a bush in Washington Square Park.

In books, clues were tidy arrows pointing toward a logical conclusion, and detectives were always in the right place at the right time. In real life, though, everything was more confusing. Sometimes there were lots of explanations for why something had happened; sometimes there was no explanation at all. You couldn't always tell what was a clue. And even when you could, most of the time those clues didn't add up to anything more than a pile of old-lady buttons.

The elevator chunked to a stop at the seventh floor.

Nobody knew how to get in touch with my dad—and if they did, they weren't telling me. Our quest to find Apollo's True Lost Love was a bust before it had even gotten off the ground. And I had no idea how to make my mom better.

The metal door scraped open, and a hungry Alex shouldered past me into the hall.

Even though I'd made fun of them, I'd kept reading those mysteries long after the boys had lost interest. (Richard's breaking point had been a particularly pathetic animatronic dragon in a cave. He has a good sense of humor about most things, but he takes his monsters seriously.) Even Alex had tired of the formula eventually, the way the kids always knew exactly what they needed to know, the way the leads always added up to a solve.

Trailing the boys out of the elevator, I had to wonder if those tidy endings hadn't been the real reason I'd kept reading.

# JUST A SKETCH

The hallway was filled with the most amazing dinner smell; I crossed my fingers that it was coming from Richard's house.

"Hi, Mom," Richard called out as he unlocked the door. "We're home."

The smell *was* coming from his house. I closed my eyes and took a deep, grateful sniff before going to say hi to his mom.

Alex says there are too many rules at Richard's house, but they're just different from the ones at his—more about everybody chipping in to help, and less about staying out of Linda's way.

I love Richard's. His apartment is the opposite of mine. When my parents moved into our loft, the bathroom didn't even have a door; Apollo helped my dad make walls for the bedrooms when I got too big to sleep in a basket. Richard's apartment is a series of little rooms, connected by passageways, every inch of them lined with books and records. Everything is white at my house, but every wall at Richard's is painted something deep and warm, the colors of the earth, and every one of them has a painting or a photograph or a piece of cloth hanging on it.

Dr. Charles collects textiles from all over the world. She hangs her favorite pieces, but she has so many that the little closet near the table where they eat is filled with carefully folded fabric. Every once in a while, you have to take everything out and wipe the shelves down with a clean rag, and then refold everything with new creases. Once a year, she uses a piece of very fine sandpaper on the cedar shelves that Mr. Charles put in there for her.

I'd clean that closet with her every single weekend if I could.

Dr. C thinks girls shouldn't always get stuck with housework, but Richard's dad had to get ready for work—he's a conductor on the subway, usually the number 2 out to New Lots. Plus, I like helping her, and Alex and Richard don't, so it was just the two of us in the kitchen before dinner.

She gave me a big pile of clean lettuce to spin dry, and then we tore it up together into smaller pieces. When that was done, she asked me to choose some fabrics from the second shelf of the closet, and then showed me how to put three different ones on the table, laying them at angles so that you could see part of each one.

Even though it's the boys' job to set the table and to bring the food, I stood at Dr. Charles's elbow, waiting for her to finish the dressing so I could take the bowl to the table. Our salad bowl at home is a big dinged-up metal bowl that my mother got from a restaurant supply place on the Bowery, but the salad bowl at the Charles' house was carved by hand from a piece of wood so dark it's almost black. The top edge dips and curves, following the grain of the wood. It even has a hole, right up near the top, where there was a knot in the tree it was made from. I couldn't wait to see how it was going to look on the table on top of the fabric we'd laid down.

When we were getting ready to call the boys to set the table, Dr. Charles leaned up against the kitchen wall and looked me right in the face.

"Is everything okay with you, Olympia?"

I looked down at my dirty sneaker and nodded. "Everything's okay. I'm hungry, that's all." I made myself smile and meet her eyes. Eye contact is very important when you're lying.

Richard's mom nodded and turned back to the stove, but not before she'd looked at me a while longer.

~~~

Dinner was a green salad and chicken in a slightly spicy red sauce with peanuts in it, which we ate on top of buttery rice with peas and broccoli on the side. Everything was so good, I filled my plate three times. I ate even more than Alex did.

Afterward, the boys cleared the table and turned on the eight o'clock movie. Richard likes to watch movies with aliens and spaceships and monsters. Alex likes anything where people run around and jump from buildings and get thrown out of speeding cars. WPIX's Saturday eight o'clock movie usually works for both of them.

I don't care about aliens *or* car chases. Also, it's difficult for Alex to stop moving long enough to watch a movie, so he was wagging one of his legs in the air, which makes me want to slap him.

I wouldn't, though. Even if it hadn't been for the ding-a-ling day.

Back when we were five, I followed Alex around for an entire day calling him a ding-a-ling. When I say the entire day, I mean The Entire Day. I called him a ding-a-ling on our way to kindergarten, I called him a ding-a-ling at snacktime, and then at recess I got everyone else to call him a ding-a-ling.

Even back then, Alex was good at tuning out, because of Linda. Still, by the time our moms had picked us up and taken us to the playground after school, he was getting pretty mad. "Cut it out, Ollie," he said, stamping his foot, and I could tell it was a warning. But the ding-a-ling thing had taken on a life of its own.

When we were little, our clubhouse at the playground was the cool, damp spot under the big slide. We used it for base when we were playing tag. That day, when we got under there, I said, "You're it, ding-a-ling," meaning I wanted him to chase me, but Alex had had enough: He hauled off and hit me, hard, on the arm.

I didn't blame him for hitting me. If it had been him calling me a ding-a-ling all day, I would have decked him flat-out before we'd gotten to school, and I probably would have tried to spit in his mouth while I had him pinned.

But Alex had made a bad mistake: He'd hit me in full view of the moms on the playground benches.

In a flash, there were twenty moms consoling me like I was going to die from the punch.

And they went absolutely *nuts* on Alex.

His own mom was the worst. "You don't hit girls, Alex," Linda hissed, over and over. "Ever. You never, ever hit a girl."

It didn't make sense. Even in kindergarten we knew it was not okay to hit a kid who was smaller than you were, but I was about two inches taller than Alex was at the time, and my feet were bigger. He was stronger, because even then he was always doing some weird trick over and over and over again, but not by much.

And I had really, really been asking for it.

Still, he never hit me again after that, no matter how much I deserved it, although I never pulled another stunt on him like the ding-a-ling day. And I never hit him, either, since he couldn't hit me back.

Sometimes, we called each other ding-a-ling as a joke. But I always let him start it.

Alex's leg wagging drove me nuts, so while the boys watched their movie, I wandered back into the kitchen to see if Richard's mom needed help.

She was putting the leftover chicken from the big red pot into a bowl with a plastic top for her lunch. I felt bad about my third helping. There was probably less left over than she'd thought there'd be.

"The movie's not your thing, Ollie?" I shook my head, and she twinkled back. I'm pretty sure Dr. Charles doesn't watch monster movies when Richard's not around. Richard's not allowed to watch them, either, unless his room is neat and his homework is done and he's finished practicing his piano for the week.

The kettle whistled, and I watched as Dr. Charles swished a bit of hot water around the bottom of the teapot, dumped that out, added a spoonful of loose tea, and poured water from the kettle over it. "Tea will be ready by the time we've turned this place over to the boys," she said, and set me up transferring broccoli and rice into Tupperware containers.

When the food was all put away and the dishes rinsed and stacked in the sink, Dr. Charles called Alex and Richard in to wash them. She said it was okay if they only did dishes during the commercial breaks as long as the kitchen was clean by the time the movie was over.

Then we took our tea back out to the table, which was still set with the three different cloths. Dr. Charles flipped over one with a sauce stain, then poured the tea through a strainer into big pottery mugs. It tasted delicious, like Big Red gum.

Full of spicy chicken and colors and cinnamon tea, I started to think that maybe I could say something to Dr. Charles about my mom. I knew that whatever she did would be the right thing; she was that kind of person. And she seemed to be waiting for me to say something.

But just as I opened my mouth—before I had any idea what I was going to say—Mr. Charles came out of the bedroom. He'd taken a shower and was wearing his MTA uniform, a blue shirt with a red tie and a blue cardigan over the top. He looked very handsome, and Dr. Charles smiled when she saw him.

"Have a good night, you," she said, as he leaned over the table and kissed her next to her eye. "A *safe* one." She worries about him working nights, but he's loved trains since he was little. This may be why he's got so much patience for Richard's monsters.

He straightened up and winked at me. "After a dinner like that, what can't I do?"

The boys came out of the kitchen to say goodbye. Alex's T-shirt was soaked through with dishwater so he just waved, but Richard gave his dad a hug, and the boys went back to their movie.

Mr. Charles nodded to me on his way out the door—"Always a pleasure, Ollie"—and then he was off, exactly like the dad on a television show going off to work in the morning, except that it was night.

Alex and Richard were lying on their stomachs in front of the TV, watching the movie. I turned my body so I wouldn't have to see Alex's fidgety leg and opened my notebook to draw Richard's dad before the image of him faded from my brain. I sketched his neat moustache and his left eye, which droops a little. I didn't look up until there was a heavy-duty crash from the kitchen, followed by an extremely loud silence. Dr. Charles shook her head at the urgent whispering that came after that, then got to her feet. I hadn't even noticed it was a commercial break.

My drawing of Mr. Charles wasn't completely done, but I'd run out of steam, and it was tricky to remember all the details of his nose and chin without him being there. I took a sip of my tea, cold now but still delicious, and flipped through the pages of my notebook, stopping to look at a drawing I'd done of my mom in her bed.

I'd made it while I was sitting outside her bedroom earlier that week, leaning against her closed door. I'd taken to sitting there sometimes after I'd dropped off her cigarettes and Tab. It made me feel like we were together, even if being in the room with her was too hard.

This drawing had come so quickly it had felt like I was tracing it, like someone else was moving my hand. She was looking up and away, one arm thrown back over her head, her eyes fixed on a spot at the corner of the ceiling. I'd drawn the dented, empty can she'd been using as an ashtray on top of the messy stack of art books by her bed, the sheets crumpled around her and her thin foot, dark on the bottom from going without shoes, poking out of the frayed bottom of her jeans.

The drawing was good, even though my dad had left right when he was starting to teach me about perspective, and I wasn't sure I'd gotten the bottom half of her body totally right. He always says practice is the most important thing, anyway. *Just draw, Ollie. Get it wrong! Who cares? Paper is cheap. Look carefully. Draw. Then do it again.*

He'd been right about practice, because I had gotten better. Since my mom had gone to bed, I'd been drawing all the time.

I pushed the open notebook away from me. As good as the drawing was, I didn't want to look at it. What I wanted was to stay at the Charles' house forever, following the rules that made things nice, sitting down for dinner as a family and cleaning up as a team and drinking cinnamon tea.

"Smaller than the Taxonomy, that's for sure."

I'd forgotten all about Dr. Charles, on her way back to the table from the disaster in the kitchen. I was tempted to close the notebook quickly, but it's better not to act like your notebook is secret. If you do, then everyone is always making a big deal out of seeing what's inside. Not that Dr. Charles would, but I knew that hiding the picture would make her curious.

She leaned over to look more closely. "This is your mom, Ollie?"

"It's just a sketch." I shrugged, sounding even to myself like she'd caught me doing something wrong. "I was just messing around."

She traced the lines with her finger without touching them. "You're getting really good. I'm seeing a big improvement, even since the last monster you drew for Richard. Leaps and bounds."

I was glad she could see it. Mostly, though, I was relieved that she wanted to talk about drawing, not my mom.

She sat down at the table again, the notebook between us. "It's miraculous to me, what you can do. You know I can barely draw a stick figure."

I brushed off the compliment. "My dad says you have to look, and then draw what you see. And practice, as much as you can."

She laughed. "I'm not sure it's that easy. Anyway, a lot of people don't see anything at all. Helping people to see what's there—especially everything they'd rather ignore—is one of my jobs, too."

I'd been one of those people. The first time we talked about Manet's *Olympia*, Dr. Charles told me, "The model's name was Laure." I'd been confused: Apollo had told me that the woman who'd posed for Olympia had been an artist called Victorine Meurent. But there are two women in that painting, and Dr. C was talking about the servant behind Olympia, the one that people—including me, until Dr. C told me her name—tended to ignore.

Dr. C looked down again at the drawing I'd made of my mom, and I saw it the way she must be seeing it: the disheveled bed, my mom's rawboned hands and her too-thin wrists, her eyes looking away. I couldn't tell what Dr. C was thinking, and I had to resist the urge to grab the book right out of her hands.

"Journalists and academics like me look closely, but we can only record exactly what we see. Other people transform their experiences, even the hard ones. They turn difficult things into beautiful ones. They're the artists. And that's what you are."

I didn't know what to say, so I didn't say anything, but the tender, careful, proud feeling she'd given me stuck with me the whole rest of the movie, like I had a kitten asleep on my lap.

# KIND OF SUSPICIOUS

There aren't very many cars on Greene Street at night on the weekends, so Alex and I walked down the middle of the street to avoid the shadowy doorways and the black garbage bags by the curb, which rustled when we passed.

Rats love SoHo.

That morning, there'd been an impatient feeling in the air, like the birds and the blossoms and the little green buds were all saying, *Come on, lemme show you what I've got.* Now that it was dark, that feeling had intensified into something urgent. Suddenly I understood why my dad always says teenagers don't have to go looking for trouble in this weather; it comes to them.

Leaving Richard's house had been awkward. Usually, my dad would come to pick me up and we'd drop Alex off on the way, but since my dad wasn't around, Dr. C wanted Alex to walk me home. Linda doesn't like Alex to walk around at night by himself;

a kid went missing down here a couple of years ago. But Alex's dad wasn't around, either, and Maggie's too chicken to be left by herself. So Linda had to settle for a call when we left Richard's to let her know we were on our way.

Alex was taking his responsibility seriously, swiveling his head back and forth like ninjas were going to swarm out of the shadows to attack us. I wasn't scared, exactly, but I didn't mind him being there until we crossed Prince and he opened his big dumb mouth.

"So how does she pee?"

At first, I had no idea what he was talking about, and then I did. Of course Richard had told him.

Shame bloomed on my cheeks.

"She probably goes when I'm out, like now. Or when I'm sleeping."

"She's not making you dinner?" I shook my head and felt a pang thinking about spicy chicken in peanut sauce on a table set with three different, beautifully colored cloths. Alex didn't even bother to check my response. We both knew that making dinner had mostly been my dad's job.

Alex had already forgotten to look for robbers and was picking his way over the cobblestones like he was on a tightrope, putting the toe of one sneaker right behind the heel of the other. We had the same shoes, from May's on Fourteenth Street, only his were red and mine were blue.

He was probably trying to imagine what it would be like if Linda stopped all her rushing around and worrying and real estate showing and community board organizing to stay in bed. It was impossible. In fact, if you hadn't seen her in her fancy navy pajamas with white piping, all smeary with face cream under a silk sleeping mask—as I unfortunately had, on a number of occasions—it was difficult to imagine Linda slowing down long enough to go to bed at all.

Then he surprised me. "I think my dad's been staying at a hotel some nights. Not just when he's out of town, but when he's in New York, too."

I knew he'd stop talking if I said anything, so I made a little growl instead that meant: *That really stinks; I'm sorry.*

I thought, too, about the neat pile of blankets stored under the couch in the studio upstairs, and the quiet *snick* of the front door closing, right before my dad came in to wake me up with a glass of orange juice.

"You think your mom isn't getting up because of your dad and Vouley Voo?" Alex asked, and I wondered if he was wondering if his dad had his own Vouley Voo.

"Yeah?" I said. But I wasn't sure. I didn't think that what was going on with my mom had all that much to do with my dad. And I wasn't a hundred percent sure how much any of it had to do with Clothilde.

My mom had said it was her work, and that seemed right. Although maybe it was that everything had happened all at the same time.

Still intent on his tightrope, Alex said, "Richard thinks we should tell someone. About your mom. In case it's like last time."

Panic grabbed at me, making it hard for me to breathe, and I stopped right in front of Alex so that he had to stop, too. My voice bounced, unnaturally loud, off the walls of the dark canyon of buildings around us.

"Alex, you can't. If you tell Linda, I'll kill you. I mean it."

A siren wailed in the distance. Alex pushed past me to start walking again, worried about getting home before Linda called in the National Guard.

"Not Linda. Someone else. What about Apollo?"

"I don't think they've talked since my dad left." I was thinking about this for the first time. "He's been busy." *And he seems kind of mad at my dad*, I thought but did not say. "Apollo introduced them, Vouley Voo and my dad. She might be mad about that?" Except that my mom hadn't seemed mad about Vouley Voo at all. She'd seemed relieved.

"We could tell Richard's mom."

I almost *had* told her, sitting at her table with the cinnamon tea; now I was glad I hadn't. My mom would hate for someone outside of our family to see her the way she was. And Dr. Charles is the kind of person who always does things the right way, the way they should be done, and I wasn't sure my mom could deal with that kind of person right now.

Besides, she was going to get up soon. She had to.

"It's going to be okay," I said. "I just have to figure out how to get my dad to come home."

"Right," Alex said. "Sure."

I was getting tired of his attitude. "What's your problem?"

But Alex just shook his head slowly like I was too dumb to even talk to.

"What?" I snapped. I was going to make him say it.

He huffed out an impatient breath. "You don't think it's kind of suspicious? Your dad disappears into thin air without telling anyone where he is, or what he's doing, or why he had to leave?"

I felt like he'd slapped me. "He's in *France*," I said, tears stinging my eyes. "With Clothilde."

"Fine," Alex said, exasperated. "Whatever you say, Ollie. Your dad fled the country in the middle of the night to be with his girlfriend." He shook his head again. "Who was already *here*."

We were at my door. Too upset to speak, I used the key around my neck to open the steel front door, jiggling the handle the way you have to. A business card, jammed into the crack, fell onto the pitted cement step at my feet.

There was writing on the back, in urgent up-and-down script.

> *Restorers: please call!*
> **V IMPORTANT**.
> *In NYC until Thursday. 555-4670*

I flipped the card over. The printing on the front read:

> *Antonin Grandjean*
> *Forgery Investigation & Art Authentication*
> *Rue de la Madeleine 3, Brussels*

"Later," Alex said, startling me.

By the time I turned around, he was gone—running, as fast as he could, down the center of the empty cobblestoned street.

# FAKE

I let myself in and made my way slowly up the stairs to our apartment, holding the forgery expert's card gingerly by the edges between my thumb and forefinger like it was coated with poison.

Except the poison wasn't on the card. It was in my head.

Inside, I dropped the business card onto the steamer trunk we use as a coffee table. Without turning on any lights, I sat down on the couch to think, but as soon as my butt hit the cushions, I popped up like a jack-in-the-box.

Sitting wasn't going to work.

I rode a wave of uneasy energy all the way across the dark apartment, opened the fridge, and stared at the leftovers inside without seeing them. I crossed over to the windows, but Alex was long gone and Greene Street was deserted again. So I surfed that twitchy wave all the way back to the couch, where the forgery expert's card sat on the trunk, pulsing and radioactive.

This was almost certainly the big guy Richard had seen asking questions outside my building. He was also possibly—probably—Apollo's mysterious caller, the one looking for a missing piece of art.

A memory pushed itself to the front of my mind, raising its hand and begging to be called on like Rowan Merody when Ms. Colantonio needs a volunteer.

Ignoring it, I rubbed my sweaty palms against the seam of my jeans and said out loud into the empty loft: "I do not want to be thinking what I am thinking."

*So stop thinking it,* I told myself.

Unfortunately, that's not how it works.

In September, right after we'd gone back to school, I had discovered that I could not draw a horse.

Carla Perrucci, who is totally obsessed with them, had whipped out a pretty good one in the first session of Art Club. I thought I'd give it a try, even though the only horse I'd ever seen in real life had a cop on it. But horse legs, especially the back ones, didn't work the way I thought they should.

Lady Day wouldn't even try. "Animals with sideways-facing eyes are *prey*," she told me, a little snottily, I thought. "A cat doesn't have to worry about what's behind her." Prey or not, I didn't like that Carla Perrucci could draw a horse and I couldn't, so I went down to the studio after school to ask my dad for help.

He'd happily hauled a big book filled with old photos of racehorses off the shelf for me, and I'd settled in with my notebook and a couple of sharpened pencils to copy some of them while he unwrapped a new job—a minor work by a well-known artist I'd never heard of.

Nudging the painting free of its bubble wrap, my dad looked at it closely, running his white cotton gloves gently over the surface. It was a small canvas, stretched on boards but with no frame. It was ugly, I thought—crude, hard lines surrounding a curvy guitar.

He flipped the canvas over to check the back, tilting it to inspect the rusty nails fastening the canvas to its wooden mount. He hit the switch on the most powerful task light in the studio and studied the painted surface under its harsh beam before carrying it back—again—to the natural light coming through the window.

I put my pencil down to watch. Something was bothering him.

Then he did something I'd never seen him do: He picked the picture up and sniffed it.

"C'mere," he said. "What does this smell like?"

I inhaled and shook my head, confused. The painting didn't smell like anything to me.

"Exactly!" he said. "What about that one?" He pointed to an easel nearby, holding a choppily painted seascape that Apollo had been complaining about all week. Not expecting much, I went over and took an obedient whiff, then looked up at my dad in surprise.

The seascape *did* smell: basement stale with a deep sweetness underneath, like Christmas Eve at Richard's grandma's church.

"Exactly," my dad said again. "A painting smells like the room it's been hung in." He lifted the new job to his face again. "And this one doesn't smell like anything at all."

He'd leaned over his little black magnifier, an inch away from the painting's surface. "It's usually the whites that get them," he said, more to himself than to me. "They get lazy, fall back on a time bomb from a tube, a formula invented long after the picture was supposed to be painted. . . ." I knew all this already from Apollo, who made his paints by hand from pigments, the way they'd been made for centuries.

Horse legs forgotten, I watched my dad's intelligent hands run over the front edge of the painting at the bottom, hunting for something that wasn't there.

"No dust," he whispered, and I understood.

How many times had I watched him and Apollo ease a painting off its stretcher, then reach for the German wood-handled brushes they'd use to lovingly sweep away the dust that had collected at the bottom? My dad would hold up the clot of grey fuzz and hair like an auctioneer: "Behold, ladies and germs, a genuwine, authentic, one-hundred-year-old dust bunny! Going once, going twice, to the lady with the butter-yellow parasol!" And then he'd chase me around the studio with it, trying to put it into my ear.

A painting doesn't kick around for the better part of a century without some dust falling into the crack at the back of the stretcher. But the guitar painting had no lumps at all in the front—no dust.

It was a forgery. A good one, maybe, but not good enough to fool my dad.

I blew air out through my lips with a loud sound, as if I could scare the memory off. Unlike my dad, though, it wasn't going anywhere. Which left me on the couch in the dark loft, sitting very, very still in front of Antonin Grandjean's card. I felt like my brain had shrunk to the size of a pea, leaving nothing but room for bad thoughts to zoom around the cavern of my skull.

Specifically, the words from my dad's note: *Not everyone thinks it's the right thing to do.*

That drove me off the couch again, but no matter how many laps I did around the big room, I couldn't get ahead of the conclusions that my busy brain kept jumping to.

The fights about money. Apollo's tight jaw as he hung up the phone. A missing piece of art.

Nobody knew better than me that my dad could draw or paint anything. He'd done a perfect *Starry Night* in icing on my eighth birthday cake, and he'd try to make me laugh by drawing Cubist and Impressionist versions of Garfield the Cat on the placemats at the coffee shop while we waited for our pancakes.

It would have been the easiest thing in the world for my dad to save one of those genu-wine one-hundred-year-old dust bunnies. I even knew exactly which spatula he'd use to cram it down the back of a painting. A painting he'd made.

A painting he'd forged.

With paints mixed from Apollo's pigments, so no time-bomb titanium white could trip him up.

The thought of Alex's told-you-so face made me want to punch the couch.

What had my dad done?

# BUTTERFLIES

Sunday was not great.

It had taken me a long time to fall asleep, but I hadn't slept in. And when I woke up, the scared, scary ache at the base of my belly was still there.

I lay in bed for a while, lost in the color study across the room, trying to figure out what there was to get up for. It was cold and rainy out. Alex had to go up to Gimbels with his Auntie Em to buy summer clothes, and I wasn't sure I could face him anyway. Apollo doesn't usually work on Sundays, and I'm not allowed in the studio when there's no grown-up. Mr. G's store is open, but it's his nephew Babak's day, and he doesn't really like it when I hang out in the store.

I could have gone up to the Met, but it's crowded on weekends and you can't be alone with anything or get far enough away from the paintings to see them without a million people getting in the way. Richard goes to church in Brooklyn on Sundays, and then his family has lunch with his dad-side grand-parents. Sometimes I go with them, but Haitian church is all in French and I didn't have anything to wear and I was still feeling shy around his mom.

So I got up and watched TV instead. Most kids would love a whole day watching TV, but I was bored and wished that someone would yell at me to clean my room.

I did try to clean up, a little. The big room had an unloved feeling about it that bothered me. I thought about how carefully Dr. Charles had rinsed and dried the giant wooden salad bowl after dinner the night before, about the tiny dot of oil she'd rubbed in with a soft cloth until the insides of the bowl were glossy with care. So I got up and pushed some of the clutter in the big room around, but I didn't make much progress.

There were two more hang-ups on the machine, and another message from my mom's gallery. Nothing for me.

I wondered what Lady Day was doing.

I lay down on the couch with my head hanging off the edge until all the blood in my body was in my head. And then I fell asleep.

It's absolutely exhausting, doing nothing all day.

                              ᧫᧫᧫

When I woke up, it was four o'clock. The whole day was almost gone, and I was glad. I went to my mother's door and made myself turn the knob.

The room scared me, filled with long shadows and lumps I couldn't identify.

"Mom," I whispered, sitting down on the edge of the bed. Her long red hair spilled out over the pillow, more witch than mermaid, and her skin looked scarily pale. She didn't move.

"Mom," I whispered again, a little louder. Nothing.

I pushed at her shoulder. "Mom, wake up and talk to me." The way she looked scared me. "Mom?"

My mother opened her eyes slowly, more like she was coming up to the surface than waking up. She shifted around in the bed, her eyes fuzzy and unfocused. "Shhh, Ollie. No noise, okay? I need to sleep."

*All you do is sleep!* I thought. *And it's freaking me out.*

My mom rolled over so that her back was to me. "Are you hungry or something? Why don't you make yourself a grilled cheese?"

"I'm not hungry," I said. Which was true, or maybe not. I couldn't always tell what I was feeling anymore.

Even when my mother was up and about, she wasn't exactly a dinner-on-the-table-at-six kind of mom, but more like a "two o'clock in the morning is a fine time to smash a mirror into tiny pieces so that I can make an empowerment mosaic of a woman's fist in the bathroom" kind of person. My dad was better at what he called the care-and-feeding stuff, but he worked a lot when he was here.

I did know how to make grilled cheese, though. I knew how to make scrambled eggs, too, but I didn't like cleaning the pans afterward; the way the egg clogged up the scrubby sponge grossed me out. So I was eating a lot of apples and buying an extra can of peanuts for myself from Mr. G's.

After another minute, my mom started to close her eyes again. She's not like Linda. She doesn't have thirty-six different questions to ask about protein.

I spoke up, louder than I meant to.

"Mom. What's going on?"

She rubbed a hand across her eyes. "I just can't, Ollie."

*Can't what?* I thought. *Get up? Or explain why you can't?*

"Try," I said, and my voice sounded like Ms. Colantonio's when she means it. But my mom closed her eyes again.

I wasn't sure what to do, so I lay down next to her. Like a lot of lofts, our ceiling is covered in stamped tin, painted white. Mostly, it's an egg and dart pattern, but there was a leak in my mom and dad's room, and the hole was fixed with a different pattern. The patch has pineapples stamped into it, which my dad told me used to be a symbol of hospitality and friendship. It's impossible to make the joins between the ceiling and the repair line up, of course, but I always close one eye and try.

"What about your show? Aren't you excited?"

I could feel her shake her head no.

"Why not?" Her new dealer had told her that there was a lot of demand for her new work. I thought that meant that my parents wouldn't have to fight about money anymore.

I closed my eyes quickly against the thought of money and my dad and everything he might have done for some. My mom's hair smelled dirty.

"What about that new piece you started? With the teabag that looks like a wedding veil?"

She interrupted me, almost mad. "It's just not the art I'm supposed to be making right now."

She was so tired, I wanted to leave her alone, but I needed to know.

"What do you mean?"

She rolled back over to look at me. Even moving that little bit seemed to take a lot out of her.

"Do you remember when Ms. Nora got the caterpillars?"

Of course I remembered. When I was in preschool, we had a fish tank filled with caterpillars. They didn't do anything but eat; Ms. Nora said it was like having teenagers. We basically forgot they were there after they turned into cocoons. Then one day after nap, Sam Weathers noticed a butterfly drying its wings on the metal mesh top of the cage, and Joseph Scarlato saw another one pushing its way out of a cocoon. After that, there was absolutely no point in trying to get the class to sit still for story time.

By the next morning, all of the butterflies had come out, and we took the tank to the park to release them. We ran into my mom on the street on the way there, and Ms. Nora said she could come with us to set them free, even though it wasn't a parent activity.

It was a brilliant, sunny, early spring day. The birds were out, and the trees were filled with new buds, and my chest felt like it would burst because I was the only one who got to hold the hand of my funny, beautiful mom.

When we got to the park, we sat in a circle on the grass, and Ms. Nora took the top off the terrarium. We'd thought the butterflies would fly right out, happy to be free, but that wasn't what happened. Most of them stayed right where they were, in the cage, so my mom taught us a song about shipwrecks and feathers and kitchen chairs while we waited. Then one butterfly flew out, and another, and another—but still, they didn't fly away.

Instead, one by one, they settled into my mom's curly red hair.

The whole class lay down on our backs in the grass, even Ms. Nora. My mom sat in the center, singing folk songs to us about shipwrecks and feathers and kitchen chairs—a queen, crowned by a cloud of contented butterflies, their orange and black wings moving lazily in her wild, beautiful hair.

It was impossible to believe that the person in her bed was the same person.

"Mom," I said. Her eyes were closed again. "*What* about the butterflies?"

She shook her head and sighed, impatient with me. "I'm about to change into something different, that's all. Like the caterpillars did."

That frightened me. "Why? Why do you need to change into something different?"

"It's part of growing up, I guess." Then she put her head back down on her arm and closed her eyes. When I put my arm around her, she pushed it away—not mad, exactly, but like I'd hurt her. So I lay quietly next to her with my hands by my sides, looking at the patch on the ceiling that I could never line up.

I didn't want to stay there in bed with her. I didn't want to leave, either, but eventually I did.

# FREE FALLING

The only thing you can see from the windows in my house is the building right across the street. It looks like ours, six stories tall and dark with city dirt, wearing its own fire escape like the hard jewelry on the girls outside the bars on St. Mark's Place.

You have to go outside if you want to see the sky. So I put one leg up onto the sill for leverage, grabbed both of the brass handles, and rolled up the big windows so I could crawl out.

The rain had stopped, but the sky was grey. Not the shiny grey it turns before a storm, reflective like the inside of an oyster shell, but flat, like an ashtray, like it was stealing the light from everything around it.

Everything I could see was grey. Apollo talks about finding all the colors in a color; he's always showing me the brown and blue in a pink, the green in a deep blue. It was true that the band around the neck of the pigeon on a windowsill across the street had some iridescent purple and green in it, and the gum stains on the patched concrete sidewalk were really battleship blue. But if I'd been drawing my block on that chilly Sunday afternoon, I wouldn't have needed anything but my Blackwing.

I leaned forward so I could see the paste-up of the egg through the bars. The colors had faded, so that it blurred into the wall behind it. One edge had come loose, tattered by the wind. I remembered how happy that artist had been when he'd seen how it looked on the wall, like it was hanging at Joyce Walker's or one of the big-deal galleries on West Broadway. He'd wanted his work to be seen. He'd cared enough to wear a suit and climb that fence. Now it was just more clutter on the street, ugly like the weeds and litter choking the bottom of the barbed wire.

It was time to face facts. My dad probably wasn't coming back. He might even be going to jail. I had a hard time imagining him as a forger; it just didn't seem like something he'd do. But if you'd asked me a couple of weeks ago, I would have told you I couldn't imagine him leaving, either.

Not to mention that my mom wasn't getting better. In fact, with every day, she seemed to be getting worse.

If I turned around, I could see the outlines of her sculpture on the workbench by the window. What had she meant, that she was making the wrong art? My dad would sometimes tell Joyce that he didn't think a young artist had found the right way to say what they had to say. But Joyce always said that the only way forward for those artists was to do the work—to keep making the wrong art, saying even a little piece of what they had to say, getting better and closer all the time.

But my mom wasn't making anything at all. It didn't seem like she could. And I knew what she'd said about growing up was wrong. Plenty of people grew up without going to bed.

A truck, the body covered with graffiti, rumbled down the street and ground to a halt at the loading dock for the textile factory next door. The cab door creaked open and slammed, and then the metal door to the factory. I didn't move. A smashed bottle trapped between the cobblestones glinted up at me like a pirate's gold tooth, the only spot of brightness on the block.

A thick twist of cigarette smoke curled up through the grating, the dirty smell hanging around me like an uninvited guest. I sat out there without moving until I heard the door bang closed again.

It's like I said: Nobody ever looks up.

◆◆◆

When it got too cold on the fire escape, I went inside to find something to eat.

But as the heavy window rolled down behind me and I started to walk across the big room toward the kitchen, the whole world started to spin.

It felt as if the floor was falling out from underneath me, as if I was walking on a tightrope instead of on the floor.

I stopped in my tracks, but that only made it worse. Standing still, I couldn't seem to get my balance at all.

Hunched over and shuffling, I made my way painfully toward the couch, each little step feeling like the next one would pitch me through to the center of the earth. Even though I was looking at the weathered wood floor, feeling it solid and ordinary beneath my feet, I could not convince my brain I wasn't going to fall through.

I have no idea how long it took me to walk the fifteen feet from the window. When I got to the couch, I closed my eyes, grabbed fistfuls of the white cotton sheet covering it to stop my hands from shaking, and breathed in and out as deeply as I could.

"Get it together, Olympia," I told myself sternly. But for a while, there wasn't much I could do except hold on.

When the spinning stopped and I could finally open my eyes again, the world seemed normal. There was the scarred brick wall, painted white, the big nail in it next to the door where I always hung my keys. There was the jam jar on the plywood counter, the one I'd had orange juice from that morning, pulp still sticking to its side. In the far corner, there was my mom's workbench, propped up on two sawhorses. Her sculpture was there, front and center, like it was asking me, *What happens to a person who has to make things, when they don't want to make things anymore?*

My hands finally stopped shaking. I lay there for a while, trying to figure out what had happened to me. Whatever it was, it seemed to have passed.

"See?" the stern part of me said. But the rest of me wasn't so sure.

# SAVING LAMBIE

The next day after school, the boys walked back to Greene Street with me. We were all going to the studio, to do our project on Ancient Egypt.

We always do our art projects at the studio. Dr. and Mr. Charles are supportive of the arts, but Richard's apartment is too small for us to leave a big project out. Alex's house is a loft like mine, except Linda has a hissy fit if you drink a glass of water in there. I can't imagine what she'd do if you got glue on one of her leather sofas, or paint on her refinished floors.

The studio, on the other hand, is already covered in paint and glue and solvent and worse, and my dad and Apollo don't care if it takes you more than one day to finish as long as you're set up somewhere that won't interfere with their work. Plus, the studio comes with everything you could ever need to make something. My dad says that Michelangelo could have made a masterpiece on newspaper he found in the trash, but Apollo says that the proper tools and materials make a good artist better.

First, though, we had to stop at Alex's house. He was going to make a mummy, only because his original idea hadn't worked out. He'd really wanted to make a canopic jar, which is the jar they put your organs in after they've taken them out to mummify you. He'd emptied out the pickle jar he uses at home for loose change, and was going to buy some real livers and kidneys from the meat section at C-Town to put in there, but Ms. Colantonio overheard him telling me about it and cut him off at the pass.

Alex's house is only two blocks away from mine, but his whole block is much cleaner. There's even a store on his block, even though we can't tell what it sells besides lamps and pillows; everything in there is white. Linda is always saying that SoHo real estate is some of the most undervalued property in the city. She calls herself a pioneer. (Say it like she does, without moving your jaw.) But my dad says plenty of people live and work here already; they're just not rich people.

Alex's building has a new coat of dark blue paint, and he has a doorbell and a buzzer system instead of a key you throw down in a tube sock. Alex's dad probably doesn't even own any tube socks, since you can't wear them with a suit.

Richard and I made ourselves comfortable on the loading dock, our legs dangling off the edge, while Alex went up to his house. Neither one of us felt up to dealing with Linda, and we had a lot of work to do on the Transformation section of the Taxonomy.

"I've divided the Transformation section into two parts," Richard explained. "Shapeshifters can go back and forth. After a Metamorphosis, you're stuck." Then he told me a story about a guy turning into a roach, but I didn't want to hear about it, so he gave me some torn-out pictures to copy instead.

I nearly jumped out of my skin when *boom!* Alex landed next to me. He likes to jump the whole last flight of stairs from the landing. Sometimes he props the door open at the bottom and lands in a roll.

With a flourish, he popped up and pulled a stuffed animal out from under his shirt, waving it at me and Richard.

"Ta-da," he said. "Meet my mummy."

I don't usually like to give Alex the satisfaction of a reaction, but I couldn't get ahead of the look of shock that crept across my face.

"Holy cow, Alex," I said, my lips thick with horror. "You can't mummify Lambie."

Lambie is Maggie's favorite stuffed animal, the one she's slept with every single night since she was born. Losing Lambie is right up there next to Getting Enough Protein in Linda's Personal List of Things to Worry About. She'd been so freaked that something would happen to Lambie that she went back to the store where they'd got her and bought a spare, but Maggie took one look at the imposter and pushed it out the window of the Fourteenth Street crosstown bus.

"Not Lambie," she'd said, before putting her thumb back in her mouth.

That had been a couple of years ago, and Maggie was nine now, but Lambie was still her most important toy. If Alex mummified Lambie, Maggie was going to lose her mind. And I didn't even want to think about what Linda would do.

I tried to communicate this to Alex. "If you mummify Maggie's lamb," I told him, "it's gonna be your organs in a jar." Frankly, I was worried about my own organs, too. Linda is always on the lookout for bad influences.

Alex held Lambie tighter and stuck out his chin. A bad sign.

I stole a look at Richard. I was hoping that he understood the gravity of the situation, but you can't always tell what Richard is thinking. I watched as he reached out with great deliberation and took Lambie out of Alex's hands. He tilted his head and turned her around slowly, looking at her carefully from every angle. Her fur was matted and sparse, and the stuffing was long gone from her ears and legs, leaving them floppy and chunking up the center of her. She was well loved, that was for sure.

When Richard spoke, it was with great authority. "The real problem is that this won't make a good mummy, Alex." He shook his head, and then shook poor bedraggled Lambie, gently and with regret. "It's going to look like a mummified dog. If your mummy is going to be convincing, you need to start out with a stuffed animal that's shaped more like a person."

I knew from Apollo and the story of Egyptian brown that the Egyptians had mummified their animals, too, but I kept my mouth shut, holding my breath. There was a long, terrible pause, the three of us looking at Lambie, limp and defenseless in Richard's hands. Then I guess Alex saw Richard's logic, because he grabbed the scruffy toy and stormed back upstairs.

A couple of minutes later, he appeared, defiant, with another stuffed animal from Maggie's stash. This one was a stiff, demented-looking pink bunny with buck teeth made out of scratchy felt and oversized plastic eyes that had been glued on crooked. It was horrible, the kind of stuffed animal you win at a street fair at the shooting game after you've had zeppole and then throw in the garbage an hour later because you're tired of carrying it around and want to get cotton candy.

I hoped it wasn't another one of Maggie's favorites. Frankly, I didn't see how it could be.

"This is a much better choice," Richard said, examining it closely before nodding his satisfaction.

I exhaled: He'd saved Lambie.

Alex grunted and set off down Mercer toward my house, tucking the bunny backward under his arm so that its horrible, violent-criminal bug eyes leered back at me the whole way.

# FIELD OF REEDS

With Lambie safe from mummification, I was free to go back to thinking about my own project.

The week before, Ms. Colantonio had taken our whole class to the Metropolitan Museum of Art to see the mummies. On the way up there, I'd sat next to Alex on the bus. Field trips are good for Alex, what with the moving around and all.

"What's this?" I asked, opening the paper bag he'd brought for lunch and sniffing suspiciously at a log of something wrapped in brown waxed paper.

"A granola bar? With spelt? And maybe carob?" he said unhappily as I took a cautious bite, then leaned back against the ripped vinyl seat to look out the window.

"Remember that playground your dad used to take us to up here?" he asked me.

But I could only nod because there was no talking around

the horrible ball of toenails and sawdust in my mouth. I don't see what Linda could possibly get out of making such a hurtful snack.

I did remember, though. My dad used to take Alex and me to the Met every Saturday. In the morning, we'd look at art, my dad keeping up with Alex so I could stop to sketch whatever I wanted to. (I was into the Dutch Masters then.) For lunch, we'd get a hot dog from the cart outside—two, sometimes three for Alex, and a pretzel with mustard for me if they looked soft and not stale. Then we'd spend the whole afternoon in the enormous new Egyptian-themed playground next to the museum. My dad used to say cheerfully it was so big that if we ever got kidnapped, it would take him an hour to notice we were gone.

Thinking about those Saturdays made my dad seem so close that I took a deep breath, as if I might catch a whiff of soap and leather. But the bus smelled like dirty metal and old gum, the way every school bus smells.

For years, Alex and I had played the same game every week at that playground next to the Met. I don't remember whose idea it was originally, or how we came up with the rules. There was no way to win or lose: The only goal of the game was to avoid all contact with other human beings. It was like hide-and-seek, except we were a team, and the people we were trying to hide from didn't know they were playing.

We'd spend hours in that playground on Saturday afternoons, ducking around corners, disappearing through the sprinklers, laying ourselves flat against the sun-warmed walls of the concrete pyramids. At the beginning, we used gestures to signal to each other, crashing back into the cement tunnels whenever we saw someone, our hearts in our mouths as if we were being chased. Eventually, though, the slightest lean was enough to tell the other person it was time to melt back against the stone.

The bus carrying our class pulled up outside the school tour entrance to the Metropolitan Museum of Art, which is much less impressive than the real entrance with all the stairs. As the teachers herded the class off the bus, Alex and I both looked over toward the playground, but the whole museum was between it and us.

Off the bus now, we lined up with our backs against the museum wall to count off.

"You think he's ever going to come home?" Alex asked me.

It hadn't occurred to me that Alex would be missing my dad, too. But of course he did. After those long Saturday afternoons, my dad would laugh with approval and say, "That boy needs to be run like a big dog." Alex's energy had never gotten on my dad's nerves the way it seemed to get on Linda's.

But it was already our turn. Next to Alex, Vivian Yi called out, "Nine."

"Ten," Alex said, still waiting for an answer.

"Eleven," I said.

"Twelve," muttered Lady Day Rodriguez, who does not appreciate being herded.

"Thirteen," hollered Rowan Merody, making sure to be louder than Alex.

"Fourteen," Richard said absentmindedly, after Rowan bumped his arm.

And so it went until it was time for the class to turn around and walk in twos into the museum. Ms. Colantonio had separated Manny Weber and Javadi Awad for slap fighting during the count-off, so I was paired with Lady Day, leaving Alex with Vivian.

That was a relief to me, because I had absolutely no idea what to say to Alex.

I didn't think my dad was going to come home. I didn't think my mom was going to get up. And I had absolutely no idea what was going to happen next.

                             ~~~

The museum, at least, was a distraction.

The Egyptian gods of the dead were terrifying, and mummification was incredibly gross. The guide didn't have any trouble keeping order; I hadn't seen my class this interested in anything since Mr. Dawson had let us look at snot under the microscope.

There was only one sixth-grader who wasn't interested in the gory details of how you wrapped a dead guy in papyrus, and that was me. The whole time we were there, I couldn't stop thinking about Egyptian brown.

"No leaning on the cases," a guard with a caterpillar on his upper lip barked at me, as if I'd been leaning on purpose instead of letting people push their way in front of me as I made my way to the back of the room.

Irritated, I gave his mustache a long look before turning around to see exactly what it was that I'd bumped into.

Behind me was a series of glass cases at waist level. Inside the low cases were five boxes, about the size of lunchroom trays, filled with little people and objects and animals. They were models, like dollhouses, except they were open at the top instead of on the sides.

I looked around quickly, then leaned down to get as close to the glass-topped boxes as I could without making the guard with the awful mustache yell at me again.

The first model was a barn. A black-and-white cow was lying down, a man kneeling at its head with his hand outstretched to feed it. I got so close that my breath fogged the glass of the case. There was another cow, too, standing up, and I almost laughed out loud when I saw the expression on her face: She was bored!

The artist who made that cow lived ten thousand years before me. But it might as well have been yesterday, the way she or he had used the expression on that bored cow's face to reach forward through space and time to share a joke with a kid in 1981.

I heard the guide telling our class about Anubis, the jackal-headed god of embalming, but I didn't hear Lady Day come up quietly behind me. Checking first for the guard, she leaned in close to the little case, too.

"They're like dollhouses, right?" I whispered. "What do you think they are?"

Lady Day didn't even need to look at the information card next to the case. "Kings were buried with everything they'd want to have in the afterlife—real food, chariots, boats, jewels. Even servants." She snorted in disgust. "They *murdered* people, just so they wouldn't have to wash dishes after they were dead."

I bet that wasn't on the card.

"Anyway, rich people copied the kings by being buried with models of the things they'd need. That's what these are."

I guess I looked surprised by how much she knew because she said carelessly, "My dad's a guard up here. Islam and the Asian galleries now, but he worked Egypt for a couple of years."

I lifted my head. The guide was telling our group about how the Egyptians stored the mummified corpse's organs in a canopic jar. (This was where Alex had gotten the idea for his first project.)

But Lady Day wasn't done. "These were only found by accident. The grave had been robbed, way back in Egyptian times, and the archaeologists who found it thought there wouldn't be anything valuable left. But someone from this museum went back to make a map of the site, and he stumbled into a hidden room, totally untouched, with these models in it." She sounded proud. "It was a real find."

A thrill went up me. A hidden room filled with treasure in a robbed tomb—that was better than one of Alex's mysteries.

Lady Day leaned close again and pointed into one of the boxes, her finger a careful millimeter from the glass.

"This is a place to store grain." Some of the little people in the model were carrying big sacks of flour; others were making notes on tiny pieces of real linen. "They're making sure the dead man will have enough food in the afterlife." She moved over so I could see into the next box. "This is a bakery, so the dead can have freshly baked bread in the afterlife." She smiled a little, remembering. "It's a brewery, too. My dad said it wouldn't be heaven without beer."

Before leaning over the next model, the box with the cows, Lady Day checked my face to make sure I wasn't bored. Then she pointed to the lying-down cow they were feeding by hand. "This guy's too fat to get up." The lying-down cow was another joke.

I flipped over the boring fill-in-the-blank question sheet they'd given us at the beginning of the tour—"_____ is the process the Egyptians used to preserve bodies after death"— so I could sketch. My pencil moved so fast, the paper was covered before I knew it.

The last box was a garden lined with trees, with terracotta tiles on the floor and a fountain in the center. Lady Day stood looking at it for a long time. She was even taller and skinnier than Alex, I realized. "This one is a garden, but there's no food growing or anything. I think it's just a place to hang out."

She was going to say more, but Ms. Colantonio had appeared behind us. I was worried she'd be mad we hadn't been listening to the guide, although unfortunately I had not been able to avoid the part about how the embalmers broke up the corpse's brain with a long metal hook and then pulled it out through his nose.

But our teacher was looking with interest into the model garden. She pretended to offer me her arm. "Care for a stroll under the sycamores, miss? A snack of figs and honey? Or a game of checkers by the pool?"

Then she held out some of the extra question sheets to me, blank-side up so I could keep drawing.

"Olympia, it looks like you've found your project. Lady Day, I will expect great things, per usual." She turned to join the group. "Catch up when you're done, okay?"

After she'd gone, Lady Day drifted away, too; a statue in a case nearby had caught her attention. I kept drawing. I drew the little bakers, their forearms white with flour, and the tiny loaves of bread they were kneading. I drew a man kneeling patiently in front of the round black oven, waiting for the next loaf to be done. I drew another tiny man, his arms curving gracefully around the wooden urn of beer he was pouring into a bigger barrel. I drew the fat cow, and the bored one. And I drew the garden, each tile meticulous in miniature, so tranquil and cool.

As I drew, I could hear the guide telling the class about Osiris, god of the dead, who greeted the newly dead by weighing their hearts. If your heart was light enough, you could go on to the Field of Reeds, which was just like regular life, except without anything to worry about. But if your heart was heavier than the Feather of Truth, then the Devourer of the Dead got to eat your heart, and you were declared completely dead.

I wondered what made someone's heart heavier than the Feather of Truth.

Eventually, the guide moved on to the next case, and I had to abandon my models to rejoin the class. But the sketches I'd made were good. On the bus ride home, while the boys talked about brains in jars like it was Christmas morning and Jennifer Kernicke got so freaked out about Osiris she convinced herself she was going to throw up and then had to go sit up front with Ms. Colantonio, I sat next to Lady Day, going through them again, adding details as I remembered them. Sketching next to Lady Day also meant I didn't have to talk to Alex about my dad.

I couldn't wait to get to the studio. For my project, I was going to make my own model of everything I'd need in the Field of Reeds—an afterlife just like my real life, but without anything to worry about.

# NO ANSWER

There was no music on in the studio when the three of us got there.

Apollo bowed to Alex and Richard. "This is an unexpected pleasure, gentlemen. Welcome." He turned to me. "Olympia, have I lost track of time? Is it one of our days?" I come in after school sometimes, to organize shelves or fold rags. Apollo and I used to mix colors together, but we hadn't since my dad had gone.

I shook my head. "No, but we have an art project to do. Is it okay if we do it here?"

"Please do. I will enjoy the company." He looked at me, making me the host. "Ask if you need help finding something?" That's the best thing about Apollo: He doesn't hang off you, trying to help like other grown-ups do.

I watched him as he turned away. I bet he knew what my dad was up to. And I bet he didn't like it any more than I did.

Richard was studying Apollo closely, too, but lost love isn't like chicken pox. You can't see when someone has it.

The phone rang, and Apollo picked it up. I got too close trying to eavesdrop, so Apollo covered the receiver and told me to scoot, but not before I'd heard him telling the person on the line—more than once—that their piece wasn't ready. I also heard the words "delays," and "unexpected complications," and that worried me, too. Apollo had been at the studio a lot, and he hadn't been making his own art at all, but I had no idea if he could do everything that needed to get done for the business without my dad.

I went to help Alex and Richard, but we'd done so many projects there that they knew the rules already. Keep an organized workspace and be respectful of your tools. Don't grind the brushes. Clean and dry the ones you use and return them to their places every night, even if you're planning to take them out again the next day. And if you use a flammable solvent to thin paint, like linseed oil or turpentine, soak the rags you use in a bucket of water before leaving them to dry. Most people don't let kids use real solvents because they're flammable and not good for your lungs. But my dad and Apollo are okay with it, as long as you follow the rules. And none of us mind following the rules, mostly because they're all the same rules that my dad and Apollo follow, too.

Collecting my own supplies, I imagined how satisfying it would be to show the studio to Lady Day. Richard and Alex have been my best friends forever, but they don't really get art.

Apollo was still on the phone; I couldn't hear what he was

saying, but I could hear his answers getting shorter and tighter. Eventually, he hung up, but the big black earpiece had barely landed back on the receiver before the telephone rang again.

Apollo grabbed it. "Restoration," he muttered between gritted teeth.

That conversation was shorter, and loud enough for me to hear. "As I have told you many times now, I am not in possession of this piece of art. However, this *is* a place of business, and your pestering is intrusive. I must ask you to stop these calls."

I froze in place as he slammed the earpiece down without waiting for a reply.

The forgery expert, looking for that piece of missing art.

Missing, like my dad.

Apollo went over to where Richard was sitting with a bummed-out expression on his face.

"He doesn't know what he's going to do for his project," I explained, still watching Apollo's face for clues, though he'd wiped his expression back to a careful neutral.

Apollo listened to Alex explain the assignment, as if Richard's project idea was the most important problem he'd deal with all day. He couldn't fool me; I knew all about the power of distraction.

When Alex was done, Apollo shrugged. "This is easy. Richard will make a monster. Of course."

Richard looked up, a little hopeful despite himself. "I'm not that good at making stuff. Also, it needs to be Egyptian."

"Yes, I understand," Apollo said, standing and swinging a big, water-damaged book of Egyptian art down from the bookshelf over Richard's head.

Richard opened the heavy cover and began flipping through the rippled pages, not convinced.

"Look." Apollo stopped the turning page with one finger, pointing at a statue with the head of a hippo, the arms and legs of a lion, the back and tail of a crocodile, and a gigantic pregnant belly. The caption said she was Taweret, the goddess of fertility and childbirth.

She was definitely close enough to a monster to be of interest to Richard. Unfortunately, she also had huge saggy boobs.

"I can't," Richard said, in a strangled kind of voice.

"Well, perhaps not that one exactly," Apollo said, separating some pages that the water had stuck together, stopping when we could hear them tear. "But we are on the right track, I think."

The phone rang again, insistent and loud. I got up to answer it, but as soon as I stood, Apollo told me sharply to leave it alone.

I sat down again next to Alex. The phone rang—five, ten, twenty times, which meant the answering machine was off, which meant that Apollo didn't want to deal with messages.

Then it stopped.

Ignoring the phone, Apollo flipped through a few more water-damaged pages. "What about this gentleman?"

He'd stopped at a full-page photograph of a wall painting featuring a sun god called Khepri. A shiver ran down my spine at the sight of him. Khepri had a man's body, but there was only a black scarab beetle where his head should have been: an eyeless mask split down the middle, with long antennae curving out from the side like horns.

Apollo was right: Khepri could have been ripped straight out of the pages of the Taxonomy.

Richard was chewing the inside of his lip and nodding. "I could make a maquette," he said under his breath. Maquettes are scale models; people who make monsters for the movies are obsessed with them.

"Good," Apollo said, pointing at me and Alex with his chin. "So. The two of you go ahead and get started. I will help Richard with the papier-mâché." But Alex waved me off as he went around the studio collecting supplies; he never wants help with anything.

The phone rang again. I looked over at Apollo, who looked away. Richard and Alex watched him uneasily as the harsh bell rang out, over and over again, into the big space.

Eventually the ringing stopped, and I was relieved, even though I knew it did not erase the problem of Antonin Grandjean.

Or the problem of whatever it was that my dad had done.

# BUNNY MUMMY

When Richard was set up, Apollo handed me a flat box filled with small tools he thought might help me work the clay—skinny picks with wedges at the ends and little bits of wire, as well as a few shreds of bubble wrap I could rest the pieces on while I was working on their other sides.

The best tool for carving turned out to be an ordinary yellow pushpin; the colored plastic hat on top made a handle and meant I could be very precise.

Even so, it's hard to make things so small. Richard and Alex and I worked for a couple of hours, long enough for the light coming through the big windows in the studio to turn blue and then black. The phone rang a few more times. Eventually, Apollo unplugged it from the jack in the wall, but I wasn't sure he wanted me to notice that.

When he threw the switch for the overheads, I straightened up and blinked hard. My back was sore, my eyes were blurry, and my hands felt crampy and tight. Richard and Alex shuffled in next to me, looking at their sneakers and trying not to laugh.

"Here, Ollie. We made you something for your model," Alex said, stifling a laugh before dropping something into my hand. He'd rolled a long, skinny strip of toilet paper into a little toilet paper roll. "You wouldn't want to be without that in the afterlife." He could barely get the words out, he was laughing so much. "Eternity's a pretty long time without any TP."

Richard was behind him, snickering, too. He usually acts more mature than Alex, but a sixth-grade boy is a sixth-grade boy. I placed the toilet paper roll next to the pile of objects I'd already made without saying anything. I knew from experience that there was no point in getting into it with them. But I did think—not for the first time— that it might be nice to be friends with a girl for a change.

From across the room, Apollo announced that he was ready for a break. He turned on some more lights before heading over to the hot plate to put the kettle on for tea. The boys were both finished. While we waited for the water to boil, we all went over to look at what they had done.

Richard's scarab-god looked great. He's not particularly artistic by nature, which is why I have to do the drawings in the Taxonomy, but he'd given the maquette a real personality. He'd painted Khepri's robe in the jewel tones the Egyptians would have used: a deep red and a bright, sunny yellow with cobalt and turquoise accents. The black scarab head, still wet with paint, made the god look both majestic and menacing.

I was impressed, and I said so.

"Ray Harryhausen says—" Richard started, stopping to scowl at Alex, who was making a face. Ray Harryhausen designed the monsters for *Clash of the Titans*, which Richard has seen twelve times.

Ignoring Alex, Richard continued. "Ray Harryhausen says that when you're designing a monster, you have to think about the way a lion can look noble or terrifying or even cute, depending on what's it doing." He stopped to see if we were making fun of him, then continued. "He says if an audience can't imagine your monster sleeping, then you haven't made a real monster."

"Then you have indeed made a real monster," Apollo said, and Richard dropped his head with a shy smile. I was happy for him. His Khepri maquette was excellent work.

Alex's bunny mummy, on the other hand, was a complete disaster.

I couldn't do anything but stare at it. Nobody else said a word, either. I think we were too impressed by the sheer awfulness of it to speak.

The rabbit looked even more deranged than it had before Alex wrapped it in layers of saggy toilet paper, grey from his dirty hands. For some reason, it was wearing a bandit's mask, so that it looked like Zorro, if Zorro had been terribly burned in a garbage can fire, then bandaged up in Scott brand single-ply.

I couldn't take my eyes off it.

Our silence made Alex aggressive. "See? It's got a death mask," he said, poking at its eye area. "Like King Tut."

A traitorous bubble of laughter rose in my chest. I pushed it down.

Apollo opened his mouth, then closed it again. He believes in being diplomatic, but he doesn't like to lie. Finally he said, "Your greatest talents, Alex, are in the realm of the physical. Perhaps next time you should research Egyptian movement. They were great martial artists, I believe."

One of the bunny mummy's nylon whiskers was sticking out, like it was smoking a cigarette. I put my hand in my jeans pocket to stop myself from tucking the whisker back in.

The big bubble of laughter down below sent a little exploratory giggle up to my throat to see if it was safe to come out yet.

I fought it down again, only barely this time.

Then the worst thing happened. Richard took the bunny reverently from Alex and held it up out in front of himself, nodding and turning slowly like he was an Egyptian priest. "Thank you, Alex," he said in a solemn voice. "You have speeded this rabbit's journey to the afterlife."

Alex looked furious. The big bubble percolated up in my chest again, treacherous this time.

Then Alex shook his head and the corner of his mouth lifted in a half-smile. Even that little bit of encouragement was dangerous, and I bit my cheek hard, still not sure it was okay to laugh.

Unfortunately, it was too late.

Apollo let rip a huge, snorting guffaw at the exact moment that I made eye contact with Richard.

After that, there was no turning back. I laughed until I cried, until my stomach hurt, until I wished I could stop so I could get a proper breath. Richard put his head down on the stainless table, shoulders shaking, strange animal sounds coming from underneath his hands. Every time I'd start to wind down, I'd look over at Apollo, bent over with his hands on his knees, tears streaming from his eyes, and I'd be right back where I started: gasping for breath and trying not to wet my pants.

The whistle of the kettle only made us crack up harder. Alex looked back and forth between the three of us and the mummified rabbit in amazed irritation, and when Apollo lay down, weeping with laughter and kicking his heels against the floor of the studio, Alex took the bunny and chucked it at him.

It didn't seem to hurt a bit.

~~~

The smoking bunny mummy joined us for tea, of course.

Still wiping his eyes, Apollo pulled a carton of milk out of the little fridge where he and my dad keep some of the more delicate adhesives, putting it down next to the chipped white sugar bowl which was marked, like everything else in the studio, with little dabs and fingerprints of paint. He put out a sleeve of Pecan Sandies, too. Alex always searched, but he never could find Apollo's secret cookie stash. I made sure to snake my hand in there to score three before the boys grabbed them all.

It had taken us all a while to calm down. My belly ached from laughing, and there was a clear, light feeling in my chest that hadn't been there before.

When the pot was empty, Richard set his cup to the side and cleared his throat significantly.

"We're trying to solve a mystery," he said to Apollo.

Apollo said, "Of course. A young man will take on any challenge to win the heart of a beautiful maiden." He winked at me, then at Alex.

Alex practically fell backward in panic.

"Wait, what? No, that's not it at all."

Richard, who has an easier time telling when Apollo is teasing, picked up the ball. "Is that your personal quest, Apollo? To find a beautiful maiden?"

"Well, sure," he said, smiling. "Always. But surely you know that it is not the point to solve the mystery—to find the missing statue or the blueprints or even the beautiful maiden. The search for her sets the plot in motion, but finding her is never really the point."

Alex looked exasperated. "If the point of the mystery isn't to solve the mystery, then what is?"

Apollo looked into the chipped mug still wrapped in his mammoth hand. "The mystery, my friend, provides an opportunity for the hero to find out who he is." He inclined his head in my direction apologetically. "Who *she* is."

"That makes absolutely no sense," Alex said peevishly, but I wasn't sure.

"It's a way for a hero to find out what's really, truly important,"

Apollo explained, in the dangerous tone that usually meant he was settling into a lecture. But I was wrong. Suddenly, he was wearing the same sad, handsome look on his face I'd seen when we were at Hwa Yuan. "Which might be something as simple as finding a way to be in the world without causing harm to yourself or other people."

I looked at Alex and Richard, but they looked as confused as I felt. We weren't getting anywhere. The mummified bunny, propped up against the paint-scarred sugar bowl, tilted dangerously to one side.

Maybe the stupid rabbit was Apollo's True Lost Love.

Impatient with all of them, I got up to take my cup to the sink. This roundabout questioning was a dead end. If we couldn't figure out how to get Apollo talking about his True Lost Love, then I might as well get back to work. The boys were done with their projects already, but I had a couple of hours left for sure.

On the way back over to my workspace, though, I practically tripped over a box sitting, ready to go, by the door. This was unusual. The studio might look like a mess, but it's actually quite orderly; everything has a place, even if it's paint-spotted. Apollo would never leave a client's work out in the middle of the floor, and it wasn't a supply delivery; those always went to the table by the far wall if they couldn't be unpacked right away.

I knew I shouldn't pry, but my curiosity got the better of me. Taking a quick look around to make sure Apollo was still sitting with the boys at the table, I eased a finger under one of the flaps.

There were jars in the box, twenty or thirty of them, each of them with a label written in Apollo's spiked black handwriting.

Jars, filled with pigments. A box of colors.

The blood rushed in my ears. Still squatting, I looked quickly at the pantry in the corner. The bottom five shelves were bare.

He was packing up his colors. And if I knew anything, I knew this: If his colors were going, Apollo was going, too.

# DRAW WHAT YOU SEE

I hardly even noticed when Richard and Alex said goodbye before heading home. I still had work to do, even if the upside-down feeling in my belly showed no signs of going away.

Apollo had put his Walkman back on after he'd cleaned up the tea things, and was back at work on the triangle painting. I could hear trumpet leaking out from around his headphones.

I headed back to my workspace and leaned in to arrange the pieces I'd made.

I placed my desk against the wall of the clean white painted box and my bed under the window, exactly as they were upstairs. I'd made myself an open notebook, which I put on the floor, plus a box of Blackwings. Apollo always made sure I had a fresh box of pencils, but I figured he'd probably have better things to think about in the afterlife.

Not to mention that I couldn't be sure he was going to stick around.

I'd also made a tiny toothbrush and a full tube of toothpaste, because I hate, hate, hate going to bed without brushing my teeth. If the Field of Reeds was going to be like real life except without anything to worry about, then I needed to bring a toothbrush, or that feeling would bug me for eternity.

I had the basics: an afterlife survival kit. But the model still didn't feel done.

I unwrapped a new piece of modeling clay, working it between my fingers to soften it.

I'd seen an orange bike with a banana seat and streamers on the handlebars in a movie once; I could bring one of those. (Bikes probably didn't get stolen in the Field of Reeds.) I could make a chest, spilling over with a million dollars in gold coins. I could make Alex a Pac-Man arcade game, like the one at Joe's Pizza. Actually, if Alex was going to visit, I should probably make a whole stack of pizza boxes and a freezer filled with ice cream.

I pushed the clay into different shapes as the ideas came, but nothing worked—probably because I didn't want to bring a bike, or a million gold coins, or a whole afterlife's worth of pizza.

What I wanted to bring was my mom and dad.

I could picture exactly how I'd make my mom's long red curls, my dad's stubbly face and faded jeans, the three of us sprawled on the couch watching the Saturday night movie with our sock feet touching. But my fingers wouldn't cooperate. The figures I made, over and over again, turned out thick and misshapen—ugly little dolls. They didn't look like my parents at all.

I closed my eyes in frustration and thought about what my

dad would say if a drawing I was working on wasn't working.

"Really *look*," he'd say. "Draw what you see, not what you think you see."

I tossed the ball of clay onto the stainless worktable, where it landed with a flat *thunk*. That was why I couldn't make my parents watching TV with me like they wanted to be a family, forever and ever—because it wasn't *true*.

Why would they want to be together in the afterlife, when they didn't want to be together in real life? They weren't happily watching TV on a Saturday night with me, feet up on the steamer trunk. My mother had gone to bed, and my dad was on the lam, a criminal.

I thought about the phone, fruitlessly ringing out into the vast space of the studio. I thought about my mom, unmoving in her bed upstairs. I saw the forgery expert's business card, dropping to the stained concrete.

And then, for one horrible moment, I allowed myself to imagine what my life would be like if Apollo left me, too. The loneliness that crowded in was almost unbearable. The dizziness that had made me feel like I was going to fall through the wood floor rushed at me, so that the ground felt like it was falling away.

I opened my eyes and picked up the clay again.

I didn't want my parents with me in the afterlife if they weren't going to be happy. But I did want them with me.

On the bus ride back from the museum, Lady Day had told me that poorer Egyptians who couldn't afford full-on models drew symbols on the walls of their tombs to represent the things they wanted to bring. They might paint a picture of a cow to represent meat, for instance, or a stringed instrument to guarantee that they'd have music in the afterlife.

I stretched my back again, rolling my neck and shoulders, and then I quickly shaped a little coffee cup with the outline of a Greek temple on it, like the one on the WILD TIMES poster. I rolled out another little tube of clay and made a can of Tab, the distinctive logo etched into the side. (This came out even better than I'd hoped.)

After those were done, I made a tiny replica of Apollo's favorite teapot, the one with the hay-colored stripes and the straight, sloping sides. Then I lined the three symbols up on the model's miniature desk.

I took my brush and tools over to the double sink to let the warm water run over them. I massaged the stuck bits of clay off with my fingers, watching as it turned to reddish-brown mud and ran down the drain. I wiped the wide stainless-steel table, then used the heavy broom to sweep a pile of discarded clay bits into the dustpan, leaning the handle against my shoulder to steady it. I cleaned until everything was orderly again and it was time to go.

At the door, I stopped to look back at Apollo, who was still working on the triangle painting and occasionally playing an invisible solo along with the music pumping out of the bright yellow Walkman clipped to his belt. When you're on a roll, my dad says, it's best to see it through.

He gave me a smile and a wave goodbye, and I waved back. All I could do was hope that I wasn't saying goodbye to him forever.

# LEAVE IT

School on Thursday was hard. I couldn't concentrate on a thing anyone said.

The thought of Apollo leaving filled my brain, pushing out all the other thoughts. Where was he going? Why was he going away? Was it because my dad had deserted him?

Was it because of what my dad had done?

The third time Ms. Colantonio caught me spacing out, she sent me to the nurse's office. I told the nurse that there wasn't anything wrong with me, but she said I didn't look right and put me on her cot to rest. I lay there and painted the pieces for my model in my mind while she did paperwork and gave out Band-Aids and checked a third grader for lice. It was pretty relaxing, actually, and I felt a little better by dismissal.

I rushed back to the studio after school, ready to paint. Apollo wasn't there, but he'd left a note on the door saying it was okay for me to go in without him. I went downstairs and got the key from the nail in the wall by our front door. But before I could get back to work on my model, I knew I had to go in to see my mom.

I sat on the couch for a little bit to gather my courage. Every day, it had gotten harder to go in there and pretend that everything was okay. Sometimes I even thought it would be easier to let her door stay closed. But some part of me knew it wouldn't, not really.

So I stood up, took a deep breath, and made myself open the door to her room.

The figure in the bed was faded, bleached out, like the cover of a book left on the windowsill too long.

"Mom," I whispered, but she didn't stir.

I sagged in the doorway. The room was a disaster. Litter covered the floor in drifts. There was a smell, too, of unclean sheets and full ashtrays and something else I couldn't identify and wasn't sure I wanted to.

Leaning there against the door jamb, a vision of Dr. Charles flashed into my head, the way she'd run her palms over the immaculate counter, checking for any last sneaky crumbs. "Kitchen closed," she'd said with a smile at me before turning out the cozy light over the stove.

Maybe I couldn't make my mom get up out of bed, but I could make it a little nicer for her to be in there.

Charged up with energy suddenly, I got a couple of deli bags from my dad's stash under the kitchen sink. As quietly as I could, I emptied the big ashtrays by my mom's bed. Ashes rose out of the bag in a grey cloud, covering my tongue with grit. When the first bag was full, I tied it tightly at the top and filled another one with Tab cans and empty cigarette packs and tissues, and then another. My mother didn't move.

Once I could see parts of the floor again, I started to enjoy myself. Cleaning made me feel brisk and efficient and competent, like a nurse in the war movies I used to watch with my dad, the kind of person who would go around saying things like "You'll be right as rain in no time, Corporal." I could almost see my crisp white uniform, feel the bounce of my clean curls under a tiny cap.

"A breath of fresh air, that one," I imagined an old-timer with one leg saying appreciatively as I carried the dirty dishes and old coffee cups and glasses into the kitchen. Some of the dishes had been sitting there for so long that the gunk at the bottom had hardened like paint. I filled the bottom of the sink with hot soapy water so they could soak.

It felt so good to be doing something that I tried not to think about the way those movies always ended: with the brave, kind nurse coming in one morning to find an empty bed, sheets neatly folded where the corporal used to be.

When I went back into my mom's room, the stale fug in the air hit me again. With a little grunt, I got the sticky window open a crack.

My mom woke up with a start.

"Leave it, for God's sake," she mumbled. "Just leave it." She didn't take her face out of the pillow to look at me.

I tried to sound upbeat. "It's no trouble. I thought I'd tidy up a little."

There was no answer from the bed.

I tried again, my cheerful voice cracking a little. "It's gotten pretty stuffy in here." And I leaned over to pick up a stained white T-shirt from where it was lying in a tangle under the bed.

"*Leave it,*" she hissed, raising up halfway on her elbows.

Rage distorted her face. She looked like she hated me.

For a minute it looked like she was going to hit me, and the shock of it pushed me back. Then I wished she would; it would have been worth it, to see her get up. But she dropped back onto the greasy pillow, her face in a crumple, and I looked away fast so I wouldn't have to see her so scared.

Two guys were unloading crates outside the button factory. I could hear the hundreds of little wheels turning as the heavy boxes shuttled down the slanted belt into the basement hatch.

"Olympia, go. Get out of here." There was no harshness in my mom's voice anymore, only exhaustion.

Desperation surged through me. "Mom, please. You have to get up. Will you get up? Please?" Another box rattled down the ramp.

My mom barely had the energy to shake her head no.

"You're better off without me." Her voice was a whisper.

"Please don't say that. It's not true." Salt dripped into my mouth. I hadn't even known that I was crying.

I allowed myself to imagine her bent in concentration over her workbench, her strong hands making something beautiful out of all this bad feeling. "What about your show?" I asked, but even before the sentence was all the way out of my mouth, I knew it was impossible.

She shook her head. "I don't make anything anymore." And her voice was bleak as she said, "This is no place for a kid, with me like this. You should go be with your dad now."

I was crying in earnest now. "No, please. I don't want to go to France. I don't want to do anything except be here with you. You don't have to get up; you don't have to do anything. Just tell me what to do, and I'll do it."

But she had already turned away.

I was afraid to stay, but afraid to go too far away, too, so I banged my way out of the room and sank to the floor outside, pressing my back against the closed door. I sat outside my mom's room for a long time, hugging my legs tight, wiping the snot and tears that wouldn't stop coming onto the knees of my jeans.

Inside, I could hear my mom sobbing, too, crying so bitterly I knew I would never be able to comfort her. Nobody would.

# MIZ MONOCHROME

It was almost dark when I got back upstairs to the studio.

*Field of Reeds*, I chanted under my breath as I unlocked the big steel door with shaking hands. *Field of Reeds*. Every bit of me concentrated on what it would feel like to lose myself in working on my model in the quiet, paint-splashed organization of the studio.

I knew it was stupid, but I felt like getting the model right might fix something.

*An afterlife just like real life, except without anything to worry about.*

Apollo had left a battered metal tray by my workstation with a note, a large yogurt container filled with white paint, and an open box of butter cookies next to a clean mug with a fresh tea bag in it.

Suddenly ravenous, I ate the cookies while I read the note.

*Olympia*, the note read in Apollo's strong, slanted handwriting. *This is nice primer. A coat before you paint will help your colors to stay true. Take a break for tea! (And don't forget to turn off the hot plate.)*

*Love, A*

My eyes welled up again.

After a while, it was a relief to turn back to my model, to the collection of little pieces waiting for paint. I arranged the notebook, the pencils, the little toothbrush. I'd have everything I needed. My mom and dad and Apollo were there, too—or their stand-in drinks, anyway.

But something was still missing.

Looking into the models at the Met, I'd felt like I was *there*. I could practically smell the fresh bread in the air and the prickly, yeasty smell of the beer, see the motes of grain sifting down through the sunlight as the model servant crushed his pestle into the nutty grains. I could smell the cows, hear them chewing, feel the warm terracotta tiles of the garden floor against my bare feet, hear the burble of the fountain and the buzz of the insects in the eucalyptus in the garden.

Compared to those, my model seemed uninhabited. It reminded me of the way my house had felt the night before.

I remembered Lady Day puzzling out the meaning of the garden—how there was no reason for it, no fruits or vegetables growing. It was a place to relax, to listen to music, to play board games and chat. That garden wasn't part of an afterlife survival kit, unless playing games and listening to music in a beautiful shady spot was something you needed to survive.

Maybe it was.

I went back to the shelf where the box of modeling clay was kept, unwrapping a small block on my way back to the table. Unlike the pieces I'd tried to make of my parents, this piece came together right away and exactly the way it had looked in my head, like there was a direct connection between my brain and my hands.

And when that last, easy piece was finished, I knew my model was done.

Then I got to work painting it all, letting my focus narrow until there were only the tiny clay objects I'd made, going from brown to a dingy beige to a chalky white. With each consecutive coat, my paintbrush turned them clean. Soon, my hands were sticky and tight with dried primer, and the little pieces were drying next to the cardboard box I'd chosen to hold them, the sides trimmed down and painted a stark, spotless white. The methodical work gave my brain a place to rest, too.

I was placing the pieces in the box when the metal door swung open behind me. I took a moment to admire Apollo's oversized green T-shirt, which had a hand-painted bronze arrow on it.

"Emerald," I said. Despite its name, Emerald Green the pigment is dirtier, more copper-colored than the gemstones. The color was only commercially available for fifty years during the nineteenth century because it was poisonous—something they didn't figure out until they'd used it to dye clothes and the wallpaper that most likely killed Napoleon.

He looked down and nodded in agreement. "Without the

arsenic that blinded Monet, we hope." He walked over to the hot plate and put the kettle on. "Now we will have a cup of tea while you show me all the progress on your survival kit for the afterlife."

We took our tea over to my workspace. Apollo laughed about the toothbrush, and nodded approvingly at the extra notebook I'd added at the last minute, worried that one wouldn't be enough.

"But this, Olympia, this is your masterwork," he said, picking up the tiny cat I'd made an hour before. She was still damp, so he held her gently in his huge hands as he examined her, appreciating each of the tiny whiskers I'd carved with the pushpin, the delicate ears, her intricate tabby stripes. Then he returned her carefully to the tiny bed, curled up neatly right where my feet would be, her triangular chin resting on her front paws.

Looking at her made me feel better.

Apollo's arms were crossed against his chest, his head tilted to one side. He nodded. "It's very good," he said, and I let his words warm me along with what I knew, which was that they were true.

We stood there for a minute more, looking at the neat clean shapes and the little shadows they threw against the bright white box. I was supposed to paint it next, but I didn't want to. I didn't want to add color at all.

The model was just right the way it was, orderly and stripped down. Pristine. Blank.

Right as I had that thought, Apollo leaned in to look again, saying, "It is going to be quite the trick for you to capture some of these details when you start the paint. I have a very small brush; expensive, one or two fine hairs. I will see if I can find it for you."

I must have stiffened a little, because he looked sideways at me and then threw his head back and laughed.

"Oh, no! Miz Monochrome. You are not going to paint it at all, are you? You've decided to leave it white."

I was glad he was laughing.

"It feels *done*," I said.

"Well, I made you something," he said. "Last night, after you left. But my feelings will not be hurt if you prefer to bring your colorless campaign with you to the afterlife."

As he crossed over to the stainless-steel worktable near the triangle painting, I noticed that he'd put hot pink laces into his worn brown work boots. And when he dropped the little object he came back with into my palm, I laughed with delight and recognition: Apollo had made me a miniature canvas, an exact copy of the blue study he'd made for me using ultramarine, the first color I ever mixed with him, back when I was nine.

"We will begin with the best," he'd told me, watching carefully as I ground the precious lapis lazuli the way he'd shown me, mixing the powdery dust with alcohol. He'd shown me how to use a magnet to separate out the metallic pyrite in the stone, and how to knead the pigment carefully into a ball of wax, and then push it through a fine metal filter so that only the purest pigment remained.

The study he'd made with our paint had been so beautiful that I kept sneaking back to look at it, even after we'd cleaned up.

He'd surprised me by giving me the color study the next day, making a joke of it by sticking one of those gaudy plastic Christmas bows on the top. But it wasn't a joke. It was the most beautiful thing I owned.

I carefully held the little canvas against the wall of the model, across from the bed. It would be the first thing I saw when I woke up in the afterlife, too.

Apollo was teasing me now. "Of course, I understand completely if my humble contribution dilutes your strict vision."

"No. I love it," I said, struggling to put what I was feeling into words. "That little bit of color makes the rest of it look right." I put a dab of strong glue on the back of the canvas and held it in place with a careful finger, counting to thirty under my breath.

Apollo looked at his watch, a massive hunk of metal in a battered leather strap, the only thing he'd kept from his time in the Polish army. "It's late, Olympia. What are you going to do now?"

I shrugged, but I knew exactly what I was going to do. Gluing the pieces in place would take about ten minutes. Then I was going to clean up my workspace and go upstairs to heat up a can of tomato soup, and then I was going to watch some stupid show on TV until I fell asleep on the couch. I didn't think I was feeling brave enough to check on my mom again.

"Nothing much," I said. And then, too quickly, "Do you want to get some dinner?"

I was mad at myself as soon as the question popped out of my mouth. It made me sound desperate, like one of his dumb girlfriends. But it was too late to take it back, and I knew that Apollo would be too much of a gentleman to say no.

He did hesitate for a minute before saying, "Actually, there's a party I have to show a face at, for an artist I know. I don't have to stay long. I know that it is a school night for you, but perhaps you would you like to come with me? We can eat a slice of Sicilian with tomatoes and onions on the way."

I nodded quickly, still embarrassed, and then turned back to my glue. I'd been eating a lot of pizza, but it would be better than soup and saltines.

Besides, a party sounded interesting. I'd gone to art parties with my parents when I was a baby, but that meant falling asleep on a pile of coats in the bedroom while the grown-ups smoked and argued about time landscapes and ready-mades. Sometimes Linda would ask me to sleep over when she was throwing a party for her real estate clients so I could keep an eye on Maggie (Alex, too, if we're being honest), but those parties were boring. The three of us would steal as many éclairs from the dessert tray as we could carry, and then we'd sit and eat them on the mezzanine, looking through the railing at grown-ups drinking wine and laughing at jokes that weren't funny.

An art party would be better than that.

And even if it wasn't, it would sure be better than going home.

# NO ÉCLAIRS

There were no éclairs at the party Apollo took me to.

We crossed Canal, passing fabric warehouses and empty lots, until we came to a loft building in worse shape than ours. The stairwell had no lights, so Apollo sang a Polish drinking song and I followed his voice up through a fuzzy black so dense it filled my mouth.

Four flights up, he stopped and banged on a metal door.

We waited, my breath coming heavy and loud in the dark.

When the door swung open, a giant woman with cheekbones painted on like knives kissed Apollo and pulled him by the hand into the squash of people behind her. She didn't even look at me.

I could tell by the way his shoulders were set that it annoyed him how bossy she was. Apollo doesn't like being told what to do.

He turned around to mouth something at me over his shoulder, but I couldn't understand what he was saying, and it wouldn't have mattered anyway. The door, covered in stickers and fat Sharpie, had slammed shut behind me, and Apollo had disappeared into the crowd.

A camera flashbulb popped. In the afterglow, the air was ghost-colored from the smoke. The big room smelled like armpits and spilled wine and perfume. Candles dripped onto the bottles they were set into, and the music sounded like someone shaking change in a coffee can to discipline a dog. I pushed through people laughing, their heads thrown back like something was going to bite their throats, or maybe they were going to do the biting.

This was no place for a kid.

On the other hand, it made me invisible. I could look at anything, everything. All the women were wearing boots, silver and covered in writing, or black with zippers all the way up. They were beautiful.

It was too hot.

A woman wearing tight leather pants was sitting backward on a chair like a lion tamer, legs spread, one knee up against an industrial sink, the other nearly touching a table crowded with bottles. It didn't look like she was going to let me through, and something cold and hard curled at the bottom of my stomach. Suddenly, she clapped her knees together against the chair back like she'd been making a joke, and I slid by her fast, half expecting her to slam her knees out again to block me. When she didn't, the thrill of a near miss shot up the back of my legs.

By the table with the bottles, there was a woman with a knob where her hand should have been. I know about birth defects because Linda is obsessed with them. This kid Kai in the second grade at our school only has two fingers on his left hand; it looks like a lobster claw. Linda always makes it sound like the claw is Kai's mom's fault, but she seems nice when I see her pushing him on the swings at the park.

The woman with the tiny fist wasn't hiding her hand, like Kai does. Instead, she'd dipped it in yellow rubber, so that her arm had a colored tip, like a match, and when she talked, she waved the yellow fist around like a scepter. People think yellow is happy, punch buggies and have a nice day, but it can be a warning, too. Wasps are yellow, and police tape. I bet the woman with the yellow fist knew that.

The skinniest man I'd ever seen swayed in the middle of the room, holding a bottle and dancing, but not to the music. I kept looking away, afraid he'd open his eyes and catch me watching, but he didn't, so I let myself stare until I felt the shock of something cold and wet on my ankle, and then an insistent, hard shove behind my knee.

There was a black and brown dog snuffling around my legs, a big German shepherd with a pointy nose and a sloping back, like the cop dogs on the train. I held my hand out to her, the way my dad had showed me. She gave a quick disinterested sniff and let me pat her thick, oily coat. It felt like petting a bear.

I wondered if the music was bothering her. It was bothering me, and Lady Day says that dogs' ears are four times more sensitive than humans'. But she didn't seem bothered; she seemed busy. She didn't let me pet her for long before she headed back off, into the crowd. When I looked up again, the dancing man was gone.

I made a beeline over to the window. I thought it would be cooler there, but it wasn't. The music kept coming loud and fast out of the black speakers. I felt like if I had one extra second I could get ahead of the noise and the heat and the smoke, but there wasn't any time. My heart kept beating too fast, or maybe it was the music.

I turned around and put one foot onto the windowsill to brace myself. Then I grabbed the brass handles and yanked. With a blast of cool air, the heavy glass panes rolled up on their counterweights, just like at home. I swung myself up and out.

# OUTSIDE, LOOKING IN

As soon as I felt the fire escape beneath my feet, the jangly feeling from the party drained right out of me, through the metal grating and onto the street.

The window rolled back down as soon as I let it. I jammed one of my sneakers in there, next to a cord snaking over to the building next door; they were stealing the electricity for the stereo. With one yank, I could have thrown the whole party into silence.

It was quiet outside, and the distant sounds of Broadway ponged around my head, filling the space where the music used to be. I rocked forward into a squat and peered down. Mica glittered in the dark pavement below. Getting down to the second floor would be easy, but the ladder at the bottom was pulled up and locked, and the last drop to the sidewalk stretched out into the darkness. Alex could have done that jump, maybe. But it was way too far for me.

I dumped my backpack off my shoulder and got my note-book out. I drew the windows first, big frames I could fill in with the black night behind, the easiest way I could think of to get across the feeling of shiny dark danger the party had given me.

Then I flipped the page and drew the dancing man in long, quick lines. I'd draw him properly later, but I wanted to remember the delicate shadows under the ribs that poked out from beneath his skin, and the careless, loose swing of his arms crossing his body as he swayed, like the sleeves of a coat with no arms in them.

My Blackwing moved until it stopped.

I'd go back inside and find Apollo. It was time to talk to him. The thing with my mom had gone too far; I needed help. I'd confess about peeking into the box and seeing his colors. He wouldn't be mad. Maybe he'd tell me where he was going. And if it wasn't too much, maybe he could take me with him.

As I crammed my notebook back into my book bag, a voice came out of the dark.

"Hey," it said, deliberately soft, but I flinched anyway.

The Wake Up Artist was sitting on the far side of the fire escape, like the statue of the Buddha that Linda has in her foyer, quiet in a dark blue suit that blended into the nighttime behind the bars. Only he wasn't a he, like I'd thought, but a she, with a necklace of green wooden beads wrapped three times around her wrist.

I wished I was wearing my other shoe.

"You spend a lot of time on fire escapes," she said. Her voice was gravelly and low.

"Usually people don't look up," I said.

She nodded. "That's been my experience, too."

Inside, the music changed. We could hear people laughing. "Were you the only kid in there?" she asked, jutting her chin at the window.

I nodded. "I came with my friend Apollo, but I got hot."

"Yeah, I know Apollo," she said. Everybody knows Apollo. That's why you have to use mind-control techniques so he doesn't stop off at Pearl Paint before dinner.

"How come you're out here?" I asked.

She didn't answer the question. Instead, she asked me one: "Did you see the dog in there?"

I shrugged. "I petted her, but she didn't seem like she was looking for company."

"Do you know what she's doing?"

I didn't, but I was curious. That dog had seemed like she was up to something.

"Watch," the Wake Up Artist said.

The two of us kneeled forward and watched through the window as the big dog moved around the outside of the room, stopping every once in a while to touch the back of someone's knee like she'd done with mine. She bumped up against a guy wearing a baby blue pirate shirt.

I sat back again. "I don't get it."

Still watching the dog, the Wake Up Artist said, "She's herding them. She'll have the whole party in one corner by midnight."

Now that she'd said it, a lot of people did seem to be concentrated in one corner of the loft. The guy in the pirate shirt had moved over, so that he had his back up against another grown-up playing dress-up, a woman in a princess's tattered violet gown.

The Wake Up Artist leaned back against the painted iron. "She does it at every one of these parties. And nobody ever notices."

"She didn't herd us," I said.

"No," the Wake Up Artist said. "She didn't."

The people inside looked like they were onstage. I got lost watching them until the Wake Up Artist got up, rising easily from her cross-legged position, and I imagined Linda's Buddha unfolding himself to stand.

"You about ready?"

I scrambled to my feet.

The Wake Up Artist pushed the window up and ducked under. I caught it and crouched on the sill to put my sneaker back on before jumping down.

It was cooler and less chaotic inside. Still, I was glad when the Wake Up Artist went first, clearing a path through the crowd. She waved at a lot of people, but she didn't stop to talk. I was glad about that, too.

I saw the guy in the pirate shirt and the woman with the yellow fist. I saw the German shepherd, quietly nosing her way through the partygoers, pushing them toward the far corner without anyone realizing. Finally, I caught sight of Apollo on a low couch along one wall. There was a woman with red lips and short black hair and a short black dress sitting on his lap. She wasn't the art critic or the sound artist or the mime, or anyone else I'd seen before.

I raised one hand in his direction and kept moving, like I'd seen the Wake Up Artist do. Out of the corner of my eye, I saw him gesture me over, then try to shift the woman so he could get up, but I was moving quickly, my eyes focused on the back of the Wake Up Artist's suit.

Thanks to the dog, the crowd was thinner closer to the door. I twisted between two guys, sweaty in white tank tops. Then I was out the door and into the stairwell, where there was no light.

# HOW I THINK

A huge moon illuminated the empty streets.

The Wake Up Artist walked easily next to me, her untied
boots silent on the uneven Belgian blocks. She stuck to the center
of the street without me saying anything about the rats.

Panic shot through me periodically, like I was remembering that
I'd left something important behind at the party—my notebook,
maybe, or the keys around my neck. But the only thing I'd left behind was Apollo, and my chance to tell him everything that was happening. I twisted to look back at the dark building where the party
had been, not sure I could trust myself to tell him tomorrow.

"He saw us leave together," the Wake Up Artist said, explaining why he hadn't followed me out. Which was something, I guess.

She didn't say anything else, so I didn't, either.

Some of the buildings we passed were bombed out, broken windows gaping black or boarded up with graffitied plywood. Piles of

tires loomed outside a single-story garage; roll-down grates protected electrical supply stores and hat factories and metalworking shops. Drifts of garbage swirled at our feet, but the Wake Up Artist ambled down the dark street like she was walking down a country lane, taking in the sights. I snuck a look at her, hunting for some sign of the electric energy that made her paste-ups so exciting. But her face was placid, her body relaxed, paint-flecked hands soft and open.

"My mom's an artist," I said, for no reason except that the little faucets weighed heavy in my pocket. "She has a show coming up in the fall."

"How's that going?"

"Not so good." The truth slipped out; it came easily with a stranger. "She's having a hard time getting up right now. Out of bed, I mean."

The Wake Up Artist didn't say anything, and I thought maybe she hadn't heard me.

After a few minutes, we came up on my block, and the empty lot where I'd seen her for the first time. I wondered if it would upset her to see her poster tattered and grey, but she smiled a little when she looked into the dark, rubble-filled lot.

"It doesn't bother you, that they get dirty and ripped up?"

She shook her head. "Nothing lasts forever."

I couldn't stop. "But nobody even saw it, just me and some guys who work in a button factory."

She smiled again. "Those guys count. So do you." A dog barked twice in the distance. "Every time I see you, you've got that notebook open. Do you show those drawings around?"

I made a face. "Sort of." It was hard to explain. It made Mr. G so happy when I gave him a new drawing that I would have brought them even if he hadn't traded me for candy. But I didn't sketch to show off. I didn't care about compliments; I knew when the drawings were good, and I knew when they were bad. And if they were bad, I only wanted to hear from people like Mrs. Ejiofor and Lady Day and my dad, who would have ideas about how to fix them.

"So how come you do it?"

Nobody had ever asked me that. My fingers itched thinking about the question, as if having a Blackwing in my hands would help me answer it. Drawing was what I did, what I'd always done.

"It's how I think," I said finally.

The Wake Up Artist nodded at that.

"Your posters—they felt like messages," I said, wanting something from her, even though I couldn't say what it was. "Like you were talking right to me. But maybe I just wasn't understanding what you meant."

She shrugged. "Doesn't matter. Sometimes the stuff we make is just for us. And sometimes we give it away, so that other people can see what they need to."

We had arrived at my door. I pulled my key out from under my sweatshirt and put it into the lock.

She didn't wait around to see that I got in, so she was already past when I heard her say, "Most people need to wake up. But some people are already feeling too much. That can be tough."

I watched her go. Halfway down the block, she waved back at me without turning around.

# JUST A KID

I let out an audible sigh of relief as I stepped into our front vestibule. A wave of exhaustion broke over me. They call New York the city that never sleeps, but I was tired.

Dreading the long climb, I looked up to the top of the steep, crooked stairs—and in one moment, all of my tiredness dropped away. There was an enormous man waiting on the landing outside the studio.

I could have turned back fast to the tricky front door; my brain was already rehearsing how I'd lift and jiggle the knob. Except that the big man didn't seem to be coming for me.

He did inch forward a tentative step or two, one hand raised unmistakably: *Harmless!* And when his face caught the light of the dangling bulb, I could see that he was at least as scared of me as I was of him.

More, probably. I'm nowhere near as fast as Alex, but I

could have outrun this guy by breaking into a brisk walk.

There was another thing, too: I was pretty sure that this was Antonin Grandjean, the forgery expert. I'm not an authority on serial killers or anything, but I'm 95 percent positive they don't go around dropping off business cards with their phone numbers on them before a murder spree.

The big man shuffled forward to the very edge of the dingy landing. Clearly, what he wanted now was to leave, if he could figure out some way to do it without passing me. I almost smiled; Joyce would have said that I had him treed.

"I'm sorry! So sorry!" His voice echoed off the painted tin walls. "I didn't expect . . ."

A kid, is what he meant. I recognized his accent immediately: This *was* the same guy who'd been calling Apollo.

I was going to have to watch what I said. I had no idea whether my dad had done the right thing or the wrong thing, but even if it was the wrong thing, he was still my dad.

Luckily, there's no underestimating a grown-up's ability to underestimate a kid.

"Are you alone? Where are your parents? It's very late, you know, and this neighborhood is . . ." He trailed off again.

Like it was any of his business. He liked scolding better than apologizing, I guess.

My own voice came out much braver than I was feeling and sounded very New York after his. "What do you want?"

"The restoration company: They're not answering their phone. Do you know the people who work there?"

I shrugged. "Not really. They're kind of weird."

His mouth twisted in disappointment like a baby's.

I moved to go upstairs, ending the conversation, but he stepped forward quickly, desperate. "There's no chance you know anything about this?" He reached into his rumpled coat for a piece of white paper in a clear plastic folder and held it out in my direction.

I climbed three steps to see—and then a couple more, not so I could see better, but so I could be sure.

The drawing Antonin Grandjean was holding was one of the hundreds of sketches I'd made of the Head.

"Where'd you get that?" I asked, buying time, although I knew with 100 percent certainty where he had gotten it. I could almost taste the Goldenberg's Peanut Chew.

"I bought it," the man said, and I did smile then, turning my face into the shadows so he couldn't see; Mr. G had always told me he was going to be responsible for my first sale. "The man at the store wouldn't tell me where he'd gotten it. But the subject is a painted carving stolen from a church near my grandmother's house in France." He added something in French I didn't catch: a name.

*Stolen.*

Antonin Grandjean wasn't here about a forgery. He was here about a theft.

Even though my heart had started to pound again, I kept my face bland, neutral—just a polite kid who knows better than to be rude to a grown-up, no matter how much he drones on.

"A place I spent summers, as a boy. You see?" He pulled an old photograph with white scalloped edges from the breast pocket of his suit jacket: an awkward boy in a neckerchief in a dark church, smiling big in front of the Head.

"I'm a forgery expert, based in Brussels, here in SoHo for work. I stopped into this newsstand one morning—for a Coke, of all things—and there she was! Tacked up to a cigarette display. After forty years, like a dream," he trailed off again, either lost in his memories or believing my disinterested face, which was nothing more than camouflage for the dominos falling fast and furious in my brain.

The Head was the piece of art missing from the studio.

The Head, which had been *stolen*.

That explained the terrible gash at the base of her. It explained why Apollo hadn't wanted anything to do with the job, even though she was old and beautiful, the kind of piece he'd always wanted to work on. It explained why she had ended up so far downtown, instead of at one of the white-glove restoration places across from the museums uptown. Whoever was in charge at the Dortmunder Collection must have thought Apollo and my dad would help them get away with it.

Another domino tipped.

The Head, which had been stolen. From *France*.

I heard Joyce Walker in Richard's courtyard: *Never one to pass up a grand gesture, your dad. The last of the heroes.*

And I heard my dad's voice, just like he was sitting on the edge of my bed the night he left: *I've got to take the lady home.*

He hadn't been talking about Vouley Voo at all.

He'd been talking about the Head.

The man cleared his throat politely, as if he knew he was interrupting. "It's a very good likeness, actually," he said, looking down again at the sketch dreamily. "She is how I got interested in art in the first place." I hadn't quite captured the Head's elusive expression, but I'd gotten pretty close on this one; I tended to give Mr. G the good stuff.

"The people at the big art supply store seemed to think these restorers were working on her. But I have been phoning all week, and the man there is very difficult; I do not think he is telling me the truth, and now he does not pick up the phone at all. I leave tomorrow, you see. So after my business for the day was done, I came in person. I thought if I could catch him, if I could explain how important she is to me . . ." He trailed off. "Nothing, though, and I have been here for hours."

Apollo had left with me, to get pizza before the party.

The forgery expert's eyes, watery and droopy like a basset hound's, slipped down to my ratty sneakers and faded jeans, the beat-up backpack where I kept my homework and art supplies. He gave it one last try anyway. "You're sure, then, that you haven't heard anything about a wooden carving?"

"I'm really sorry I can't help you, mister," I said, letting his hope bounce right off my blank, perfectly pleasant, know-nothing kid face.

His round face crashed in disappointment. I knew the feeling; he'd run out of leads.

Brain still racing, I shifted on the creaky stair. "I should probably get home now, so my mom and dad don't worry." Even though I was just acting, hearing myself say "mom and dad" gave me a mini zap I didn't like.

"Of course. No, of course. I just thought perhaps . . ." The fat man shook his head to clear it, embarrassed by his own wish, and started off down the wide stairs toward me on his tiny feet. He held out a business card to me as we passed awkwardly on the stairs, and I made a show of looking at it before tucking it into my notebook, like the words printed on it weren't already burned into my brain.

Of course I'd call him if I heard anything. Of course I would.

I turned around at the landing to watch him go. He was standing in the dim light at the bottom of the stairs by the taped-up A.I.R. sign, looking mostly like a comfortable sofa and staring down at the old brown photo with the white edges and at the drawing—my drawing—in his fist.

He was in love with the Head, too.

I felt bad for him. Not so bad that I didn't take my shot when I saw it, though.

"'Scuse me? Sir?" He turned around, surprised to find me still there. "I'm actually doing a project on France, for school." He smiled up at me, and I could see him younger, thinner, the boy in the photograph. It had been a happy place for him, back then.

"What did you say was the name of that town?"

# AND THEY DANCED BY
# THE LIGHT OF THE MOON

I practically floated the rest of the way up the stairs. The fat man's cold trail meant mine had heated up again.

The Head had been stolen from a tiny church in Écalles-Sainte-Catherine, a tiny medieval town in central France. The fat man had even spelled it for me, told me where to put the accent. She'd been a gift to the church from a famous sculptor who'd fallen in love with a shepherdess in the town. Most people thought the shepherdess had been the sculptor's model for the Head.

I was willing to bet a case of Blackwings that the Head was back there now, in Écalles-Sainte-Catherine, with my dad.

My dad, who wasn't a forger after all.

Of course, it did seem like he'd stolen the Head. But if you stole something so you could return it to the people it had been stolen from in the first place, was that really stealing?

I thought triumphantly about the look I'd see on Alex's face when I told him.

*The last of the heroes.*

I threw myself on my bed, the lamp on my desk casting shadows onto Apollo's color study. Though it was late on a school night, my brain raced with plans. All I had to do was find him. There probably weren't a lot of hotels in a town the size of Écalles-Sainte-Catherine. I could call every one of them; Richard could help me with the French. And once I found him, my dad would know what to do about my mom.

The night had caught up to me, and I struggled to keep my eyes open. I wanted to get up, put on some pajamas; Alex would totally sleep in his clothes if Linda let him, but I didn't like the idea of all that street dirt in my bed. Plus, I hadn't brushed my teeth. I lay there for a long time, dreaming of squeezing the center of a full tube of toothpaste, laying a thick line of gel onto my red toothbrush, a neat curl on top like in the commercials. Then I'd wake up again with my parched, gummy pizza mouth, wishing the dream had been real.

I guess I was asleep, a little bit.

The bag of faucets made an uncomfortable lump in my sweatshirt pocket. What if my mom got up tomorrow and wanted to work? I could leave them out for her, on her worktable, like a present. Maybe they'd be the inspiration she needed.

I gathered my energy and rolled up to sit. The loft was completely quiet as I padded toward the big room in my bare feet, thinking about how good it was going to feel to brush my teeth.

But as I pulled back the curtain that separates my room from the big room, I stopped.

The big room was flooded with a shivery, magical light from that huge full moon. Panels of ghost beams crossed the floor and illuminated the walls. We'd lived in that apartment my whole life, and I'd never seen anything like it before. The watery moonlight had transformed the big room into a place of enchantment. This wasn't light to walk through; it was filigree—light you danced through, or swam.

*And they danced by the light of the moon, the moon.* It was a song my dad used to sing to me when I was little.

I stood there for a long time, my exhaustion forgotten for the second time that night. I could feel, more distinctly than I ever had before, where my body ended and the cool air began. I thought about grabbing my notebook, but I knew I'd never be able to capture that light so that someone looking at my drawing would have the feeling I had, like every hair on the back of my neck was standing up in wonder.

And so I willed myself to remember all of it, even the feeling of the bag in the pocket of my sweatshirt against my fingertips, the brown paper velvety soft from being carried around, the heaviness of the little gold faucets a contrast to the silvery light. If I could remember every single detail, maybe someday I'd be able to make a piece of art that would give someone else this feeling, too.

It was the way my mother's sculptures made people feel.

At the thought of my mom, my eyes turned to her workbench, and in a single second, that fairy-tale light turned from magical to menacing—from something beautiful into the light that fills a forest when you're running as fast as you can from a monster in a dream, branches reaching out like bony fingers to grab at you.

*Looking is easy. Very few people see,* my dad always said. I'd wanted to be one of the people who saw, and so I'd turned every walk into a memory exercise, noticing details that nobody else did, memorizing the way light reflected off a greasy puddle, the cornice above a doorway cocked like an eyebrow, the faded shadow of an old advertisement for hats painted onto the bricks between buildings.

But for all the time I'd been standing in the doorway of my bedroom, drinking in every detail of the big room bathed in that glorious light, I had not noticed the most important thing.

I had not noticed that my mom's sculpture was gone.

"Oh, no," I breathed—out loud, even though there was no one there to hear me. "Oh, no, no, *no.*"

My mind scrabbled for an explanation like a dog taking the corner too fast on a slippery wooden floor. Maybe her dealer had come to pick it up. Maybe she'd sold it. Maybe she'd moved it into the bedroom so she could see what it looked like in different light. Maybe she'd taken it to the studio because she needed to use a tool up there.

But even as I was saying those things to myself, even as I was crossing through that bewitched light toward her workbench, my breath coming fast and shallow and loud, I knew that none of those things had happened. And when I slid to a stop, I saw that I was right.

The sculpture wasn't gone. It had been destroyed.

Pieces of it were broken up and scattered across the surface of the workbench and the floor beneath it. The crumpled sign was against the radiator, like it had been kicked. The tiny fan was at my feet. I knelt to pick it up, turning it in my hands, hoping I would see a way to fix it, but it was bent and twisted beyond repair. Worse, it had lost its magic. It had gone back to being garbage.

The wrongness of it made me feel sick.

I never touched my mother's work without permission; I'd known not to do that since I was a baby. But I wouldn't leave those pieces—the fan, the embroidered tea bag, the button marked PUSH with the wire trailing out behind it like a mermaid's hair—lying all bent and broken and scattered like that, the precise, intricate clockwork of the story they'd begun to make ripped apart.

My dad kept old newspapers in a cardboard box by the door. I emptied it and bent the flaps down so they'd stay inside. Then I picked up all the pieces of my mom's sculpture and placed them carefully inside.

I left the box in the center of her workbench. As I was turning away, I felt the bag of tiny faucets, heavy in my pocket. I took them out and put them in the box, too. And then I brushed my teeth and went back to bed.

# FOR A GHOST

The next day was Friday: Our projects were due.

Eyes sandy with sleeplessness, I took my completed model to school.

My dark mood didn't match the festive feeling in the classroom as everyone milled around before the bell, looking at the Egyptian-inspired projects set up on people's desks. Even though I felt rotten, I was still interested to see what other people had done.

Nat Franklin had built a precise replica of the pyramid site at Giza out of papier-mâché. It was terrific; the Sphinx looked exactly like the real thing, down to the smashed-up nose. Nat wants to be an architect like his dad, so he's got practice with models. He'd glued real sand down, and made a tiny camel out of folded paper right by the pyramid where Khufu is buried. I was really impressed.

Erin Rizzoli had used salt and baking soda to mummify some apple slices. She'd stuck the long brown leathery chunks to a paper plate so they looked like fingers. No thanks.

Melanie Geller had drawn hieroglyphs onto a long piece of printer paper that she'd dipped in weak tea to make it look like papyrus. Mrs. Ejiofor had let her use special gold paint from the art room to do the outlines, and she'd rolled the ends of the scroll around two dowels from her dad's hardware store. There was a rumor that the hieroglyphs were coded messages about people in our class, but Melanie only looked sideways at him when Richard asked her about it.

Rowan Merody had made a life-size sarcophagus from a refrigerator box with real hinges so you could climb inside. Alex said Rowan's mom had made it for him, which was probably true, but that didn't stop everyone in the class from wanting to climb into the box so they could lie with their arms crossed over their chests like real mummies. I didn't climb in. Nat's project was better; Rowan's was just big.

I was happy to see that Richard got a lot of attention for his Khepri maquette. It was great: scary and beautiful. Alex's mummified bunny didn't look any better than it had at the studio, but Jerome Jacobson had mummified his sister's Wonder Woman Barbie and it was even worse, especially the wrapping in the armpit area.

"Bad week to be a little sister," I said under my breath to Lady Day.

She looked at Jerome's Barbie with visible distaste. "Or a doll."

Lady Day's project was, not surprisingly, the best one in the class. She had done a sculpture of Bastet, the Egyptian goddess who appears as a black cat. Lady Day's Bastet sat, calm and attentive, on a painted plinth made of a boot box, her front paws lined up neatly beneath her.

Posted on the box base was an information card, just like in a real museum:

*Bastet: Late Period (Ptolemaic) 664–630 BC*
*The protector of women and children.*
*Also goddess of domesticity, fertility, and wom-*
*en's secrets. Benevolent, but wrathful when crossed.*

I stared at the graceful black cat, keeper of women's secrets. She was gorgeous: elegant and a little mysterious, with real gold hoops in her ears.

Kind of like Lady Day herself.

"Elmer's wood filler and three-hundred-twenty-grit sand-paper," Lady Day said, tall behind me, explaining how she'd gotten the papier-mâché as lustrous and smooth as the original bronze. "Melanie's dad gave me this beeswax-dipped cloth to pick up the dust between coats. I have to go back, tell him how great she came out."

The cat statuette must have taken hours of work. Not for the first time, I wished Lady Day had been making her project at the studio with me.

I put my model on the radiator, out of the way. It didn't look very Egyptian, compared to all the others. Most people stopped by quickly, admired how small everything was, and moved on. That was fine with me. I didn't need them to look.

Ms. Colantonio spent a long time with it, though, moving around the box so she could see from every angle.

"Tell me why you didn't use color?"

I liked the way she asked me, not like I'd gotten lazy or run out of time, but like she knew I'd made a choice.

"Once I saw it with the primer on, it was just *done*."

She nodded. "That's a good thing to know, when something is done." And she kept looking, even though she'd spent more time with my project than with anyone else's.

Lady Day joined us.

"Tell me what you see, L.D.," Ms. Colantonio said, still bent to look.

Lady Day didn't have to think: "At the Met, there's a replica of a room from the town next to Pompeii. It got wiped out, too, when the volcano erupted. People were eating, talking, playing with their kids when the lava came, too fast for them to escape. It caught a dog mid-bark."

Ms. Colantonio looked up at her, listening intently.

"They're just stopped there, in time," Lady Day said.

I thought about a volcano erupting over downtown Manhattan, freezing my mom in bed, Mr. G selling magazines under the Optimo sign, Manny Weber lying on his back in the sarcophagus Rowan Merody's mom had made, hands crossed over his chest.

Archaeologists were detectives, reaching back through time to sift ruins for clues, but they had the same problem real detectives had. If you found us all after a thousand years, you'd learn some true things. But you'd get a bunch of stuff wrong, too.

Lady Day shrugged. "And everything's white. Anyway. That's what your model reminds me of. That room."

Across the room, Rowan shrieked in protest: Javadi had closed the lid of the sarcophagus on Manny and was holding it down while Manny tried to punch his way out of the buckling cardboard.

Ms. Colantonio straightened up and turned in their direction, but she was still looking into my model even as she started to walk away, so that I barely heard what she said:

"She's right. It's like you built a room for a ghost."

≈≈≈

After Manny had been rescued and everyone finally got back to their seats for roll call, Ms. Colantonio made an announcement:

Our projects would be on display in the school's lobby until summer vacation.

The smaller ones could go in the glass cases on the walls where the sports trophies would have been kept if we'd had any of those. Bigger projects, like Richard's and Lady Day's and Rowan Merody's, would have their own special spot near the principal's office.

Excitement buzzed around the classroom again, and not much got done in math.

At the end of the day, Ms. Colantonio asked everyone to collect their coats and backpacks and then return—"in a civilized manner, please, ladies and gentlemen"—to the classroom so that each of us could take our project down to the lobby on our way out. She led the way, lifting one end of Rowan's sarcophagus and calling out yet another reminder behind her. "Careful, please, and with a minimum of noise?"

For all the reminding, there was still a noisy swarm of kids and coats and papier-mâché and backpacks, so I took my time getting my coat. The classroom was empty by the time I was hefting my diorama, hot on the bottom from its spot on the radiator, into my arms.

On my way out the door, I almost bumped into Bill the janitor, pushing his cleaning cart. A lot of kids are scared of Bill because of the livid red scar that slices down the center of his face, but he's interested in monsters and likes to talk to Richard about them, so we know he's nice. Bill waited patiently until the box and I had gotten safely all the way through the doorway, then moved carefully past me into the classroom, leaving his cart in the hallway.

"Richard told me you two are getting into shapeshifters these days," Bill said as he leaned over to pick up the heavy metal trash can next to the classroom door.

With the Transformation section in full swing, the Taxonomy had taken on a new life. We couldn't find pictures of a lot of the monsters Richard had researched, so we had to rely on what details we could gather from the stories about them, and on our own imaginations.

"Metamorphosis, too," I said.

"He keeps you busy!" Bill said over his shoulder, the red cord of the scar lifting up the corner of his lip in a smile. He headed into the classroom, calling back, "You get home safe and have a good night, now."

"Thanks. You too," I replied automatically.

But the thought of going home sat in my stomach like stones. I stood by Bill's cart, the after-school smell of glass cleaner and heavy-duty disinfectant crowding my nose and my diorama suddenly heavy in my arms.

I looked down at the Tab can, the coffee cup, the little cat.

*A room for a ghost.*

Balancing the box precariously on my outstretched left hand and forearm like I was carrying a tray, I used a fingernail to pry Apollo's color study from the side of the box. Still balancing the diorama, I shoved the little canvas quickly into the pocket of my jeans.

Then, curious, I tilted my hand a smidge, like the worst coffee-shop waitress in the world. It wasn't a lot, just enough for the model and everything in it to slide off my arm, right to the bottom of the big black plastic garbage can on Bill's rolling cart.

# SATURDAY (AGAIN)

"I have to be home in a couple of hours," Alex told me on Saturday morning. "My mom wants to open the house this weekend." He meant their house on the Island. "I packed already, but she wants to be in the car around two."

My heart beat a little faster. By two—as long as everything went as planned—I'd already have talked to my dad. I'd gotten ten heavy dollars in dimes from Mr. G after school, and Richard had agreed to do the talking in French. We'd call all the hotels near Écalles-Sainte-Catherine while Alex was on the Terrorpole.

And once I found him, my dad would know what to do about my mom.

"Richard slept over at my house again, but I couldn't deal with waiting for him to get ready. He'll meet us later." Alex noticed the goose pimples on my bare arms. "You're sure you're warm enough?"

He was right: Just like last Saturday, I'd forgotten a sweatshirt.

Just like last Saturday, he said, "Race you," and didn't even wait for me to get my key out from around my neck before he'd started climbing the front of the building. Just like last Saturday, I ran as fast as I could and found, just like last Saturday, that Alex had beaten me.

But unlike last Saturday, I'd left the window open.

So when I swung open the door, breathing hard, there he was, standing right there in the middle of my living room, looking around.

"Ollie," he said, in a voice I didn't recognize, "What's going on?"

At first, I didn't know what he meant. Then I looked around, too, and I could see the room the way Alex was seeing it.

It was a mess. There were apple cores and peanut shells on the trunk we used as a coffee table, and a lot of my books on the floor, and I'd made myself a kind of nest on the couch for when I fell asleep in front of the TV. I'd washed out some of my underpants so that I'd have some clean ones to wear, but I couldn't reach the shower rod easily, so I'd put them on the backs of the chairs to dry.

I wasn't crazy about having Alex see my underpants, although I'd seen his Spider-Man ones plenty of times. But I could tell how freaked out he was by the fact that he wasn't making fun of them.

"Where's your mom? Is she here?"

I felt a flash of panic. "She's here; she's in her room. I already told you. She's not getting out of bed right now."

The doors to my mom's room are double French doors, with the glass panes painted so that you can't see in. Alex was most of the way to my mom's room when I caught up with him. As fast as he was moving, for once I was faster. I slid in front of him and pressed against one of the doors, covering the faceted knob behind my back with my hands. The glass was cool, and I held onto it tight.

Alex looked at me steadily.

"You can't go in there, Alex. It's not going to be forever, she said so. But she needs to be alone right now." My heart was beating so fast, I thought I'd see it bumping through my T-shirt when I looked down. "She needs to rest."

At that moment, I was sure that if Alex opened the door to my mom's room, I would kill him for sure. But when he slowly and deliberately reached around me and took my hand away and turned the doorknob, I didn't do anything at all.

The door to my mom's room swung open. Once again, I saw everything through Alex's eyes. The shades were down so the room was dark, but you could see a lump under the covers. My mom didn't move, even when the sunlight from the big room crossed the bed. There were new cigarette packets and Tab cans on the floor. There were stains on the comforter I hadn't noticed before, and where it had pulled up at the bottom, you could see that there wasn't a bottom sheet on the bed at all; she was sleeping on the bare mattress. The pizza slices I'd brought for her a couple of days before were still on the table next to the bed; I hadn't gotten to the plate during my cleanup before she'd yelled at me.

It didn't smell very good in there at all.

Alex stood there for a minute. Then he backed out of the room quietly and closed the door behind him. When he turned to me, he looked like Linda.

"How long has it been like this? How long has *she* been like this?"

I pushed him away from the door, catching him off guard. He stumbled back.

"Why are you doing this?" I pushed him again, harder. "You knew she wasn't getting up. Why are you acting so surprised?"

I pushed him again, even harder this time. This time he was ready for it, so he didn't stumble, which made what I was doing even more like hitting. But he didn't do anything except look at me.

"How long, Ollie?" he asked again. Instead of answering— and for the first time since ding-a-ling, almost the whole time we'd been friends—I hit him on the arm. He didn't even flinch. I pulled my arm back to do it again, just to see if I could make his face change, but his hand moved out fast to catch mine before I could.

Alex is so skinny, it's easy to forget how strong he is. I tried to yank my arm away, but he was holding my wrist tight, the same serious look on his face. I struggled for a minute, and then I didn't. As soon as I stopped fighting, Alex let go.

When he said, "We have to tell someone about your mom," he wasn't asking me, he was telling me. And then he brushed past me, moving toward the window again.

# DOUBLE TROUBLE

By the time I got back out onto the fire escape, Alex was halfway up the stairs to the studio.

I called his name, once, even though I hated the desperation I could hear in my voice, but he didn't stop.

Maybe I could have stopped him, if I'd really tried. But I didn't.

Twenty-two stairs later, he was bent over, knocking on the studio window to get Apollo's attention. I could tell by the set of his shoulders that he was in Linda mode. I bit my tongue; I wasn't going to beg like a baby, even though that was what I felt like doing: *Stop, listen to me, give me a little more time to fix it.*

He didn't look at me when he straightened up, but put his hands in his pockets and looked off into the distance down Greene Street like he was expecting to see someone he knew there. That made me furious, as if the errand he happened to be running had nothing to do with me, as if he was letting me tag along like Maggie while he went ahead with the important work of ruining my life.

Except that this wasn't what was supposed to happen. I'd *solved* the mystery; I knew where my dad had gone. I even had a plan: The only thing left was to get Richard and the dimes to a payphone.

Except that Alex was dead set on ruining everything.

It was sunny on the fire escape, but not warm; a cold wind had come up from the river, and a hard light bounced off the window. We could see Apollo striding across the studio, a rag in his hand, squinting out in our direction without seeing us through the glare. His face brightened when he got close, though, and he bent down to grab the window's handle.

As the big window rolled up, the smells of the studio—solvent, paint, a freshly brewed pot of coffee—gusted out on the cloud of warmth that greeted us. It was the smell of happy afternoons spent quietly drawing at one of the big tables while my dad and Apollo worked and talked quietly to each other about restoration problems that had solutions: alkaline baths and vacuum suction and wool felt blotters and the careful application of the right percentage of hydrogen peroxide. I wished I could curl up on the windowsill at the edge of that warmth and stay there.

"Ah, double trouble today," Apollo said, extending his arm. Alex shouldered me aside to go in first, putting a quick hand on Apollo's arm to steady himself before jumping down.

"And how was your bunny received, Mr. Alex?" Apollo teased, giving me a wink and offering me a hand as I followed Alex through the window. But I ignored his outstretched hand and dropped clumsily to the floor without meeting his eyes. Once inside, I stood very still against the radiator, arms crossed tightly over my chest and my jaw tightly shut, my molars grinding into one another.

Apollo registered the grim look on Alex's face and looked at me in surprise, trying to figure out what was going on between the two of us. I looked away. If Alex wanted to spill the beans about my private life, then he could do the talking. Avoiding Apollo's gaze, I ground the toe of my sneaker into an ancient piece of masking tape on the floorboard in front of me. I worried at it until the blackened strip lifted at the corner, revealing the pale, untouched floor beneath.

The window was still open wide, and a harsh blast of wind blew through the studio, ruffling a client's prints laid out on one of the worktables. Apollo, distracted, looked back at the prints, and then turned quickly to close the window. It hadn't rolled down evenly, catching before it had closed all the way, and I knew from experience that he'd have to shake it loose and then roll it back up in order to get it back on the track.

He dropped the rag in his hand onto the slanted drafting table by the window. It was one of my dad's old navy T-shirts, cut up and soaked through with turpentine, the smell so strong my eyes pricked with tears.

I watched in silence as the rag tumbled slowly down the angled surface and came to rest on the wooden seat of the bar stool below it.

I should have said something.

I knew it was dangerous.

But I didn't.

While Apollo was still working to free the window, Alex addressed his back.

"Apollo, we have to tell you something. But you have to promise not to freak out." He took a deep breath. "It's about Ollie's mom."

I could only see the back of Apollo's head, his shoulders tense as he struggled with the window against the uncooperative track, but still I could tell that he was suddenly listening carefully. He yanked at the handle one more time and the window came unstuck, the big panes of glass rumbling down fast to shut with a bang.

Alex kept talking: I could tell he was scared he wouldn't get it all out unless he kept going.

"She went to bed, and she won't get up. She's not working or making dinner or doing anything except sleeping." He stopped again, trying to decide what to say next. "It seems pretty bad."

Apollo turned around and looked directly at me, not at Alex. There was no teasing left in his face. Very softly he said, "How long, Olympia?"

I shrugged, my jaw set. He couldn't make me tell him. But his ugly face was gentle and kind, and I looked away again, this time so I wouldn't cry.

He moved to put his massive lion head right into my line of vision, and asked again. "How long, sweetheart?"

I wouldn't meet his eyes. "Two weeks. About," I said, and saw his eyes widen in shock.

There. It was out, gone, done, like water running through my fingers. I sent a silent message to my mom: *I'm sorry*.

Just then, the door to the studio crashed open.

Richard was standing in the doorway, glaring daggers at Alex, who looked alarmed to see him. We were all alarmed when Richard started yelling.

"What, you just *forgot* about me down there?"

He must have been sitting on the loading dock, waiting for us to come down so we could go to the park.

Except that we hadn't come down. We'd gone up.

"I didn't forget. I mean . . ." Alex waved his hands vaguely in front of him, then crossed his arms against his stomach. "The thing with Ollie's mom? It got bad." And the three of us watched the mad go out of Richard with a whoosh.

Then, as if one stupid, bossy, busybody boy wasn't enough, Richard turned to Apollo and said, louder and faster than I'd ever heard him say anything before, "Ollie can't stay there anymore. Her mom needs help. Real help. We should have told someone when it started; I knew we should and I wish we had. But you've got to do something now."

I'd thought I could trust Richard. But he was a traitor, too.

# SOME ISLAND

Apollo had been standing still, his big body frozen in place. Richard's speech seemed to thaw him out. He walked swiftly over to the big black phone hanging on the wall by the door and cradled the receiver on his shoulder while he rifled through the notebook he'd pulled out of his back pocket for a number.

He'd plugged the phone back in. The calls from Antonin Grandjean must have stopped when the big man had gone back to Brussels.

"Whoa, whoa." Alex said, jumping in front of him. "Who are you calling?"

Apollo picked up the phone and started dialing.

"I am calling your mom." Which was pretty much the last thing on earth I thought he was going to say. It also might have been the worst.

Alex also seemed genuinely alarmed by the idea of involving

Linda and went so far as to reach up to try to grab the receiver from where it was sandwiched between Apollo's shoulder and his ear, but Apollo gently blocked him with one enormous paw and turned away.

Alex came back and stood next to me, visibly upset. I was glad. I stared at the blue rag where it lay crumpled on the wooden seat of the chair, feeling the ugliness beating around my chest and pushing up through my throat. I kept my face expressionless; if you'd been looking through the window, you wouldn't have been able to tell that anything was wrong.

Alex and Richard could tell, though.

Linda picked up right away. We could hear her tinny voice through the old receiver—not the words, but the tone—and when Apollo said who it was, I could hear her switch to the icy, professional voice she uses when she calls a company to make a complaint. That made me feel hopeful; maybe she wouldn't want to get involved at all. But Apollo is Apollo, and by the time he'd growled his way through some flirty hellos, we could hear Linda softening up and laughing.

Then he got down to business. "Linda, I have a favor to ask of you. You're opening the house on the Island this weekend, is that right?" Every year, Alex spent the whole summer out there with his aunt. Usually, I missed him. At that moment, though, I didn't care if he moved to Mars for good.

Linda whinnied something back, and Apollo nodded. As if it had just occurred to him, he asked, "I don't suppose you could find a spot in the car for Olympia?"

A bubble of disbelief rose up the whole length of my body. I couldn't go away with Linda to some weird island. What would happen to my mom while I was gone?

There was a brief silence on the other end of the line, and then Linda asked a question. Apollo turned to the wall and hummed some confirmation, which freaked me out more than anything that had happened yet.

Without Apollo saying anything, Linda knew what was going on with my mom.

Then Linda said something else, and Apollo's jaw tightened. His voice sounded different, too. "When did Cornelia call you?" he asked.

Richard's head shot up; Cornelia was his mom.

"I wish you had let me know."

Linda twittered on for a while, and Apollo kept shaking his head, even though she couldn't see him. Finally, he interrupted. "I'm not sure yet. I need some time. And Olympia could probably use some . . ." He glanced at me, then trailed off.

Linda was uncharacteristically quiet on the other end of the line. I couldn't make out what she said next, but what I could hear was worse: the singsong of pity. Tears of rage bit at my eyes, and I sucked my cheek in tight between my teeth so that I didn't start yelling. If I started, I'd never stop.

Apollo wanted to get off the phone. He thanked her and said, "I'm sending the three of them to you now, Linda. Thank you. I'll call you later tonight when I know more." Then he hung the heavy black phone back onto its cradle, squared his shoulders, and turned around. He looked tired, but his voice sounded ordinary and purposeful.

"Alex, will you please take Olympia downstairs so she can pack a bag? She's going with you to the Island this weekend. You're leaving in less than an hour." To me, he said, "Don't forget long pants and a sweatshirt, Ollie—it's still cold out there at night."

I shot lasers out of my eyes at him. Alex moved quickly toward the front door, relieved to have told someone, happy to have a plan, and glad to be out of there. Richard was behind him.

I shot Apollo one more filthy look over my shoulder. He spoke so quietly that only I could hear. "I know this isn't what you want. But don't be too angry with Alex, okay? He did the right thing."

And he rested his huge hand on my shoulder quickly, taking it away before I could have the satisfaction of shrugging it off.

# TRASH

We went down the regular inside stairs. The fluttery panic I'd been feeling had turned into a cold, hard nugget of anger sitting high in my chest. Alex pretended he didn't notice me glaring at him as he moved to the side and waited for me to open the door.

Richard kept going down the stairs; he'd wait for us outside.

I went into my room and got the duffel bag I used for sleepovers from its spot underneath my dresser. I stuffed a couple of T-shirts and my other pair of jeans into the bag, grabbed my toothbrush from the bathroom and a couple of pairs of underwear from where they hung on the chairs. I put my notebook in the duffel, too. I couldn't imagine drawing anything, but I couldn't imagine being without my notebook, either.

At the last minute, I threw in an almost-full can of peanuts from the kitchen counter. Four days with Linda, and who knew what kind of wacky diet she was on right now? When we were in third grade, there had been an entire month of sardines from a can you had to open with a key, which she ate with dark mustard on crackers that looked exactly like the inside of a corrugated cardboard box. Alex had practically starved.

Alex was still waiting for me by the door, the energy radiating off him in spiky waves. He couldn't wait to leave, but he wasn't about to say anything to me, which was wise. It was going to be a quiet trip overall, because I'd already made up my mind: I was never going to speak to him again.

I waited for him to go downstairs, but he'd obviously taken it upon himself not to let me out of his sight. Fine. I turned my back to him and walked toward my mom's room.

I knocked gently, once. There was no answer from inside.

"Mom?" I whispered, leaning my head against the painted panes. Still no answer. I desperately wished Alex wasn't there.

"Mom?" I whispered again, more urgently this time, and put my hand on the knob that Alex had opened half an hour earlier, but the handle wouldn't turn. I tried again, with a little more force. The handle did not budge.

I backed away as if I'd been electrocuted. She must have gotten up to lock the door while we were up in the studio with Apollo.

When I turned around, Alex's face was terrible.

"Forget it," I said shortly, storming across the big room toward the door. "Let's go."

I shouldered past him toward the door, then turned back to see him furtively pushing the notebook on the counter away. He looked up at me guiltily. "I left the number of the house on the Island, in case your mom wants to . . ." he said, but his voice petered out by the time he got to the end of the sentence.

I headed out the door past him and ran headlong down the long, crooked grey stairs. At the bottom, on my way out the door, my shoulder brushed against the plastic-covered A.I.R. sign taped to the front wall.

It felt like a bad joke. Artist-in-residence? My mother wasn't an artist. She was barely even a person right now.

I got my fingers between the duct tape and the window and pulled. It hurt to do, but I was glad; I would have ripped the whole world apart with my bare hands if I could have.

The last bit of tape came off all at once, and I stumbled back, breathing hard, the thick wad of plastic and tape and cardboard crumpled in my hands. I smashed the sign into a ball, dropping it on the unswept tile floor of the foyer before bursting out onto Greene Street, kicking it out to the gutter as I went.

I didn't look back once. Not at the cast-iron building I'd grown up in, my mom motionless upstairs behind the locked doors of her room. Not at Richard, watchful by the curb, his shoulders hunched with worry.

And especially not when I heard the heavy metal front door clang shut behind Alex, because I didn't want to see what he knew, what we both knew, which was that my mother was not going to call me while I was gone.

# NOTGUN

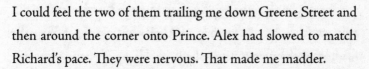

I could feel the two of them trailing me down Greene Street and then around the corner onto Prince. Alex had slowed to match Richard's pace. They were nervous. That made me madder.

I hoped we'd have to go up to Alex's room, where everything was matchy-matchy and his Star Wars figures were arranged just so above his bed. Linda had told us once that they'd have to take apart the built-ins to get anything that fell back there. As soon as I got the chance, I was going to knock Han Solo behind the shelf. Maybe Chewbacca, too.

But as we turned onto Mercer, I saw the station wagon parked outside Alex's building, the doors and back open, a heap of bags piled on the sidewalk next to the car. Which comes from Sweden, as Linda will gladly tell you, like anyone cares.

Linda and Maggie were waiting for us, and Alex ran ahead to them. I could see his relief in the way he ran.

As soon as he got close to the car, Maggie called shotgun. "Shotgun, Alex! Shotgun! Ollie, I get shotgun!" She did this every single time we went anywhere together. She had never—not one time in her whole life—noticed that we *always* let her call shotgun because we'd rather sit together in the back seat than up front with Linda. Alex always said we'd probably be in college before she figured it out.

That afternoon, though, I wished I'd thought to call it. That's how mad I was: I would have voluntarily signed up to listen to Linda yammer on about aerobics classes and loft laws all the way out there rather than spend a single second longer with Alex the disgusting traitor. Unfortunately, the one time I wanted it, Maggie beat me to it, so I was stuck with him in the back.

Linda gave me a big, suffocating hug and told me in a bright, chipper voice to give my bag to Alex, who had taken over the loading of the trunk. Then she kept talking at me in the same voice she uses with Maggie's friends, telling me all about how she liked to open the house *before* Memorial Day, so she could be ready and relax and just *enjoy* Memorial Day, like I knew when that was or cared about any of it.

She stopped talking when she saw the blankness on my face. Linda's big on manners, so I made sure to say, "Thank you for having me," in an automatic way, like everything was normal, like the invitation had been her idea, like she'd wanted me to come.

Then I saw the sadness in her face, too, and I felt bad.

I took my bag to the back of the car where Richard was helping Alex wrestle about twenty navy and white canvas tote bags into the trunk. I'd never seen anything in my whole life like those tote bags: all different sizes, but identical otherwise, with names sewn on the side of them. Two of them belonged to Alex. I knew they were his because they said so, right there on the side: ALEX, in neat, navy blue embroidery.

I'd sworn never to speak to him again. For this, though, I would make an exception.

"Nice tote bag," I said, my voice dripping with mean. He turned away from me without saying anything, but I saw the ugly flush crawl up his neck. The cords stood out on his skinny arms as he shoved the big bag into the back. He didn't look at me the whole rest of the time it took him to pack the car.

Fine with me.

It was time to go. Linda was in the front seat, checking her mirrors like she didn't drive this car all the time; Maggie was next to her, rooting through the snack bag. Alex and Richard did a lackluster version of their secret handshake—their hearts weren't in it—and then Alex went around the far side, got in, and slammed the door.

That left Richard and me on the sidewalk.

"I can't believe this is happening," I said, unable to keep the rage out of my voice. "We were *so close*. All we needed to do was call my dad. He would have helped."

Richard nodded, unconvinced, and I'd almost given up on him saying anything back when it came, soft. "Some things are just too big, Ollie."

He reached around and opened the back seat door for me, gentlemanly like a boy in an old movie.

I slammed past him into my seat next to Alex without looking at either one of them.

~~~

The inside of Linda's station wagon is all black leather. It's like Darth Vader's bathroom in there.

Linda started the engine, then leaned over to help Maggie open a bag of yogurt-covered raisins from the health-food store, reminding her to offer them around the car before taking one herself.

I said "No, thank you" to the bag she held out instead of what I was thinking, which is that I would sooner lick a dog's eyeball than eat a yogurt-covered raisin.

Richard was propped against the door of the building next to Alex's, arms crossed, watching us go. Alex's building might have been a freshly painted navy blue, but the one next door had peeling iron columns out front, covered with graffiti and posters. Linda put the car into gear and Richard raised one hand in farewell, but I didn't acknowledge it, or him.

My other former friend sat next to me, staring out his own window, air-drumming against his leg, oblivious to the poisonous thoughts I was spitting his way. Then, right when I thought I couldn't possibly hate him any more, Alex started to bounce his leg.

Already as far over on my side of the back seat as I could go, I turned my whole body away, pressing my forehead against the cool of the window as we crossed the Williamsburg Bridge into Brooklyn.

# REAR WINDOW

It troubled me, how quickly the streets I knew were replaced by ones I didn't. My dad took me to Brooklyn sometimes for art supplies, but we always went the same way, and it wasn't this one. I looked out the window as Linda's station wagon climbed up from the grimy, grey city streets onto a highway that cut through them, with five- and six-story buildings on either side. The top floors were the same height as the road, so you could look right into the windows.

I kept my eyes peeled; in this Hitchcock movie my dad loves, Jimmy Stewart and Grace Kelly accidentally witness a murder through somebody's window. But all I saw was a woman yelling at someone I couldn't see while she was making a pot of coffee, and a guy by himself on a couch, watching TV and picking his nose.

Looking into those rooms made me think of my model bedroom, of the sound it had made when everything I thought

I needed hit the bottom of Bill's can with a hollow thump. I thought of the big room at home, the stale, abandoned feeling it had gotten when I'd stopped cleaning up. It was completely empty, now that I was gone.

The short, narrow buildings gave way to wide industrial ones, buildings that had once been factories, like mine. Some of them still were, but lots of the big windows were smashed and broken, and I watched a pigeon fly right in through one. Maybe I'd come home to find pigeons filling the big room, adding my discarded peanut shells and pieces of my mom's sculpture to their nests. I imagined red-tipped matches twined into a tidy pile of twigs, lengths of knotted butcher's twine lacing together a system of tiny branches, the embroidered tea bag flying on top of the nest like a ship's flag. My mom would like that.

Alex was looking out his own window, checking out the graffiti scrolling by. Sometimes you could see how the artists had climbed onto a roof or scaffolding nearby; other times, the brightly colored scrawl looked like it had gotten there by magic. I knew that Alex wasn't looking at the art, but figuring out how he'd get up there, finding foot- and hand-holds in the brickwork where a normal person would only see a crack.

Then I thought about the way I'd hit him outside of my mom's room, and the hollow feeling in my gut got worse, as if I'd hit myself.

I turned back to my own view, suddenly restless. I didn't want to climb, like Alex—I wanted to run, as hard and fast as I could, my lungs pumping furiously to keep up with my legs so I could whistle by all these feelings before the sour egg of anger and regret and guilt and fear in my chest made a permanent home there.

Except that I was stuck in the stupid back seat.

What was Apollo going to do now? Would my mom think that it was me, not Alex, who had told? Would she be angry? Would she get up? Would my dad come home? Could he?

After a few minutes, the buildings outside my window gave way to shabby little two-story houses, and then finally to trees. We were on Long Island, Linda said. It looked like the country. I watched the highway signs pass by, silently repeating the unfamiliar names of the towns we were passing through: Merrick, Wantagh, Massapequa, Islip. The words had a weight in my mouth.

I leaned my head against the seat back and closed my eyes, feeling the doorknob to my mom's room in my hand again, the way it had refused to turn. But it's too easy for tears to leak out when your eyes are closed, so I opened them again and looked out the window, watching the poles go by.

~~~

"Get a twenty out of my purse, Alex. I'll drop the three of you at the terminal so you can buy tickets while I find parking." Linda met my confused eyes in the rearview mirror. "We take a ferry over, Ollie. There are no cars on the Island."

We got out of the car, and Linda and Alex unloaded that mountain of tote bags. I thought a ferry terminal would look like Grand Central or Penn Station, but it was nothing more than a couple of benches facing the water underneath a broken-down-looking metal roof.

Tired and distracted as I was, I was curious, too. Maggie showed me everything she thought I needed to see: the little hut where you could buy clam chowder or an egg-and-cheese sandwich; the machine that squashed pennies into souvenirs; the ticket booth, like at the movies, with two bored teenagers chewing gum behind the glass as they pushed our tickets through the mouse hole.

The biggest surprise, though, was Linda. As soon as she came back from parking the car, she turned into a different person. The sadness and tension were still there in her face. But she knew everyone, the girls selling the tickets and some older people already waiting on the benches. While Maggie was leaning out to toss the Cheerios she'd brought to feed the ducks, Linda wasn't yelling at her to sit quietly or telling her to be careful, even though the only thing between Maggie and the water was a skinny piece of rope. Instead, she sat on a bench with her eyes closed and her face tilted up to the sun. She didn't even look like herself.

I'd never been on a boat before, but I didn't say that to anyone. And, as committed as I was to having a terrible time, the boat ride was amazing. We sat up top, where the wind whipped the words right out of Maggie's mouth once we got out of the harbor and started going fast. I tried to copy Linda by closing my eyes and letting the weak spring sun warm my face, but I couldn't keep my eyes closed. There was too much to see.

Just when I had started to get used to the rush of the black water churning up white foam and the wind on my face and the loud motor underneath me, the boat slowed down again. We were coming up to a long dock. Little houses dotted the land behind.

Two little girls in pastel sweat suits were jumping up and down and waving at the end of the dock. Maggie wormed her way through the grown-ups to be one of the first ones off the boat, and we were still waiting at the top of the stairs when we saw her burst out from below. One of the girls pulled up her sweatshirt to show Maggie the turquoise bathing suit she was wearing underneath, even though it wasn't anywhere near warm enough to swim, and then the three of them ran off, without Linda or any other grown-up.

Forgetting that I wasn't talking to him, I looked over at Alex. When we were together, it was our job to worry about Maggie. Linda was there, but she was talking to an old guy in a tan vest with a million pockets.

Alex shook his head, exasperated, like I hadn't been paying attention. "She's fine."

I stomped past him, down the metal stairs and off the boat.

A friend of Linda's was waiting for us on the dock, holding the handle of a little red wagon. She was tan, with long hair, flowy blue clothes, and lots of silver jewelry, including a delicate toe ring on one of her bare feet. She hugged Linda for a long, long time. She smiled at me but didn't introduce herself.

Alex didn't acknowledge her, either, but she poked him in the stomach as he passed, and I saw him smile as he twisted away; ignoring each other must have been an old game between them.

It was cutesy and I hated it.

Linda and her friend walked ahead with the wagon piled with tote bags, already talking intently and leaving me with Alex. Even though he was mad at me, he was happy to be there, I could tell.

I was, too. This is why it's hard to be a curious person. I wanted to scuff my feet, ignoring everything like a furious teenager on TV, but I couldn't stop myself from looking around.

Since there weren't any cars, there weren't any roads, either—just narrow weather-beaten wooden pathways weaving their way through the houses. There were lots of greys in the washed-out wood shingles and the damp sand in the front yards, but they couldn't have been more different from the greys on Greene Street.

I could feel my brain flooding with details. Drawing is all about details—the details you put in, and the ones you choose not to include, too. But everything I was looking at was so new, so unfamiliar, that I couldn't sort through what to leave out.

Linda and her friend stopped the wagon and started to unload the grocery bags Linda had brought from the city. I knew I should help, but I was too busy staring in astonishment at the tiny house they'd stopped in front of, which looked like the kind

we used to make out of construction paper in kindergarten: a triangle roof on top of a fat square, with a paned window on each side of the front door.

Alex grabbed a few of the bags out of the wagon and went up a little ramp to the front door. Even the doorknob was tiny.

"Up," Alex said. I retrieved my duffel and followed him up a narrow wooden staircase off the living room.

The little room at the top of the stairs looked like it was straight out of a fairy tale. The ceiling was pitched so steeply that I couldn't stand up except in the exact middle of the room. There was a twin bed pushed up against each of the sloping walls, each one of them with its own patchwork quilt. In between them was a table with a white lamp on it. Above it, right up near the peak of the roof, was a tiny round window.

Alex threw his bag on the bed on the right, and Linda's voice came through the floorboards at us. "C'mon, guys; people are heading down to the dock."

# WATCH THE BLUES

I followed Alex downstairs. Linda was in the kitchen, pouring herself a glass of white wine. There were pots and pans hanging from nails on the walls, and the stove only had two burners, like the hot plate in the studio. It surprised me how different the house was from Linda's loft, which was all white leather and glass and metal, everything super clean and modern and untouchable.

This house was lived-in. I loved it.

The toe ring lady, whose name I still didn't know, grabbed three cold cans of apple juice out of the fridge for us, the skinny ones with a sticker on top. I helped Maggie pull hers off.

When we left the house, I turned right, the opposite of the way we'd come in. Alex went the other way. "The sun sets on the bay side," he told me, like I knew where that was. He was barefoot. I thought about leaving my sneakers in the pile of shoes outside the door but worried about them getting stolen; I only had one pair with me. I left them on.

The dock was a wooden platform over the water where a cluster of grown-ups were drinking wine. There weren't a lot of people there, maybe because it was the weekend before Memorial Day. Maggie went over to some kids fishing off the end of the dock, using pieces of what looked like raw chicken, although I chose not to investigate further. She squatted next to one of the boys, looking into a deep white bucket at the fish he'd caught. I could see its shadow flitting around inside.

Alex walked along the railing of the dock. The railing was a flat board, wide enough to sit on, but only just. There was a ten-foot drop from the railing to the water. He sped up, leaping like a mountain goat along the edge, going faster and faster. I couldn't believe he was doing it in front of Linda—and that she was seeing it and wasn't screaming her head off—but it didn't even seem like she cared. When running along that rail got boring, Alex turned upside down and walked along it balanced on his hands.

The dad with the fish was impressed, and he nudged Linda to look over.

I thought he was going to get it then for sure, but all Linda said was, "Oh, Alex. Please." It was more of a grumble than a real complaint, and she turned away and walked toward a small group of laughing grown-ups at the edge of the dock without making him get down.

We were there for about an hour. I sat on the high, splintery bench, swinging my legs and wishing I'd brought my notebook. If I'd had it, I would have drawn the loose coil of skinny rope wrapped carelessly around a pole, like it wasn't the only thing holding a shiny white and royal-blue boat called *Seas the Day*. I would have drawn the pool of water under the spigot where Maggie rinsed off her feet, and the pair of twisted purple sunglasses someone had stepped on, resting on the rim of the trash.

When Linda made her way back toward us, her empty wineglass dangling upside down between her fingers, the sun had started to set, and the sky was filled with bands of lavender and orange and pink. "Still dry, I see," she said to Alex, who took a little bow. "We're going to get dinner started. Merle's going to stay down for a little while. Come on back after the ball drops, you two."

I watched Maggie and Linda walk away, holding hands. Maggie said something that made Linda crack up, a real belly laugh with her head thrown back, and I understood that Linda wasn't holding Maggie's hand like she does in the city, worried about kidnappers and cars, but because she wanted to.

I turned away fast before I could miss my mom.

The group of grown-ups down by the water had thinned out a little, and they were quieter now, too, maybe because the sky was getting wilder with every minute. The sun was the least of it; the sky was flooded with bands of color now, the clouds shaping the stripes of light.

Merle—the lady with the toe ring—was standing beside me. "Watch the blues," she said, and she was right. The oranges and pinks might have been stealing the scene, but the blues were incredible. I named every one I could see under my breath: celadon, aquamarine, cerulean, but there were hundreds of blues in there that I had no words for, smoky purples and faded teals, colors even Apollo might not have known the names for.

The ball really did drop. The huge orangey sun turned into a half, then a quarter, then a sliver. A minute later, it was gone, and the ferocious pink glow peeking out from behind the horizon was all that was left of the day.

A handful of the people still watching clapped.

I felt embarrassed for them. "It goes down every day," I said to Merle.

"Maybe it's a way to say thank you," she said.

I scowled. There were a lot of things about this day I didn't feel particularly thankful for. "To who?"

Merle was still looking at the sky. "It's not the worst thing, is it? To celebrate the extraordinary in the ordinary?" I knew she was teasing me, but it was also the most perfect description of my mom's art I'd ever heard.

"How come you're friends with Linda?" Even as it came out of my mouth, I could hear that it was the wrong thing to say, and I started to apologize, but she stopped me.

"Linda's all right. Anyway, as you've probably noticed, you don't get to choose your family." My face flushed, even though she smiled to let me know that it was okay.

Of course. Merle was Alex's Auntie Em—Linda's sister.

Alex wandered back over to me. "I'm ready to go," he said, rubbing one bare foot over the other and looking off at the water.

"See you back at the house," Merle said, still looking at the dramatic sky. I was sad to leave her. It was a relief to spend time with someone I didn't have to act mad in front of.

Alex and I set off down the boardwalk, passing clusters of teenagers bundled up in jean jackets against the evening chill. Excitement crackled off them.

The walk back was longer than I remembered. Alex moved quickly, and I hurried to keep up. I'd been walking around SoHo and the Village by myself for a couple of years, but I had no idea where Alex's house on the Island was. All the streets were boardwalks, and they all looked the same to me. I couldn't remember the name of the street that their house was on; I didn't know if the streets had names at all.

Alex walked quickly past little houses, private but set close together. Most of them had lights on in them now. I could hear people laughing and setting the table for dinner. Kids with hair wet from their showers hung off the front porches in pajamas and rode their bikes around slowly, trading candy. Alex waved and said hi to some of them. He stopped to talk to one boy for a while, but he didn't introduce me, so I hung back.

Even if I lost him, I told myself, I'd be okay. The streets were laid out in a grid, like midtown. I'd know the house again, even if I had to walk up and down every one of those streets. Still, I was relieved when Alex turned the corner and I recognized a red wagon planter in the front yard of one of the houses. His house was on this street.

He was ahead of me when a flock of small black birds emerged against the streetlight. There were lots of them—too many—making fast, deep swoops almost to the ground. I hesitated, unwilling to walk toward the swarm, but they came for me anyway, fluttering so close I couldn't stop myself from flapping my arms in terror.

Alex kept going, ignoring them and me.

"Alex," I yelled.

He looked back, saw me standing stock still as the terrifying birds plunged around me, then turned around and kept walking.

"They're going to smash right into my face!"

"They won't hit you, dummy. They use sonar," Alex said over his shoulder.

I was sick of not knowing what was going on. "I don't know what you're talking about," I snapped. Alex didn't stop.

"What kind of stupid bird uses sonar?" I shouted down the dark boardwalk at him. There were hundreds of these crazy birds ducking and diving, some of them so close I could feel the wind from their wings hushing my face.

Alex walked up the ramp to the door of the little house. The porch light was on behind him so that I couldn't see his expression. I was sorry then that I'd been so pigheaded because, as mad as I was at Alex, I didn't think I was going to be able to get through this insane corridor of birds all by myself.

His voice drifted back toward where I was standing. "They're not birds, Ollie. They're *bats*."

Then the screen door slammed behind him.

I have never ever beaten Alex in a race, and I probably never will. But I can tell you that if he'd been running alongside me through the curtain of bats on the dark boardwalk that night, he would have gotten a workout.

# SICK

Bats, apparently, are good to have around because they eat mosquitoes.

I can tell you: There were still plenty of mosquitoes on the deck that night.

Apollo had been right: It did get cold. But it was beautiful, too, especially after Linda and Merle lit tiny candles in glass jars and placed them on the round table, which was covered with a waxy blue-and-white-checked tablecloth.

I had planned not to eat anything as part of my silent protest, but I lost my willpower as soon as I smelled the food. Linda's diet did not appear to be in effect. There were hot dogs, smoky from the grill, along with toasted buns and baked beans and sauerkraut and salad and grilled ears of corn with butter. I was so glad to eat something that wasn't a peanut or pizza or leftover Chinese, I couldn't stop myself from loading up a huge plate, and then another.

It was hard for me to stay mad with such a full belly, so I settled for not saying much. I didn't have to. Linda and Merle and Maggie talked about the people they knew on the Island—who was coming out over the weekend, who would be renting a different house that summer, which of the older kids they knew would be counselors at the camp Maggie went to. Linda's face was still tense and tight, but she put her bare feet up on the table while we were still eating, which I could not imagine her doing at home.

Alex didn't talk much. That was my fault. He didn't look at me once.

After dinner, Merle turned off the Christmas lights strung on the fence so we could look at the stars. She showed me how to poke a marshmallow on a stick and hold it over the dying coals in the barbeque so that it turned golden brown on the outside without catching on fire. Then she smeared it off the skewer onto a square of chocolate waiting on a graham cracker. The toasted marshmallow was almost liquid inside, and when I made a sandwich with another graham cracker, it melted the chocolate.

They're called s'mores because you always want some more. I had three.

Maggie fell asleep, still dressed, on a bed in the little room next to the kitchen while the rest of us were clearing the table. Linda washed; Merle dried. To be polite, I asked Linda if they needed help, but she shook her head, and the two of them started singing along with the song on the radio.

Alex and I climbed the narrow staircase to the room in the attic and turned our backs to each other while we were putting on pajamas. I got into bed and realized how tired I was.

Alex reached over and turned out the little white light.

The dark was extreme. There were no streetlights outside, and the smells of the bed were unfamiliar. I wondered if I'd ever be able to fall asleep.

It was then that I realized, to my horror, that I had not brushed my teeth.

Alex hadn't brushed his, either, but it never bothers him like it bothers me. Ordinarily, I would have gotten up, even if it meant he'd tease me a little. But there was so much bad feeling piled up between us that I couldn't make my legs move.

I tried to distract myself with all the noises I could hear. There must have been a million bugs out there. I could hear the ocean, shushing from a few blocks away, and the wind in the tree outside the little window, and something in the front yard that might have been a frog.

Nature is *loud*.

Apollo had told me that Alex had done the right thing, which really meant that I'd done the wrong thing by not telling. I'd thought I could fix it if I had more time. But what if not telling had made whatever was happening with my mom worse?

I rolled over. Alex's legs were bent as if he was running, and he had one arm thrown over his head. Even when he was sleeping it looked like he was moving.

I felt a pang. I didn't want to be mad at him anymore, and I didn't want him to be mad at me, either.

Like I needed one more thing to feel bad about.

⟨ ⟩

Ten minutes later, I had run out of distractions.

I *had* to brush my teeth.

I slipped out of bed, as quietly as I could, snuck my tooth-brush from my duffel, and tiptoed to the top of the stairs. I could picture the little bathroom, the sink the size of a dinner plate and the mirror above it so crazed with black marks I could barely see my face. As tiny as the house was, the bathroom seemed very far away, with a lot of creaking wood in between. I tried to feel light as I moved across the complaining floorboards, focusing on the minty relief I'd feel once I got down there.

I hadn't heard any sounds coming from downstairs for a while and assumed that Merle and Linda had gone to bed, but when I got to the steep wooden stairs, I could hear they were still moving around the kitchen.

I paused halfway down. Something was wrong.

The radio was off, and the easy rhythm between the two grown-ups had changed. I could hear Linda flouncing around, slamming cabinet doors and huffing the way she did when she was mad.

"You see the way she looks? Silent and starving, like something out of Dickens."

I held my breath.

Merle didn't say anything. A plate clattered loudly onto the stack as Linda built up steam. "Like a street urchin. Totally neglected."

Merle still didn't speak.

"I just can't understand it. Graham jumping ship for another woman is one thing. But Doll is her *mother*."

Graham was my dad; Doll was my mom. Linda *was* talking about me.

Merle spoke up, finally. She sounded exasperated, which is the effect that Linda has on a lot of people. "Leave her be, for God's sake. She's a good kid. We'll get some food into her, fresh air, a little sun. She'll bounce back."

But Linda barreled right along as if Merle hadn't said anything at all. "I wish I knew going to bed was an option. It sure must be nice to be an *artiste*. Maybe I'll just ignore all my responsibilities—my children, my home, my clients—and wait for someone to roll around to pick up the slack."

When Merle responded, her voice was pure acid.

"Doll is *sick*. You don't think that woman would be doing something different if she could? All you can do is step in and hope that someone would do the same for Alex and Mags if you ever needed them to. Which, by the way? *God forbid*." She might have said more, I don't know, because I turned around, hoping to creep back up the steps without them seeing me, but as soon as I shifted my weight, the wooden step I was standing on let out an unmistakable creak.

There was a sudden silence below me. I couldn't see them, but I knew the two of them must have been looking up at the bottom of the stairs where I was standing. I could imagine the horror on their faces. A drawing of the scene popped into my head, and I almost laughed at the image, the three of us standing frozen like statues, our mouths frozen into little shocked o's.

I stuck my toothbrush in my mouth, taking some comfort from the little bit of minty paste left on it from the last time I'd used it. Then I turned and clomped my way back up the stairs to the little white bed.

# THE GAME

When I woke up the next morning, I had no idea where I was.

Nothing I could see—the white-painted wood of the sloped ceiling, the patchwork quilt on top of me, the unfamiliar morning light filtering through the thin cotton curtains—made any sense, and for a second or two, I felt like I was falling through space and time before I landed back into myself.

I rolled over. Alex was lying on his back. He opened his eyes, looked at me, then pulled the pillow over his head to block out the sunlight. But after a minute or two, he swung his legs onto the floor, turned his back to me, and started getting dressed. I wasn't sure what I should do, but as he headed toward the stairs he looked back for me impatiently, so I got up and pulled my jeans on fast.

Something had shifted between us. When we'd gotten onto the ferry, I'd been mad at him, madder than I'd ever been at anyone. By the time we went to bed, though, Alex had turned into the one who wasn't talking.

When I got downstairs, he was in the kitchen, his hand in a tin on the counter filled with muffins. He grabbed one in each hand before moving toward the door and used his knuckles to throw open the screen door. Maggie, sleeping in her pretty bed near the refrigerator, didn't stir.

Was one of them for me? I couldn't be sure, so I grabbed another, pushing the sweet cake gratefully into my mouth. And I wasn't sure if I should follow, but Alex bent his knee to stop the door with his bare foot a split second before it slammed closed. He was holding it open for me. Then he headed off down the boardwalk, the opposite of the way we'd gone the night before for sunset.

Neither of us was wearing shoes, and the weathered wooden boards were cool and wet beneath our feet. The small front yards we passed were mostly sand. WELCOME, spelled the seashells in one yard. LIFE'S A BEACH, read a hand-painted sign sticking out of a grassy patch in another.

We went up a hill. Alex picked up speed, making it tough for me to keep up. He knew it, too. And so I was puffing a little as we came over the rise of the hill, when I stopped dead.

The boardwalk ended at a short flight of stairs that led down to an empty expanse of sand.

Beyond that, there was the ocean.

I'd never seen the ocean before. I'd seen the Hudson when my dad and I woke up early and went to the meatpacking district for Dominican stew with eggs and toast alongside the club kids who'd been out all night. I'd seen the East River sluggishly passing under the Brooklyn Bridge when my dad borrowed his friend Leon's car so he and my mom could take a trip out to the art supply store they liked in Brooklyn. I'd seen the bay when we crossed it on the ferry, and at the dock the night before. But I'd never seen the ocean. I'd seen thousands of pictures and postcards of the ocean, but not a single one of them could have prepared me for the way I felt looking at the real thing.

I looked over at Alex—*are you* seeing *this?*—but he'd stopped where the sand was getting darker to roll up the cuffs of his jeans. I guessed it was old news to him. Anyway, he wasn't talking to me. The wide cuffs of his jeans combined with his strong, skinny arms sticking out from his white T-shirt made him look the way I imagined Huckleberry Finn.

I bent over to roll my own jeans, feeling the sand crunchy and cool under my feet, and then the delicious shock of the cold water as it rolled up and over my toes, scary white in the bright morning light. When the wave pulled back out, my feet sunk into the sand, so that with three or four cycles of the ocean, my toes were buried and I was rooted in place.

Alex was beside me, a little ahead. I don't know how long we stood there watching the waves pull in and out over our feet, but it was a long time, long enough to get used to the cold. Then, abruptly, Alex turned his back to me and headed down the beach at the water's edge. Again, he seemed to wait for a second so I could follow, and I didn't know what else to do, so I did, a few paces behind.

We still had not spoken a word.

A woman and a man held hands with a happily squealing toddler, swinging him up and over the waves when they broke near his feet. A lady did tai chi like the old people in Seward Park. A man in a wide-brimmed yellow Curious George hat walked slowly, swinging a dark metal detector in front of him. I would have liked to ask him about the coolest thing he ever found, but Alex was ahead of me, and I hustled to catch up.

The beachfront houses thinned out after we'd been walking for a few minutes, and Alex turned up the beach to head into the scrubby forest past the dunes. I hesitated. City kids don't have a lot of experience with forests. Plus, there had been a sign on the fence where we'd first come down to the beach: DUNES OFF LIMITS. I did not think that Linda, even the relatively new and improved Relaxed Beach Linda, would be happy about bailing us out if we got caught.

I dithered, unsure whether to follow or not, so that Alex was almost all the way up to the tree line by the time I broke into a run, I didn't want to be left alone on that beach. The incline was steeper than I'd thought, though, and the sand softer. I couldn't get any traction, and the sand kicked up uselessly behind me, like a dream where you're running through quicksand. Embarrassed but desperate not to slip back to the bottom, I clawed my way up the last third, crawling on hands and knees.

When I got up there, breathing heavily, Alex was gone.

"Alex?" I said quietly, hating the quaver in my voice.

The forest wasn't dark and foreboding like I had pictured it at all. It was quiet, though I could hear the lazy heaving of the ocean and the chattering gossip of the insects in the trees. The trees themselves were short and twisted, some of them growing almost sideways, a lot of them not that much taller than me. I liked the rusty mat of pine needles covering the sand, as well as all the colors I could find in the rough, peeling bark.

Forgetting about Alex for a moment, I put my hand out to touch a gnarled, ugly branch with knobby bumps, big and raw and swollen at the knuckles like Joyce Walker's hands. My own fingers twitched, sketching those bumps in the air. For the first time since I'd left home, I felt like I could draw.

And then, out of the corner of my eye, I caught the faintest movement. Alex was there, leaning against a tree, his back to me.

"Hey," I said, absurdly pleased to see him. But he was already moving again, deeper into the trees. "Wait up," I said. He glanced back at me, then kept going.

He blazed a trail for us, vaulting over low, weathered fence pickets strung with wire and trotting between tall tufts of beach grass. I ran to catch up the way I'd thought about running in the car, like I was leaving something behind, my feet and heart suddenly lighter than they had been in weeks. Twigs and pinecones and tiny stones crunched beneath our feet, but we didn't step on anything long or hard enough for them to hurt. We ducked under low branches, twisted and leapt over shallow roots, picking up speed as we went. The day was heating up, but the sweat on the back of my neck dried fast.

Occasionally, Alex would dip out of the forest, running at an angle along the very top of the dunes. There weren't many people on the beach, mostly people walking their dogs or hanging out with their kids, but nobody looked up at us anyway. We were invisible.

A black lab, out for his morning walk, trotted up the dunes to say hello. Alex froze before taking off, leaving the big dog whining anxiously at the edge of the forest before his owner whistled him back.

We were playing The Game, the disappearing game we'd played for years at the playground next to the Met. No talking, to anyone else or each other.

When we hit a bare patch of beach with no people at all, we'd run quickly into the water, wetting our feet in the cold waves with the tiny birds. I didn't feel bad anymore about walking on the dunes. Those OFF LIMITS signs were for grown-ups, trudging heavily through the sand, weighed down by their ugly coolers and plastic beach chairs. We didn't move like that.

We ran for what felt like hours. Then, hot and tired, I bent over with my hands on my knees to catch my breath, and my stomach growled—the first audible communication that had taken place between us all day. Alex didn't say anything, but when I was ready to go again, he'd turned around so that we were going back the way we'd come, all the way back to the little house.

Nobody was there. Maggie's bed was empty. There was a half-drunk cup of coffee on the little table and nothing in the muffin tin. Still without speaking, Alex pulled a small pot off its nail on the wall in the kitchen, filled it with water, and put it on one of the burners, where it rocked back and forth on its warped bottom. After he put eggs in the pot, he laid soft slices of potato bread on the counter. I watched as he chopped a big pickle into little pieces with a steak knife and put them at the bottom of a blue metal bowl. He silenced the chipped white timer right before it went off and peeled the eggs hot, tossing them from hand to hand, too impatient to wait for them to cool. Mayonnaise, a handful of crushed potato chips, and, almost before I knew it, I was back in the dunes with a messy, heavy waxed paper bundle in my hand.

I squatted like Alex did to eat, wiping my hands on my jeans and my mouth on the shoulder of my shirt. All this without a word. After that, it seemed like the most natural thing in the world to lie back, cushioned by that mat of fallen pine needles, and close our eyes against the afternoon heat.

I slept long and hard. When I woke up, Alex was already awake, lazily peeling the bark from a stick. He had waited for me.

And just like that—still without a word—whatever had been broken between us was fixed.

# SLOW TIME

We stayed on the Island for three more days.

Monday morning, Linda called school to excuse our absences. "A family emergency," she called it. True in my case, and more and more, it seemed like it might be true for Alex, too.

Linda didn't seem to care what we did. The whole time we were out there, she didn't mention protein once. She stayed up late with Merle, the two of them talking in quiet, urgent voices. They weren't talking about me—I checked. Mostly, they were talking about Alex's dad. A couple of times, it sounded like Linda might be crying.

Time moved differently on the Island. We ate when we got hungry, slept when we were tired. One day, I slept until eleven in the little white bed upstairs. Another night, Alex and I woke up while it was still dark and went down to the ocean and lay on our backs in the cool sand, looking for shooting stars. There were too many to wish on. We fell asleep on the beach and woke up with sunburns on the sides of our faces to the sounds of families setting up their umbrellas next to us.

That afternoon, it finally got warm enough to swim. We let the waves slam into us for hours. Afterward, we let Maggie bury us in the sand.

We ate ice cream every day, sometimes twice. The teenagers behind the counter gave us tastes of the day's special flavors on tiny, flat wooden spoons. If they were bored, they'd even let us taste the regular ones, like chocolate and vanilla.

Alex and I walked down to the lighthouse and talked our way into going up to the top—242 steps—even though we didn't have any money for admission. When we came down again, the lady at the desk gave us each a certificate and a lighthouse pin.

I got a postcard at the general store while Alex was buying one for his grandma and sent it to Richard. I didn't sign it, but I made a pretty good drawing of a sea monster on the back so he'd know who it was from.

We saw the sunset every night, and I didn't feel silly clapping when everyone else did.

The whole time, I drew. I drew a pile of UNO cards scattered on the deck, abandoned after Maggie caught Alex cheating. I drew a jellyfish Alex found on the beach that looked like a giant contact lens made of clear Jell-O. I drew two broken sand dollars and a piece of seaweed like a strand of beads. I drew Linda's elegant feet in flip-flops with woven leather straps and the rusted red bike with the cracked white vinyl seat that Maggie had gotten too

big for, and a forgotten yellow
coffee cup with a daisy on
it, wedged into the sand
of the front yard.

I hadn't forgotten
about my mother. I did
think about her, and about
Apollo, and about my dad. It was
just that the rest of my life—Greene Street;
Apollo's jars in a box, the colors trapped inside them; my mom's
bed—it all seemed impossibly far away.

I knew it was silly, but I felt like if that world, my world at
home, was real, then the world on the Island couldn't be.

And I really didn't want that to be true.

❧

Our last full day on the Island, it rained.

Merle and Linda put on giant yellow slickers after breakfast
and disappeared into the mist. Alex and Maggie and I relocated
to the front room, snug in the lamplight with only the screen
door between us and the rain, to do a jigsaw puzzle. We finished
it—another lighthouse—but there were three pieces missing.

Afterward, Maggie got up and made everyone tuna salad
sandwiches with bits of celery and onion. At some point, she had
turned into a bona-fide person.

After lunch, she brought an antique wicker sewing box from
her room back to the rug, where Alex and I were reading through

a pile of old comics we'd found stacked under the stairs. Interested despite myself, I watched over the top of my *Archie's Joke Book* as she emptied the contents of the box onto the rough white rug.

She made neat rows of wooden spools stamped 15 CENTS PURE SILK, wound with thread the colors of gowns in old movies—periwinkle, moss green, seafoam, cerise. Next to them, she set out a strawberry pincushion, a silver thimble, and my favorite: a pair of delicate gold scissors made to look like a stork, the blades forming its long beak.

A red tin, the lettering long scratched off, held buttons; Maggie dumped them onto the carpet and started sorting them into matching piles. Most were ordinary, the white kind you see on a dad button-down, but some of them were treasures: a clear Lucite dome studded in rhinestones; an iridescent opal sliver with a gentle depression my finger could barely resist; a set of six made from dusty pink satin, each one padded and tufted like the back of a couch.

And a couple of ugly mauve ones, too—dead ringers for the old-lady buttons Alex had found behind the bushes in the park.

I nudged Alex's leg with my foot. He looked up, annoyed at the interruption until he caught sight of the buttons.

Dropping his comic, he leaned forward to pick one up. "Hey!

Where'd you get these? We found some like this in the park," he said to Maggie.

Who started to shake with laughter.

Alex looked at me and then back at his sister. "Wait. What's going on?"

Maggie only laughed harder, and as possible explanations poked out at me, I started to laugh, too: "She was there with us that day. You already forgot poor Rolando?"

Alex looked at Maggie like he was going to throw something. "Hold on. You set us up?"

"I didn't mean to!" Maggie protested, bringing her giggling under control enough to explain. "I mean, I meant to leave the buttons. It's a thing the pigeon lady does, when an animal she's taking care of dies. Like a memorial."

Ugh. It hadn't occurred to me there might be a rotting bird under there; we'd used our hands to dig.

Alex's voice was at least two octaves higher than usual. "But we dug it up! There wasn't anything there."

Maggie looked at him with contempt. "It's illegal to bury animals in the park, dumbo. She drops the bodies off at a vet's office," she said. "Then she leaves a ring of buttons where she found them. That bush was where I'd found Rolando; I thought leaving the buttons would make me less sad."

Alex glowered at her.

"But then you guys found them and got all sleuthy about it," Maggie said, failing to keep the amusement out of her voice. "And that *did* make me less sad."

I thought Alex might explode.

"'Let's secure this perimeter, folks,'" Maggie choked out, imitating Alex in Official Detective Mode. "' We gotta maintain a clean chain of custody on this evidence!'"

I may have snickered a little; her Alex imitation was almost as good as my trademark Linda.

Alex jumped to his feet, disgusted with us both—embarrassed, too, if I had to bet. He threw the screen door open and headed out into the drizzle, his bare feet smacking the soaked boardwalk outside.

The screen door swung back behind him, hung for a moment, then slammed shut.

Maggie yelled after him, "You should have let me play with you guys! I would have told you, if you'd let me play!"

She shrugged one shoulder at me then, a wicked grin splitting her funny, freckled face.

*"Probably."*

# THE WALK BACK

The sunset was gorgeous that night. Merle told me that it always is after it rains.

I watched her and Maggie teasing each other down the boardwalk on their way back to make dinner, and realized that I didn't want to go home. I made Alex stay down at the dock until it was almost dark, but eventually, his growling stomach drove us back toward the little house.

The walk back had become easy; I couldn't believe it had ever been unfamiliar to me. There was the house with the rainbow flag, the light green house with the fishing poles out front, the dark blue one with the fat orange cat in the window whom I had not been able to befriend.

I was wondering how I could feel the grain in the worn boards of the walk beneath my bare feet when Alex, a couple of steps ahead of me, gave a quiet "Hey" and stopped so quickly that I practically plowed right into the back of him.

I opened my mouth to protest, but he shushed me with his hand.

We were standing in front of a parcel of land without a house on it. The greenery had gone wild, and the only thing I could see were tall green fronds, like stalks of corn. But Alex was looking intently into the lot and didn't move, so I didn't, either.

It took a minute for my eyes to adjust to the darkness. When I could see, there, right in front of us, was a deer, so close I could have reached right out and touched her.

She was still and silent and watching us, ready to run at the slightest noise or sudden movement. But not running, not yet.

"Baby," Alex breathed, so quietly I almost didn't hear. For a second, I thought he was teasing me, but then I saw her. In fact, I couldn't believe I hadn't seen her right away, but I guess I was too distracted by the giant deer right in front of us to notice that the deer was in fact two deer, and that one of them was a little tiny baby deer, with white spots on her butt like Bambi.

The baby stopped eating to look up at us. Her nose twitched, and her ears and little fuzzy tail were going crazy. But after two seconds she put her head down again. The mother was still looking at us, chewing at the grass still in her mouth every once in a while, trying to decide whether or not we were something to worry about. Ultimately, she put her head down again, too.

Alex and I stood as still as statues. I couldn't believe I was close enough to a deer to hear it swallow. The mother was pretty rough-looking; her coat was kind of chewed up and she was really skinny.

But the baby was perfect and downy soft, like something out of a picture book.

Alex and I watched, breathing in the smell of the green, wet earth. The baby nosed through the grass, looking for one kind in particular, ripping up mouthfuls when she found it. Every time the baby moved, the mother moved, too. She always made sure that she was between us and the baby, protecting her. I did notice that.

I watched them and thought about Merle saying my mom was sick. I thought about how sure my mom had sounded when she'd said that I would be better off without her. For the millionth time, I thought about the feeling I'd had when the knob to her room had refused to turn in my hand.

It had felt like she'd been locking me out. But what if the opposite was true? What if she'd been locking herself in?

Eventually, the deer worked their way through the patch of deliciousness in that yard, and the two of them walked off in search of more. They passed so close to us we could have bent our knees and touched them.

It was so dark by then that we couldn't see much past the ends of our noses, but we watched them go, their silhouettes moving down the boardwalk until they were mere specks, and then gone.

And the last little bit of whatever had been so hard and mean in my chest went with them.

# MAYBE

We left late the next afternoon.

It was not a happy car.

That morning, Linda had put on a full face of makeup for the first time since we'd left the city. While we were still on the Island, it made her look out of place; people barely wore pants there, let alone lipstick. In the car, it looked like armor.

Maggie had fled the little house at dawn to play in the ocean with her friends. Still wearing a damp bathing suit underneath one of Alex's old sweatshirts, she fell asleep in the front seat as soon as the car started to move. Sweat and salt curled her hair; tearstains marked her cheeks.

That morning, I'd slipped the color study I'd saved from my model out of my jeans pocket and into her box of buttons. A little mystery for her to solve, someday.

Alex stared out the window in the back seat next to me,

playing drum solos on his legs until Linda snapped at him. While we were waiting for the ferry, I'd gotten up the courage to ask him what was going on with Linda and his dad. "She's not sure they're going to stay together," he said, kicking at one of the tote bags by our feet. "Not like it'll make a difference, like he's ever around anyway."

I'd looked off down the dock at two seagulls fighting over somebody's dropped bagel in case he started to cry.

An hour later, I was sitting next to him in the back seat, watching the fake green of the suburbs pass by and hating myself for getting sucked into the world of the Island as if it had been real. It wasn't that I hadn't wondered what would happen to me when I got home while we were there; of course I had. But every time the thought had occurred to me, I'd pushed it back down.

Like a bath toy, it was popping up again now. My mind galloped through the possibilities as if I could make up for those four careless days. There was no way they'd let me go back to living at home if my mom wasn't better. So where could I go? Whatever was going on between Linda and Alex's dad probably meant I couldn't live with them—not that I'd want to; not that they'd offered. Richard's parents didn't have room for me, and they didn't really do things outside the rules, which was both the good and the bad thing about them.

I chewed at a cuticle. Maybe I could live with Apollo for a little while. Linda frowned at me meaningfully through the rearview mirror, and I dropped my hand back into my lap. Except that Apollo was already more involved than he wanted to be in my family's mess, which was probably why he had one foot out the door.

Four days was long enough for my dad to have gotten back from France. Maybe I'd walk in to find the apartment all tidied up, my mom sitting on a stool by the counter with a jam jar of red wine, waiting for a spoonful of his famous Bolognese. It was a nice thought, but I shook my head impatiently to clear it, startling Alex out of his own reverie. We were getting close to the city, already driving past warehouses and burned-out buildings; there wasn't time for little-kid fantasies of everything being okay. My parents weren't getting back together. Even if she was out of bed, my mom would be mad at me for telling. And my dad, though he'd never show it, would probably be mad at me for making him come back from France.

And if he wasn't coming back, then I'd need someplace to stay.

Growing more frantic with every mile, I sped through my options over and over again in case I'd forgotten one. But I hadn't.

It was late afternoon and the sun was fading by the time we got back to the city, but I knew that wasn't why the streets seemed so dark. I'd spent four days surrounded by a brand-new palette: whitewashed walls, sunlight sparkling on water and green grasses waving in sandy dunes. But here we were, back in the charmless grey, and I had absolutely no idea what would happen when I got home.

The dirty darkness was a shock, but the noise was even worse. The loudest sound I'd heard in four days had been the kid next door dumping his bike with a crash on his way back from the beach. So when a fire engine screamed past the car, with the heart-attack siren they use for real emergencies, I felt like I was hearing it for the first time.

Another fire truck hurtled past us, a minute later, with the same urgent wail, and I started to feel like they were giving voice to the desperate, trapped feeling in my chest.

"All right, Ollie," Linda said, sounding fed up as she turned up Prince heading toward Greene. "Start getting your stuff together."

Dread is a word that sounds like how it feels.

I reached down between my feet to shove the comic book I'd tried to distract myself with into my duffel. "Oh, for Chrissake," Linda barked, braking so abruptly that my shoulder slammed into the back of her seat.

"What's going on?" Maggie asked sleepily from the front seat, at the very same time as Linda said, in a totally different voice, "What on earth?"

I straightened up and looked out the front window. It wasn't the flashing lights or the hulking fire trucks that caught my attention, but the sky. After four days of sunsets, I'd trained my brain to look out for them, and that's what I thought it was at first—a strange sunset, an ugly one, the sickly greenish orange purple of the bruise that Manny Weber gave Alex on his arm after Manny's dad left.

"A fire," Maggie said. "Wait. Ollie! Is that your building?"

Alex was leaning forward between the two front seats, his

head tilted to one side. "The sign," he said wonderingly to himself. "They won't know she's in there."

Linda couldn't have known that he was talking about the A.I.R. sign I'd ripped off the wall, but her spidey sense must have kicked in because she turned around to yell "Stay in the car!" at the precise moment that the door on Alex's side flew open. She reached her arm out into the back seat as if she could catch him, but he was already out of the car, dodging around the blue police barricade set up to block the end of my street. A cop tried to grab him, missed, and then headed over to his car, radio up by his mouth.

By that time, my door was open, too. And I barely heard Linda screaming after Alex or felt the cop's rough hand slipping off my own shoulder because I had already started to run.

# CLIMB

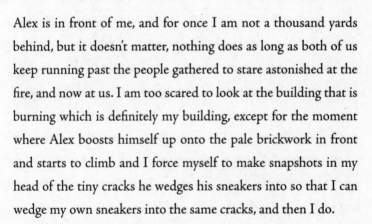

Alex is in front of me, and for once I am not a thousand yards behind, but it doesn't matter, nothing does as long as both of us keep running past the people gathered to stare astonished at the fire, and now at us. I am too scared to look at the building that is burning which is definitely my building, except for the moment where Alex boosts himself up onto the pale brickwork in front and starts to climb and I force myself to make snapshots in my head of the tiny cracks he wedges his sneakers into so that I can wedge my own sneakers into the same cracks, and then I do.

I am climbing, and it is hard; in fact, if I thought about it I would know that it is the hardest and most frightening thing I have ever done in my life, but I do not think. By the time one of the firemen on the ground sees us through the smoke and darkness and shouts, my fingers are bleeding and one nail is gone, not a hangnail but ripped right off, and my right sneaker is heavy with the blood filling it even though I do not remember smashing the toe that throbs like a heart.

It is difficult to hear the firemen shouting at us because it is difficult to hear anything. The thing you do not know about a fire—the thing I did not know—is the huge angry howl of it that reaches straight into your skull and grabs hold of your brain by both shoulders and screams right into its face. The only sensible response is to turn and run in the opposite direction as fast as your feet can take you, but that is not what Alex is doing: Instead he is moving right into the heat and the smoke and the terrible sucking rage of it, and so turning and running is not what I do, either.

The men below me have started the massive hose. It takes four of them to control it, and I look down at them and then up at the spray of the water on the flames and all I can think of is how beautiful it is, the fire dancing in what looks like wicked delight and the spray from the hoses making rainbows against the bruise-colored sky behind.

None of this matters, either, because we have done it, we are fifteen feet off the ground, at the level of the top of the first-floor windows and Alex above me is reaching out into the darkness to catch a trapeze I cannot see. I am barely holding on but then he is on the bottom rung of the ladder that leads up to the fire escape, and he is calling back for me, one hand outstretched.

I am scared, not just scared that he will not be able to support my weight but that I will not be able to take one hand off the wall, and scared that the rusty bolt that keeps the ladder secured so that burglars can't climb up from the street into our house will give way and send the two of us plummeting down to the sidewalk like when someone gets off the other end of the seesaw. But

this is not the right thing to be thinking because Alex is screaming for me and so I close my eyes and ignore my finger as I take
one hand off the wall and then he has it, he has me, and the pain
is very bad and there is a sickening moment where I am dangling,
but then there is a thin metal bar cutting into my hands, and Alex
reaches down and grabs the back of my jeans which used to be his
jeans and so are big enough that there's some fabric there to grab,
which he does, and his strong, skinny arm hauls me up.

The ladder should be easy compared to the brickwork, but I
am already so tired and there is no time to rest. It is hotter here,
which I did not think was possible, and louder, and the ladder
shudders horribly under our weight. Breathing is too hot so I sip
air through my nose, but there isn't enough. The people below
are not too small to see, and they are coming after us. I can smell
the tiny hairs on my face burning as the two of us climb, so close
together that Alex almost kicks me in the face.

We're at my floor now, and Alex swings aside to make room
for me on the fire escape which leaves me in front, leading the way
as we inch down the narrow walkway next to the building like it's a
tightrope, the open hole of the fire escape stairs gaping open beside.
My right foot is not working very well, I notice, and then I stop
confused in front of the window of the big room, familiar even behind its curtain of smoke, because there is someone in there, a massive figure weaving through the big room like a minotaur in a maze.
But there is no time to find out who or what it is because we have
to do what we climbed to do which is to get my mom out of bed.

I keep pushing right into the dragon's breath, and the

fire escape railing bites into my hipbones as I lean out over it to see into her room. The window is closed again but the curtain is where I left it, tucked behind the art books on the sill, and through the heavy smoke I think I see the shape of her in the bed and the shape is not moving. My heart beats like a rabbit's then, tears of rage and frustration filling my scorched eyes and burning away just as fast, because we have climbed so far and have gotten so close and yet—like always—I have no idea what to do next.

Just then, a fireman shouts from below so I look down, then startle back when I catch a sudden movement from my mom's room out of the corner of my eye: the wood frame around the French doors splintering as the glass-paned doors fly open. And then the minotaur is there, dropping down to one knee by the bed.

It's Apollo, a dark bandana over his mouth like an old-timey thief. I cry out to him but he can't hear, so I watch the silent movie from the noise and heat outside as he scoops my mom up and staggers back through the smoke with his burden towards the broken doors. My mom is not small, but she is small in Apollo's arms, and the man's shirt she is wearing trails beneath her.

Desperate to get their attention, I hit the hot glass of the window with my open palms but Apollo does not see or stop and I smell my hands sear like meat.

A millisecond later, the whole world explodes with a blast of heat so intense that my eyelids are no protection against it. I cower away in confusion and fear.

And as I turn my head away from the inferno, I feel rather than see Alex as he falls.

# WHAT I SAW

After I get out of the hospital, I lie in the dark for a long time.

The room I'm in belongs to one of Joyce and Peter Walker's sons. He's grown and married, but the room is still a boy's room. The walls are covered with maps. I avoid looking at the map of the moon hanging beside the bed. Even in the half-dark, the vinyl background is a queasy teal, and the Sea of Tranquility looks like a chicken pox scar.

I never know what time it is here. I could ask for a clock, but I don't.

Joyce brings me soup and grilled cheese sandwiches. Sometimes I eat some soup before pushing the bowl away. My throat is too sore from the smoke for sandwiches, even melted American on squishy bread.

Joyce brings me chocolates, too, and eats them when I don't.

Apollo spends most days in the beaten-up armchair on the other side of my room, reading the newspaper or a book by a Polish poet with a name like a sneeze. He sleeps in the chair, too, although I'm pretty sure he has a bed in another room. I do not want to talk, so we do not talk, but I do not like it when he leaves. When I have bad dreams, he tinkers over a little table with a clip-on utility light.

Saint Fall is there, too. She smells like corn chips and sleeps at the foot of my bed and licks my face when I cry.

I do not talk, but people talk to me. That's how I know my mom is okay. She got out of one hospital for smoke inhalation and went to another one for depression. Depression is why she went to bed.

Alex is also okay, if breaking one of your legs in two places, your arm, and three ribs can be considered okay. Apollo had pretty bad smoke inhalation, which is why he sounds like a bear growling from the chair in the corner of my room when he breathes, but he was out of the hospital first of all of us.

My dad calls Joyce's house every day, sometimes more than once, but I do not talk to him. Joyce drags her son's old baby blue slim-line phone over to the bed, and I turn my face to the wall. I want my dad to come home, to wrap me up in the warm leather coffee smell of him, to scratch my back hard the way I like it, and to tell me everything is going to be okay.

If he's not going to do that, then I don't want anything from him at all.

It's not that I can't talk; it's that I would rather not. Right now, I see a series of pictures in my mind, complete and fully formed. I hold on to them, tracing the details, wearing grooves in my brain in the shape of the memories. Talking about what happened will spread the story out, and what I remember will get mushy and bloated with other people's thoughts and impressions.

I need what I remember to stay tight and precise. I need to know what I saw.

Sometimes, late at night, when there's nobody in the armchair in the corner of the room, I raise my bandaged hands and sketch what I saw into the air, pawing out the corners of these strange drawings I will never make.

I draw the stiff collar of a fireman's black coat, and the mask that prevents me from seeing his eyes, held on by rubber straps that cut into the grey and black stubble chafing my cheek.

I draw Linda running toward the gurney loading Alex into an ambulance. His feet, the only part of him that I can see, jerk side to side with the rolling wheels. One of his red sneakers is gone.

I draw a forgotten rag, soaked in solvent, as it tumbles down a slanted drafting table before settling onto the seat of a wooden stool.

I draw the rough loose crumple of a cardboard sign wrapped in plastic, trampled on the floor. I draw firemen standing on the street, while a building that should be empty burns.

I draw a broken door, swinging jauntily on its hinge as a massive minotaur lifts a woman from a bed. The oversized white men's shirt she wears trails behind her like a wedding dress.

This is the hardest memory to draw, because of the smoke that is everywhere, and because of the look in the minotaur's eyes. The look is none of the things that you would expect. It is not determination, or horror, or fear.

The look is love.

# PROOF

Exactly one week after the fire, I woke up again from the dream.

I must not have cried out, because Apollo was still working at the little tray table by the time I'd calmed down enough to speak. A small circle of light illuminated his hands, but his face was in shadow and I was glad; it would be easier for me that way.

"Why hasn't he come home?" I spoke to the ceiling, in a voice creaky with disuse.

I saw Apollo stiffen in surprise, but he didn't look up. "Your father is still in France," he said in an everyday tone of voice, as if I'd been chatting away the whole time.

I knew what he was doing. You get a wary deli cat to come over to you by pretending the whole thing is no big deal—you, the cat—*whatever, man*. Apollo was the one who taught me that.

I said, "He should have come back."

The words came out like bullets. Apparently, I was angry.

Apollo didn't disagree with me. All he said was, "I am not sure that he can, just now."

"How come?"

"He is in a bit of trouble."

"Because of the Head?"

Apollo sighed then, one of those massive Polish sighs my dad used to make fun of him for, and placed the small tool he'd been holding back onto the tray. "You know about that?"

"The guy with the accent was waiting for you, in the hallway. Grandjean."

Apollo shook his big head. "Relentless. I cannot think how he found us."

"He was buying a Coke," I said, and Apollo stared at me. "He saw a drawing I gave Mr. G."

Apollo threw his big head back and laughed, delighted by the coincidence. He hadn't expected that.

But I wasn't in a laughing mood. "Was it the wrong thing to do, what my dad did?"

Apollo didn't say anything for a long time, and I let him think. Finally, he responded, directing his answer to the stamped tin ceiling above us. "Returning the head may have been the right thing to do. But stealing was almost certainly the wrong way to do it." Another sigh. "By disappearing, he was trying to protect you two—from lawyers, the police—but this did not work, either." Yet another sigh. "He has made a terrible mess. And for nothing."

I sat up straight in the rumpled bed. "What do you mean, for nothing?"

Apollo rubbed a hand over his eyes. "Well, she was not destroyed in the fire, so that is something, I suppose. But nobody can prove definitively that the Head came from this church in France. So back it must go, to the Dortmunder."

I felt like someone had shot an arrow, pinning me to the headboard.

"Art goes missing, art is hidden, art changes hands—this is what happens during wartime, the man at the museum tells me." Apollo's voice had ice in it. You wouldn't want to lecture him about war; he was hungry in Poland for years. "But it is not right."

I lay back against my pillows, heartsick. So much disruption and confusion and secrecy—and for nothing. Just another stupid mystery, sputtering out.

I couldn't let it go. "But there must be some people there, who remember her from before she was taken? Don't they want her back?"

"Of course, yes, the people who live there are sure. But France is not going to pick a big fight with the United States over this—a little piece of art, stolen from a church with three pews in the middle of nowhere and vouched for by a bunch of farmers." Apollo sounded as bitter as I'd ever heard him. "And your father, well, he is caught in between. In France, he is okay for now. But he cannot come back to the States."

*Ever?* I thought but didn't say.

My plan wouldn't have worked anyway.

I looked down at my useless, bandaged hands. I'd drawn the Head over and over, dissatisfied every time. Now I wasn't even sure if my hands would ever heal enough for me to do a drawing I hated. As if he knew what I was thinking, Apollo leaned forward, elbows on his knees. "All of this? You do not have to worry about any of it. All you have to do is get better." I see him shake his massive lion's head out of the corner of my eye. "This mess is not your fault, Olympia. None of it. You must understand that. And it will get sorted. Everyone is, or will be, okay."

He was wrong, of course. The fire *was* my fault. But I couldn't tell him that, not yet.

I flipped over onto my side, my face just inches from the wall, while thoughts gathered like thunderclouds.

Fine. So the Dortmunder would get the Head. Maybe it didn't matter that she was stolen; at least lots of people would get to see her there.

I flipped over again, onto my back.

Except that it *did* matter. Some Egyptian noble had commissioned careful replicas of everything he'd need in the afterlife— cows for milk and little loaves of bread and a beautiful garden with terracotta tiles. Why was it better for a museum to steal those things than the grave robbers who'd come to take his gold? Because of the fancy glass case and the information card? It *wasn't* better—not to the people who'd lost the art, anyway.

I thought of farmers coming to kneel at the foot of a beloved, butchered statue. And I saw the big man's sad, hopeful face looking up at me from the bottom of the stairs, my imperfect sketch clutched in his fist, the old brown photo under his plump thumb.

A space opened up in the center of my chest and I turned my head slowly toward the chair where Apollo sat, staring moodily off into the middle distance.

"Let's say there was a photo," I said. "An old one. Of the Head *in* the church, with her body. From way back when." Apollo's eyes met mine, one side of his mouth starting to curve up into the smile that meant he was ready to make some trouble. "Would *that* count? As proof?"

# MAKE SOMETHING

While he was getting the big man's business card from my note-book, Apollo told me not to bother getting my hopes up. But he spent a long time on the phone.

When he was done, Joyce came in with plates of lasagna and salad. She tried not to show how happy she was that I was sitting up and talking—in fact, she was practically whistling with nonchalance—but I saw the look she shot Apollo.

We probably hadn't been fooling the deli cats, either.

I couldn't hold the fork with my bandages, so Apollo fed me like a baby. I ate every bite of lasagna on my plate, and a big piece of Apollo's, too. Peter is a good cook, and it was the first time I'd been hungry since the fire.

After we'd eaten, Apollo sat back with the beer that Joyce had brought him.

"Well, we will see. Are you okay, little bird? There has been so much."

I thought before answering, looking up at the official photograph of Buzz Aldrin that Joyce's son had hung above his desk. The astronaut was wearing his puffy white space suit, his arm resting proudly on the enormous fishbowl of his helmet. I wondered how you went back to being a normal person after you'd walked on the moon. He looked like he couldn't quite believe it himself.

"Olympia?" Apollo nudged gently.

The truth was, I was tired of sleeping. "I'm bored," I said, and Apollo smiled, for the first time in what felt like a long, long while.

He held up one finger. Saint Fall, excited by the change in the air, struggled to her feet and galloped out of the room after him, her back legs working in a slightly less coordinated rhythm than her front ones. When the two of them returned, Saint Fall almost underfoot, Apollo was holding a plastic bag with Pearl Paint's red logo on it, and a thin strip of leather with a buckle, like a short belt.

He moved the little tray table over from its spot by his chair, pulling it right up next to the bed and swinging the tray in front of me while Saint Fall clambered awkwardly up onto the bed next to me, huffing as she went.

"Saint Fall's old collar," he said, holding up the length of leather. And then, pointedly, to the dog: "From before she was fat."

Delighted by the sound of her name, Saint Fall bounced on her hind legs like a sea lion and licked the air around my head. Dogs can smile.

Apollo wrapped the strip of leather carefully around my bandaged hand, and buckled it before slotting a brush in there. It didn't hurt. Then he filled two empty spaghetti sauce jars with water from the bathroom sink before producing an expensive watercolor pan set and a thickly textured pad of paper from the bag.

He laid the white enameled pan on the table and placed little squares, no bigger than a thumbnail and wrapped in different colored papers, into the depressions. They looked like Joyce's chocolates, but I knew they were cakes of color, the names printed in heavy black ink: Sap Green. Burnt Sienna. Winsor Lemon. Raw Umber.

"I don't want to," I said.

Ignoring me, Apollo opened the pad and unwrapped one of the little blocks of color. It was French Ultramarine, the first color we'd made together, the color in the color study he'd given me—kind of a low blow, if you ask me. He grabbed my bandaged hand and dunked the brush into the water in one of the jars before working it into the cake of paint.

I watched as the tiny cube filled with a slurry of pigmented liquid. Then, still holding my hand with the loaded brush, Apollo drew a fat, wet, intense blue line right down the center of the white page.

We looked at it in silence together. It was the first mark I'd made in more than a week.

I contemplated the line for a while, then pulled my hand back. "I don't want to."

Apollo's jaw set stubbornly. "I think you should."

"I don't use color, remember?" The tone of my voice was not nice.

Apollo was undeterred. "You will not be able to use your Blackwings until your hands heal. Watercolor, you can do now."

More gently, he took my hand again, and together we dunked the brush into the jar. The water turned a bright, clear blue.

Apollo unwrapped another small square—Alizarin Crimson, a red more orange than blue. Using the brush strapped to my passive hand, he made another slurry. I watched with detached interest as he moved it over to the pad and drew an orange-red circle next to the blue line. We watched together in silence as the creamy paper absorbed the liquid. The colors spread, creeping slowly toward each other before bleeding together, creating a narrow purple line where they met.

Apollo ripped the paper off a yellow cube, a green, and a brown, and dropped them into the depressions in the tray. He pointed at the jars. "Clean water, for dilution. Dirty, to clean brushes."

Then he got up to go. At the door, he paused.

"Please. Stop thinking and make something."

And then he was gone.

# BLUR

I wasn't going to. I didn't want to.

But I had been telling the truth, before: I was bored.

And I discovered, once I'd started, that there was a lot to learn. We'd used watercolor in Mrs. Ejiofor's class, but the colors in the plastic sets were pale and lifeless, and the cheap, thick brushes had scratched at the paper instead of leaving a clean line. The colors Apollo had brought me were beautiful, pure and deep, and I discovered that, even though many of the cubes sat unwrapped and inaccessible to my bandaged hands, I had lots of combinations right in front of me if I mixed the open ones together on the glazed white back of the open palette lid.

I filled that first page, adding water to the shapes we'd begun. I liked the way the color flowed out of the brush, changing as I altered the position of it, how I could control the intensity of the paint with just water. Colors I didn't think would work together—

pinks and oranges, green and purple—mixed together in a soft haze.

When that first page was completely saturated, I ripped it out and let it slide to the ground, starting another one right away. I heard my dad again: *You learn by doing. Paper is cheap, Ollie. And so is time, when you're young.*

In one corner of the new page, I drew a slash of plain water, then added a drop of yellow, using my brush to draw the pigment out to the dry spots. I created a moat in wet green paint and let it dry, protecting the white space it surrounded when I added a forest of colors to the periphery. I learned that if I held the brush at the very end, where an eraser would be on a pencil, and made a lazy stroke with my whole arm, I could lay down a luxurious swath of color.

Once I got a little more confidence, I realized I could actually draw with the paints. I sketched the room using the brown Apollo had left me, blocking out the wall of astronaut and space shuttle pictures, the way the smaller squares echoed the huge panes of the windows reflecting the streetlamp opposite. But I didn't fill them in, less interested in the details than in the shapes I could make with the color.

I flicked the brush, first by accident and then on purpose, and delighted in the perfect round dots of different sizes that splattered the paper—messy, but effective. The bed sheets, dark navy with little white dots spaced randomly to look like stars in deep space, didn't show much paint. Anyway, I had to believe Joyce wouldn't care too much about sheets: There was still a bullet stuck in the bathroom door downstairs from the time she let an artist shoot a gun in the gallery during a show.

I hobbled to the bathroom to change the water in the jars every once in a while, but mostly I let my mind rest while I lost myself in the physical pleasure of the brush moving over the textured paper, the colors blooming beneath it on the pad. An explosion of orange and red made me think of the fire, but I dropped a bomb of blue on top and let it turn into something completely different.

It was a relief to let things be a little blurry. I liked how forgiving the watercolor was, how easy it was to pretend that you hadn't made a mistake.

By midnight, Saint Fall was snoring on top of my feet, and the better part of the pad, rainbow-colored and wavy with water, littered the floor around my bed. The pages didn't look that different from the first ones I'd made, but I had more control.

Sandwiching the jars between my bandaged hands, I carried them to the bathroom and emptied them, and let water run over the brush in the sink. I clumsily ran a damp washcloth around the back of my neck without looking at myself in the mirror, and found that Saint Fall's old collar fit a toothbrush perfectly.

I knew Joyce could hear me—I could practically hear her listening—but she left me alone.

While I'd been painting, I'd made a decision—or maybe, I'd come to terms with something I'd known I'd have to do all along.

I was going to have to tell Apollo what I had done.

# THE MAKING OF
# A BRAVE MAN

I had fallen asleep waiting for Apollo, but I woke up right away when he came in. The clock by the bed said it was two in the morning.

He shrugged off his brown leather jacket, folding it and placing it over the back of his chair. I saw him note the drifts of watercolor paper around my bed.

"Hey," I said softly so I wouldn't scare him.

"You had fun?"

I nodded. It was the truth. Painting with watercolor had been the first thing I'd thought of when I'd opened my eyes.

"Yeah. But I don't really know how to do it yet. And I think I got paint on the sheets."

He shrugged. "Like everything else, it will take a lifetime. Still, it looks like you have made a good start. Go back to sleep now. I have some tricks in my sleeve that I can show you in the morning." He settled into his chair, picking up the magazine he'd left on the arm of it.

The second thing I had thought about when I'd opened my eyes had been everything I had to tell him. I took a deep breath and looked at the wall for courage. The astronaut John Glenn had been on the cover of *Life* magazine in 1962, under the headline *Making of a Brave Man*. He was wearing his helmet in the photograph, and he wasn't smiling.

"I think I started the fire," I said.

Apollo put his magazine down again.

The words rushed out of me before he could speak. "When Alex and I came in from the fire escape, you put a rag on the drafting table so you could close the window. I saw it roll down and land on the seat of the stool. I should have said something, but I was so mad at Alex and Richard. And then later, I was mad at you."

The light was behind him, making Apollo's expression unreadable.

I couldn't stop talking. "I'm so sorry. I can't stop thinking about it. I'll go to the police if you think I should."

"Oh, Olympia," Apollo's voice was calm and strong. "There's no need. They are not sure what caused the fire, but it was something in the apartment—a cigarette, maybe, or the wires in the walls. It did not start in the studio, the fire."

Suddenly, I couldn't talk at all.

Apollo kept going. "It was not caused by the rag you are talking about, definitely, because I disposed of that rag properly after the two of you were gone."

I sat back against my pillows, stunned. I had been so *sure* that it had all been my fault. But it hadn't been my fault at all.

Too late, I realized Apollo was still talking. "Olympia, are you listening to me?"

I shook my head. "No. I really thought . . ."

"I understand what you thought. But it was not true."

All I felt was exhausted. I leaned back against the pillows and looked back up at the portrait of John Glenn on the cover of *Life*. His eyes looked like he had seen some things he'd never be able to explain.

"I ripped down the sign."

It took him a minute to figure out what I was talking about. In the pause, I saw the ARTIST-IN-RESIDENCE sign again—crumpled into a loose ball on the tiled foyer floor, then the blue of my sneaker kicking it out to the curb with the rest of the trash.

"You were angry." He was only offering an explanation for this incredibly dangerous thing I did, not an excuse.

"I'm sorry," I said, but he shook his head. That apology wasn't his to accept.

A minute later, Apollo leaned forward to gather the color-stained papers from the floor at his feet. "Listen. Since we are exchanging confidences in the dark of the night." He sat up and clasped his big, rough-looking hands in front of him, then clasped them again the other way. "There is some news. I talked to your dad tonight. We think the best thing is for you to go over there, to be with him for a month in the summer."

I noticed, with some surprise, that my first response wasn't an automatic no.

"But isn't he in trouble? What if the photo isn't enough?"

Apollo gave a quick, sharp laugh. "He is not in trouble in France. Even if the photo of the young Monsieur Grandjean does not force the museum to return the Head to the church, your father is still the big hero there. He can't come back here—although we will see what happens with that when the French government finds out about this photo. But in the meantime, you can visit, no problem."

A pang went through me. "What about my mom?"

"She believes it is the right thing, too, for you to go." Apollo's voice got soft when he talked about her. I couldn't believe I'd never noticed that before. "And it will give her the chance to get back on her feet."

"Will she be okay, without me?"

"She will miss you very much. She already does. But I will be here, to look after her. And it will be good for you. They are staying in the country, your dad and Clothilde, on a farm that belongs to her family. It is beautiful there—you'll eat fresh eggs for breakfast, from the chickens in the backyard—and close enough to Paris that you can go in for the weekend."

I wasn't sure about the chickens, but Apollo knew how to sweeten the pot.

"You can go see Manet's *Olympia*. And thousands of other pictures you've seen in the books."

Everybody knew the museums in Paris were almost as good as the ones here. Still, I didn't say yes or no.

"You will like Clothilde, I think." Apollo bent to retrieve the watercolor palette from the floor. He placed it on the tray table and moved it to the side. "I do." He folded his magazine, then leaned over the arm of his chair to turn out the light behind him.

"Also, she is a grown-up, and making a better job of it than the rest of us. It might be nice for you, for a change, to be a kid for a little while."

# OURS

Two mornings later, Apollo came in, holding a foil-wrapped egg-and-cheese sandwich in one hand and a folded newspaper in the other.

Joyce had cleared her son's desk and moved it in front of one of the big windows so I could paint. Apollo had brought me some watercolor books, along with a new pad. One of the books was all about Winslow Homer, whose work I didn't like until I kept looking and then I did. I hadn't been sure how I could make art out of the way the ocean made me feel that first day on the Island, but Winslow Homer helped.

Apollo put the newspaper down to the left of the watercolor I'd been working on. He'd folded it so I could read the article on top without having to use my bandaged hands.

There was a photograph of the big man with the Head, right next to a reprint of the old one he'd shown me in the stairwell, of him standing in front of her when he was a kid.

Then Apollo opened the foil package and held out half of the sandwich for me to take a bite.

# Looted Carving Returned to Church in Rural France

Associated Press, Écalles-Sainte-Catherine, FRANCE

Home—at last.

The cows grazing in this field of wildflowers seemed bemused by the crowd of eager onlookers who gathered today to witness the return of a piece of painted wooden statuary to the tiny church behind them.

The exquisitely carved representation of a woman's head surfaced earlier this year in the previously undocumented holdings of the late industrialist and philanthropist George C. Dortmunder.

Concerns about the provenance of the piece came to light during a routine cleaning prior to display. With the help of Antonin Grandjean, a Belgium-based art expert who spent summers in the area as a child, French officials have now confirmed that the Renaissance-era piece disappeared from the church sometime during the German occupation of Écalles-Sainte-Catherine during the Second World War.

A professional from New York–based firm Greene Restoration was hired to transport the piece, and will stay to supervise its reinstatement onto the badly damaged remains of the original sculpture.

Art historian Peter Blakely believes the work would not be out of place in one of Europe's grand cathedrals. "The quality of the work—the artistry—is absolutely extraordinary."

Its reappearance gives weight to long speculation that famed sculptor Paulo Marconi travelled to the South of France early in the sixteenth century, possibly to recuperate after a mental health crisis. According to local lore, the visiting foreigner fell in love with a shepherdess—perhaps not surprising, in a village where sheep still outnumber people three to one. The shepherdess's name is now lost to history, although her face is not: The carved head is believed to be her likeness.

The Dortmunder Collection was, of course, eager to avoid any taint associated with artwork stolen during the Nazi regime. Alastair Tronk, a spokesman for the collection, issued this statement from New York: "We are grateful to be given this incredible opportunity to right the wrongs of the past."

Lucille Mayer was baptized in the church seventy-four years ago, and has come almost every morning since to attend Mass. When told that auction houses estimated the worth of the piece at over a million dollars, Madame Mayer seemed as bemused as the cows grazing outside.

She responded simply. "But she is not for sale. She is ours."

# THE MEANING OF MAYDAY

We went back to the hospital to get my bandages off the next day.

I was still moving slowly, because of my foot, and the sunlight seemed unfamiliar. The air outside still smelled a little bit burned, but that might have been my imagination. When we passed my block, I turned my head so I wouldn't see.

I didn't like being in the hospital again. The doctor was pleased by how I was healing, even though my hands looked awful. She gave me a cream and some exercises to do so I could draw again. I started doing them even before she stopped talking.

After my appointment, Apollo took me down to the fifth floor, where Alex's room was. "I'll be in the lounge," he said, gesturing with his newspaper at an open area at the far end of the floor, and I felt a flutter of panic as he ambled away down the hall.

I stood in the doorway of Alex's room, screwing up the

courage to go in. He looked tiny in the bed. Straps and poles came down from a web of shiny struts above his bed, and his left leg hung from one of them, encased in a thick ugly cast. He lay there, stock-still, looking out the window on the other side of his bed.

I turned away, sick at the sight and sure I was going to cry. It was too awful. Alex, the boy who never stopped moving, was lying there immobile, trapped in some bizarre contraption. Who even knew if he'd ever be able to climb or jump again?

I couldn't do it. I just wanted to find Apollo and get out of there. But right as I turned to flee, Alex swiveled his head toward the door.

"Ollie?" he called out, and I had no choice but to go back.

"Hey," he said, grabbing at the steel triangle dangling down in front of him and swinging himself up to sit.

"Wow," I said, because I couldn't think of one single other thing to say.

"I know! Isn't it cool?" The ropes in his forearms stood out as he lifted his body again, showing off for me, his injured leg sawing back and forth like he was living inside his own personal jungle gym.

"You see my muscles?" His skinny arms looked the same to me, even when he showed me how he could do dips on the bed's steel frame. He cycled through all the tricks he'd learned, hauling himself up by the triangle. He could, it turned out, pull himself almost to a standing position on the bed by manipulating the complicated bars and straps into different configurations.

I never imagined I'd be so happy to see him doing some dumb trick.

"You look like Wile E. Coyote," I said, cracking up a little when he narrowed his eyes at me. The Road Runner is one of Alex's heroes.

Then, without warning, he let go of the pole he'd been hanging from with a loud clatter and lay back quickly with an innocent expression.

I turned around. Behind me was an enormous woman, her nurse pajamas covered with approximately twelve thousand teddy bears.

"I thought we weren't going to touch those straps, mister," she said to Alex, checking something on the chart hanging at the bottom of his bed.

"I was just showing my friend," he said weakly, but his cheeks, flushed with effort, betrayed him.

She looked at him, expressionless, until he squirmed. "Sorry."

"Mary," she said, introducing herself to me with a wink while she was plumping the pillows behind him. Then she came around front and stuck her finger right into the center of his chest, pushing him back into the pillows she'd fluffed.

"Now that your friend has seen what you can do, you stay put. Your ribs can't heal if you're climbing around like a drunken monkey."

To get out of her way, I sat down on the slick plastic chair next to the bed. Alex rubbed his chest, aggrieved, like she'd mortally injured him with her finger. "You better not forget that you promised me an extra pudding with lunch," he called after her broad back. "Remember? Mary?" She didn't bother turning around.

There was writing all over his cast. Apollo had signed it. So had Manny Weber and Javadi Awad. Richard had drawn a little monster, like the rubber puppets you put on top of a pencil. It wasn't bad, actually.

"Want to draw something on it?" Alex handed me a Sharpie from the tray by his bed. I hadn't held a fat pen yet, and my hands stretched uncomfortably to accommodate it.

"How are they?" he asked me, looking at my hands.

"Okay, I guess." I showed him the splint I had to wear to stretch the scar tissue. "The doctor said I'll probably get full range of motion back if I do my exercises. She said I could draw now."

Could I? I looked, unsure, at the cast. Whatever I chose to do would have to be pretty easy. The plaster was super bumpy, and Sharpies weren't great to draw with in the best of circumstances.

I thought about Saint Fall napping on my legs the night before, remembering the heavy, solid warmth of her and the comfort I'd taken from having her there, licking her chops and grumbling softly in her sleep. There was a big blank spot on the cast around the fattest part of Alex's calf, and I thought maybe I could sketch a cat, as if she'd fallen asleep on him.

Honestly, it was a little bit of a cheat. I'd drawn a thousand cats in my life. Even if the conditions weren't ideal, I could draw one with my eyes closed.

Alex picked up a candy bar from the pile by his other leg. "Apollo brought me these yesterday," he said, ripping it open and offering me a bite.

I chewed slowly. Apollo's name hung out there in the air between us.

"It was my mom," I said. "His True Lost Love."

Alex nodded, not surprised.

"When did you know?" I asked, uncapping the Sharpie.

Alex opened his mouth to lie, then changed his mind. "I ended up asking Linda after all." I concentrated on the sleeping cat taking shape over his plaster shin, careful not to show any expression on my face. "She wouldn't tell me, but I overheard her when we were on the Island, telling Merle."

"What did she say?" I asked, even though Alex hated talking about this stuff.

"That Clothilde had been a blessing in disguise." My hand was sore and tired already, but I kept my head down, grateful to have the drawing as an excuse. "That your mom and Apollo would never have had a chance if your dad was still in the picture, so it was good that he'd met someone."

I filed that away for later and let him off the hook.

"Linda must be really upset about all this," I said, nodding at the contraption above us.

He exhaled sharply. "Yeah, it's pretty bad right now. But at least there's food in here. Maggie says that Linda is on the Beverly Hills Diet now." He answered the blank look on my face. "Fruit is okay, but that's it. Maggie said she ate five pounds of grapes in one day."

I winced. "Gross." My stomach hurt thinking about it.

"Yeah." Alex was playing with the straps suspending his legs again. "Anyway. I don't think my dad's going to be living there, either, when I get home."

He must have seen a look on my face because he spoke quickly. "It's not because of this. Maggie heard Linda say she'd made up her mind by the time we'd left the Island." He brightened a little then. "She says she's going to spend the whole summer out there with us this year."

"Yeah?" I was surprised he seemed so happy; one of the things Alex liked about the Island was the lightened Linda load. As if he could read my mind, he said, "She's different out there."

I had one more question. "How did you know my mom was still in there, that night?" The night of the fire.

"I don't know," Alex said, looking genuinely perplexed. "I just did. I guess I thought Apollo would let her stay. He'd help, but he'd let her get up herself, if she could."

I nodded. That was right.

"You saved her life," I said to Alex.

He scowled at me. "Apollo was already up there."

"But the firemen didn't know about either one of them." I watched as understanding broke over his face; I couldn't believe he hadn't known. "Remember? They were just standing around; they thought the building was empty," I told him. "You're a hero."

Alex turned away from me, pretending to need a sip of water from the pink plastic cup on his bedside table, but not before

I'd seen the twist of pleasure and pride on his face.

The silence between us might have gotten awkward if Richard hadn't turned the corner, pushing a bald man I'd never seen before in a wheelchair.

"Ollie!" Richard looked incredibly happy to see me, and I knew that if Alex hadn't been there, he would have given me a hug.

"Olympia did most of the drawings in the Taxonomy," he told the man. To me, he said, "Ollie, this is Stuckey. Mary the nurse introduced us. Stuckey's a stuntman."

Stuckey raised one hand, then dropped it again to continue drumming on the arm of his wheelchair.

"We have the same physical therapist," Alex explained. "Stuckey has broken twenty-seven bones over the course of his career."

"Twenty-eight, as of this morning," Stuckey said. "They missed one of my metatarsals when they admitted me."

"Stuckey knows Ray Harryhausen," Richard said. "He played Triton in *Jason and the Argonauts*, even though he was only there to do stunts."

"They needed someone with long arms," Stuckey explained modestly, holding one of them up for me to see. I didn't know what he was talking about, and anyway, his arm looked regular to me.

Alex narrowed his eyes. "Hey. Stuckey. How'd they do that thing where the skeletons attack Jason?"

"Well, it was animated, but that didn't make coordinating seven skeletons any less complex. . . ." Stuckey leaned forward in his wheelchair and started walking Alex through the scene, using his hands to explain.

Richard tore himself away to ask me how I was doing.

"I'm okay. I can draw again, anyway. Sort of. But I won't be able to help you with the Taxonomy this summer. They're sending me to France, to see my dad."

"My mom told me," he said. "She's been calling Apollo to check on you. She can't forgive herself; she knew something was wrong that night you had dinner at our house."

That felt like a slap. It hadn't occurred to me that Dr. C would feel bad.

"I'm sorry," I said, and meant it.

Richard leaned against the wall and plucked at the seam on his jeans. It took him a long time to ask.

"How come you didn't want to tell anybody?"

"I thought I could fix it," I said. Richard wrinkled his forehead. *I wanted to be the kind of person who could.*

"Next time, I'll send up a flare, okay?" I waved my arms like I was hailing a helicopter. "Mayday!"

Alex and Stuckey stopped talking to look over at me flailing, but Richard didn't laugh. "You say it three times," he said quietly. "Mayday. Mayday. Mayday. So it can't be confused with another call."

I was thinking about it for the first time. "It's a weird thing to say, right? I mean, why *Mayday?*"

"It's French," Richard said. "*M'aidez.*" He sounded like his Brooklyn grandma, Violine.

I changed the subject back. "Anyway, I'm sorry to leave you with the Taxonomy. We were just getting started on Transformations."

He looked down, shy suddenly. "I've been doing some stuff on my own. After Khepri, I made a couple more maquettes; Mrs. Ejiofor helped. And Stuckey's going to be in a monster movie next year. He can't tell me anything about it now, but he said he'd take me with him to the company that makes the prosthetics, when they cast his face for the mask."

"That's great," I said. "I can't wait to see your maquettes."

His face got serious again. "Are you okay? About going to France?"

"Yeah. I really want to see my dad." There was a lift in my chest at the thought, and I realized it was true. "I kind of wish I spoke French, though."

Richard smiled dangerously. "Yeah, be careful what you point at. They eat snails there, for real. And horses." I shuddered. I thought French food was supposed to be good, but maybe it was the kind of good that kids don't like.

Apollo's bulk filled the doorway. He tossed a bag of chips at Alex in the bed, then bent over to shake hands with Stuckey.

I got up to go, then turned back to Richard. "Are you going to tell me what 'Mayday' means?" I tried to pronounce it the way he had, but it came out more Pepé Le Pew than Violine.

Richard didn't say anything for a little while, and I wondered if it would always take him so long to do things, or if that would have to change when we grew up.

"*M'aidez*," he said again, the Haitian-flavored French rolling out of him. "It means 'help me.'" He left it there, his brown eyes meeting mine.

I ducked my head. And I didn't mind at all when he reached out to give me a hug goodbye, even though Alex made gagging noises behind us.

# TWO GIFTS

"Your tail is back up," Lady Day said.

She was perched on the wide windowsill in my room at Joyce's house, her long skinny legs in a spiky pile, while I used the bed to fold and pack the clothes Joyce had bought me for the trip.

Joyce had told me she'd waited thirty years to buy clothes for a girl, so I felt a little bad that the only things I'd wanted were jeans and T-shirts and shorts. She did buy me a dark blue dress, though, in case things got fancy in France.

Lady Day meant that I was feeling more like myself. Cats don't vocalize at other cats, unless they're warning them off; meowing is strictly cat-to-human. Instead, they communicate with one another (and with us) with their tails. A lowered tail means a cat is scared or aggressive; a bristling one means she's alarmed; thrashing means she's mad. But a straight-up tail means a cat is relaxed and content and happy to see you.

Lady Day was right: I did feel better. My hands were healing, and I could draw a little, even though it made me tired and my hands cramped after a while. I'd kept playing with Apollo's watercolors, too, layering a forgiving wash of color on top when my pencil sketches looked rough. The night before, I'd finally talked to my dad, who was so happy I was coming to France that I thought he might have been crying on the other end of the line.

And my mom had gotten out of the hospital. She was staying with a friend of Apollo's in Brooklyn. He was going to take me to see her on our way to the airport.

"You're so lucky to be going," Lady Day said. "I'm dying to know what it's *like*." Lady Day is going to be a world traveler when she grows up, but the only place she's gone so far is Puerto Rico, where her grandparents are. "Are you going to open this before you go?"

There was a package on the desk addressed to me, wrapped in brown paper and covered with stamps from France. It had been there for a couple of days.

"You can, if you want."

Lady Day checked my face, then nodded and leaned over to pick at the thick tape holding the brown wrapping closed.

Inside was a big art book: photographs of Paris. The note on the inside cover was short: "Dear Olympia: I look forward to meeting you," it said, in handwriting that looked a little like Apollo's. "Your friend, Clothilde."

I was going to have to get out of the habit of calling her Vouley Voo.

Lady Day flipped through the pages. The photos had been taken a long time ago, but the introduction said that Paris hadn't changed much. "It doesn't look all that different from New York," she said.

That was what I thought, too. There were pictures of parks, and restaurants with tables outside. There were impressive buildings with columns and marble stairs, and rough-looking industrial parts, too. There were cobblestones. There was even a picture of the photographer's studio in there, a familiar mess.

Looking at it, Lady Day asked me, "Will Apollo keep the studio? Are you going to move back into the loft?" I shook my head; I didn't know. Nobody knew what was going to happen next, even though they all wanted to tell me they were sure it was going to be okay.

Lady Day had stopped at a photograph of a not-very-clean little boy in a cap and boots, waiting outside a doorway. Her right hand was moving, a gesture so small I'm not sure I would have noticed if I didn't do exactly the same thing: She was air-sketching, translating what her brain was seeing into something her hand could understand. She stopped when she caught me looking, but I smiled and she smiled back, and I felt a little sad that the first time we'd ever hung out outside of school was the day before I was leaving for France.

"Can we go to the Met together some Saturday, when I get back?"

Lady Day shrugged like she didn't care, but I could tell she was pleased. "Sure. We could bring sketchpads even, if your hands are better." And I imagined being there, drawing, with a friend who was a girl, who knew about art.

"Hey," Lady Day said, looking out the window onto Broome Street. "There's a guy putting up a poster down there."

I joined her at the window. The Wake Up Artist was across the street, wearing the same brown suit and wide-brimmed hat. She was applying a poster to the wide, empty brick wall of the one-story mechanic's garage that sat catty-corner across from Joyce's house.

"She's not a guy," I said absentmindedly to Lady Day, trying to see. "What's on the poster, can you tell?"

She shifted a little, but the angle was wrong. "Not without falling out. Let's go down."

"We'll be right back," I called out to Joyce, the big metal door of the loft banging behind us as Lady Day and I flew down the industrial stairs—me a little more slowly because of my sore foot and shorter legs—before bursting out onto the street below.

It was beautiful out. There was none of the restless feeling of the last few weeks in the air: Spring was officially here, and pretty soon summer would be, too. I inhaled deeply. Even in SoHo, it smelled green.

Lady Day checked fast both ways for cars and headed toward the poster. The Wake Up Artist had disappeared. The poster was there, though, vivid colors standing out against the faded red and brown brick.

The image was a painted woman, two fingers pressed to her forehead in a waggish salute that matched the mischievous smile she wore. I caught my breath, my eyes widening in surprise and delight.

It was the Head.

The Wake Up Artist had captured the sweetness I hadn't been able to nail in the hundreds of drawings I'd done. But in the Wake Up Artist's version, the sadness was gone, replaced by a naughty, winking, do-you-think-we're-going-to-get-away-with-it? look that had me smiling on the street.

Lady Day read the yellow comic-book speech bubble running along the top of the poster:

STAY COOL!

Hearing it made me laugh out loud.

Lady Day moved in for a better view while I stayed behind on the sidewalk, looking around.

The Wake Up Artist had reappeared up the hill, just off Mercer Street. She was watching us. I waved a thank-you, and she swept off her hat, holding it in front of her as she folded into an elaborate Shakespearean bow.

I looked back at the poster then, the smile still broad on my face. And when I looked back up the hill, the Wake Up Artist was gone.

# BROOKLYN

The next day, Apollo borrowed Joyce's car so he could drive me to the airport. But first, we were going to Brooklyn, to see my mom.

Joyce calls her car the filing cabinet, so I had to clear some of the bills and art magazines onto the floor before getting into the front seat while Apollo put my new suitcase in the trunk.

My stomach fluttered. It was weird that I was more nervous about seeing my mom than I was about going on an airplane. But after a few blocks, I realized: I wasn't nervous about seeing her. I was scared that I was going to be mad.

It's easy to talk in the car because the driver can't look at you for long.

"Is my dad why my mom got depressed?" It was the first time I'd said the word out loud. *Depressed.* Like the snake in *The Jungle Book.*

Apollo shook his head.

"Not really, no. She has struggled with this for a long time."

I knew that was true. Not everybody who gets Vouley Voo'd goes to bed.

"But everything that happened probably did make it worse—even the good things, like getting the big show."

"Is she going to get better?"

His voice was soft again. "She can, with the right doctor, and some help. I think she will."

"You rescued her," I said, trying it out.

Apollo shook his head without taking his eyes from the bridge in front of us. "You cannot rescue somebody, little bird. You can help them. But they must rescue themselves."

Alex had been right. Apollo had been letting my mom do it herself.

"Are you going to be together now?"

He shook his head. "She needs to get better, stronger. Then maybe we'll see."

It wasn't a yes, but it wasn't a no, either, and I was glad for him, and for my mom. I was happy for me, too. Apollo feels like home to me. He always has.

We were quiet for a while, crossing the bridge. Then I asked, "Is she working right now?"

I could imagine art being the kind of thing my mom's doctors didn't want her to do. But, as I could have told them, it was when she wasn't working that you had a problem.

"Yes, but the work is different now." Another kind of happy look. "It's good, I think. You'll see."

We were driving through an industrial area, the kind of abandoned neighborhood they use for car chases in the movies. The buildings were mostly one story, with metal roll-up grates in front. I read the signs to Apollo as we drove past: "Custom-Crafted Tables and Chairs for the Hospitality Industry," "Full-Service Machine Shop and Mechanical Contractors," "Low-Cost Iron Work, Residential and Commercial." There was a lot of sky because the buildings were so short.

Apollo pulled up outside a nondescript building on a corner, a little taller than the rest. He rang a bell and the heavy metal door buzzed open for us. The elevator was enormous, big enough for a car, with metal accordion doors you had to open and close yourself, and a lever you pushed down to make it go.

Apollo let me do the lever, which was the kind of thing I would ordinarily like, except that my stomach felt very bad suddenly and I got worried about lining the elevator up with the fourth floor, which was where we were going, so Apollo helped.

The hallway was clean: battleship grey and lined with metal doors. Apollo stopped in front of one of them and knocked his big cop knock.

The door opened. And just like that, I was in my mom's arms.

# OFF THE GROUND

I have no idea how long we stood there. My ear was squashed and a piece of my hair was caught in the button of her shirt, but I didn't ever want her to let me go.

She was very thin. But she felt strong, too, and she smelled clean. I closed my eyes and let her hold me. I wasn't mad. Or maybe I was, and it didn't matter. It didn't matter at all.

I finally opened my eyes, still in my mom's arms. We were in a loft with windows on two sides like our apartment at home. But in the center of this one, there was a huge sculpture, if sculpture was even the right word. It looked like the cyclone in *The Wizard of Oz*—a tornado of tiny objects. Dense at the center and sparser at the edges, the sculpture whirled with barely contained energy, as if a nudge would break the whole thing apart, sending each piece spinning off into space.

"Whoa," I said, into my mom's sweet-smelling hair. "Is that yours?"

"Yeah," she said. "Want to see?"

Holding hands, we walked over to look. The objects were suspended and tied together with fishing wire so thin I could barely see it. Some of the pieces were held tightly in place. Others dangled free, moving with the currents in the air. I blew gently, just to see it move.

"You made it so fast."

"I had a lot of time to think, in the hospital. When I came out, I knew exactly how I wanted it to look. I had to get off the ground," she said. "Move into space."

I walked around the cyclone. Every angle gave you something different to look at.

"I'd made a lot of it already, too," she said, pointing to the PUSH button, and the dangerous little lady's fan.

I turned to her, confused. "Wait—how?" I had no idea what had survived the fire, if anything.

She shook her head, sad. "Apollo found the box and brought them here. Before. He was making a studio here." She looked at Apollo, and I understood that there was a whole secret language between them now. I thought it might make me feel left out, but it didn't. "For the two of us."

Seeing her art felt like being reunited with an old friend. My brass faucets punched through dark blue velvet. The tea bag was there, too, a needle suspended in midair from the unfinished embroidery, making you worry that it would slip the needle's eye.

There were hundreds of details I hadn't seen before, also, mostly taken from nature: acorns and leaves and whirligigs and bits of rock wired like precious jewels. My mom said, "There's lots more to do, but I'm on the right track, I think. We go for a lot of walks. The trash is good here in Brooklyn. So are the parks."

I didn't want to let go of her hand, so I pulled her backward so I could take the whole thing in again.

"Watch," she warned softly, and I looked behind me. There was Apollo's box of colors, the same box I'd nearly tripped over at the studio.

I thought about the two of them here, making work together. I thought about Apollo's kettle whistling, reminding them to take a break, and a secret stash of Pecan Sandies somewhere Alex wouldn't think to look. I thought about mixing colors with Apollo, maybe making a color study with him to replace the one that had hung across from my bed.

I looked back toward the muscular twist of the sculpture.

"It's beautiful."

My mom dropped my hand to hug me again then, and I let myself rag-doll in her arms. Then she stood me on my feet, and the mischievous look in her eyes was not unlike the one the Wake Up Artist had given the Head on her poster.

"Come," she said, heading toward the door. "We've got one more thing to show you."

# SOMETHING TO LOOK FORWARD TO

We were out in the hallway, still holding hands, and my mom was aiming for the door at the very end.

It was the longest time I'd ever seen her without a cigarette.

The door at the end of the hallway opened as soon as we knocked. The sound artist, Sari, stood there.

She hugged my mom, and I could tell by how gently she shook my hand that she knew the whole story. (Either that, or she's the kind of person who shakes hands like a dead fish. Joyce says it's important to have a solid handshake, but not a bone-crusher. We spent an entire afternoon working on mine when I was eight.)

I wasn't that surprised to see Sari; Apollo always ends up friends with them after they break up. I *was* glad to see a guy on the couch in his pajamas, though, who looked up and waved before going back to his book. At least Apollo wasn't Sari's True Lost Love.

"We wanted to introduce you to someone," my mom said, looking behind Sari to the most beautiful cat I'd ever seen, stalking across the bare wooden floor of the loft like a model on a runway. She was a brown tabby, covered in light and dark stripes, with eyes the color of the jade fish necklaces you can buy in Chinatown.

"Her name is Artemisia." My mom raised her eyebrows. "Bet you can't guess who named her." Artemisia Gentileschi was an Italian painter at a time when there weren't that many women painting; Apollo finds her work nuanced and expressive.

A beat later, something struck me. "Wait. Are you saying that Apollo named *me*?"

My mom laughed. "Let's say he consulted."

I looked back down the hallway, but Apollo was nowhere to be seen. "Then why Olympia?"

"We hoped you'd be clear-eyed." She paused. "And unafraid."

As if she knew we'd gotten distracted, Artemisia brushed by my mom's legs, her elegant, striped tail lingering behind to wrap in a question mark around her calf. She had a white chin and elaborate black and white stripes around her eyes that made her look like she was wearing Egyptian makeup.

Sari sat down cross-legged on the wide wooden floorboards then, patting the spot next to her. I sat, admiring the thick, comfortable socks she wore, and my mom dropped down beside me.

"She's playing hard to get," Sari said, looking at the cat, who was sitting a little ways off, tail curled primly around her neat paws. Without thinking, I held up my fist, and Artemisia came right over to bump my hand with her head as if she was saying hello to another cat. Then she let the whole soft, warm length of her graze my knuckles, her tail curling around me like a lady with a feather in the movies.

Sari looked surprised. "My friend Lady Day taught me that," I told her. "A fist is the shape of a cat's head. It looks scary to us, but it's friendly to them."

"I didn't know that!" Sari said, impressed. She held up her own fist, and Artemisia came over to say hello to her, too.

Sari asked me, "Do you know about the blink of love?"

I shook my head, and so did my mom. I bet Lady Day knew.

"That's what I call it, anyway," Sari said. "Cats indicate trust by making eye contact," she looked meaningfully at Artemisia, "and then closing their eyes in a long blink." She closed her thickly lashed eyes for a moment to show us. "Between cats, it means, 'I trust you enough not to watch you every second.' But when domesticated cats do it to their people, it's more like blowing a kiss."

I looked at the tabby cat and closed my eyes, feeling like a complete idiot. When I opened them, Artemisia was looking at me like she thought I wasn't entirely wrong to feel that way. But then, a few seconds later, she closed her eyes in a long blink, too, and a thrill went up the back of my neck.

"Ha!" my mom said triumphantly, and I saw a flash of her old self.

I made the fist again, and Sari said, "She likes her head scratched hard."

"Like you," my mom said, using her nails on my back.

I pushed into my mom's hand, and Artemisia pushed her head back into mine, eventually flopping over to lie on her side. I looked at her greedily, marveling at every perfectly symmetrical stripe, wishing I could draw her and pet her at the same time.

The cat's eyes were closed, and the motor of her purr was so loud it was almost a growl. Without looking up, I said, "Lady Day also told me that purring doesn't necessarily mean that a cat is happy. It can mean she's scared, or hurt, or sick, too."

Sari's voice was careful.

"I didn't know that. But I can tell she really likes the way you're scratching her head." Hearing that, I could have sat in that patch of sunlight forever, especially after Artemisia fell asleep, her head resting on the arch of my hurt foot. The center of her paws moved from dark to light—*ombre*, I could hear my dad—with pads the exact color of dark chocolate. I committed every whorl to memory so I could draw them later.

Apollo came into the apartment behind the three of us, still sitting in the sun around the sleeping cat. "It's almost time to go," he said gently. "We don't want you to miss your flight."

"She's so beautiful," I said, turning around to show him without moving my foot.

"Yes," he said, "she is a good-looking beast." A glimmer of conspiracy passed between him and my mother. Then my mom squeezed my leg and said, "And she's going to have some good-looking kittens. In about a month, when you're going to be getting back from France."

Sari said, "The babies have to stay with her for a bit after they're born; I was hoping you'd come and help me with them."

I nodded yes at Sari as if it was no big deal, but my brain went *kittens kittens kittens kittens kittens kittens kittens kittens kittens kittens kittens kittens kittens kittens kittens*.

My mom reached over to push a strand of my hair behind my ear. For the first time, I noticed that the area under her beautiful eyes looked bruised and tired, but her smile was real. "And once you've gotten to know the litter, we thought maybe you could pick the one you like best."

I looked up at Apollo, then back to my mom for confirmation. They were both smiling like they were the ones getting the present. Apollo said, "We don't really know how any of it is going to work, Ollie, but we will find a way for you to have a kitten. I promise."

I leaned forward and gave my mom another big hug, awkward because of the way we were sitting. Between us, Artemisia opened one eye and shifted as if we had ruined everything, then went back to sleep on my foot.

"Something to look forward to," my mom whispered into my hair. "For when you come home."

# THE BLINK OF LOVE

My mom walked me and Apollo down to Joyce's car. On the way out, I noticed what I'd missed on my way in: a red plastic A.I.R. sign on the door, the letters official, indented and white.

"I'm glad you're going to see your dad," my mom said. "He misses you so much."

"You've talked to him?"

"Sure. I miss him, too." She looked away, down the deserted, industrial street shining in the sun. "Anyway, it'll be fun for you to see the Head where she belongs. He's going to spend the summer putting her back onto the altar they stole her from."

"I drew her a thousand times," I said, "but I never got that expression exactly right."

"Your dad will help. And it might be useful, to see her in place," said my mom.

I scuffed my sneaker into the sidewalk, not sure. "Maybe.

At least I'll find out what she was looking at."

My mom's head tilted to one side. "You don't know?"

I shook my head. "No! Do you?"

"Yes," she said, turning away to look down the empty street, but not before I saw that she was trying not to cry. "She was looking at her baby."

She looked back at me then, and there it was, the Head's expression on my mom's face.

Apollo was already in the car; he looked at his watch, then leaned over to open the passenger side door. I had to go. I hugged my mom one last time, burying my face in the warm, sweet smell of her, then got into the front seat next to him.

As Apollo started the engine, my mom raised one open hand in a wave, and I put my own scarred-up open palm against the window. She was smiling and crying at the same time. And as we pulled away from the curb, past her and into the Brooklyn sunshine, I saw my mom close her tear-fringed eyes at me in a long, slow blink.

# AWAY

The stewardess in charge of me was called Rita. She had a southern accent like Joyce and high heels and a nice face, framed with the kind of round sausage curls I've always wanted to pull. She gave me a wing pin from the pilot that I put on my sweatshirt to be polite, but secretly thought I'd save to send to Lady Day.

Once we'd taken off, Rita showed me how to lower the tray table attached to the seat in front of me. There was a round depression in the pebbly beige surface that made me think of the indentations in the watercolor palette Apollo had brought me.

The watercolors were packed in my suitcase. Still, I imagined filling the dent with a thick slurry of pigment and water, of dragging a brush across the tray table and then the back of the seat, over the strange round windows and up to the curved ceiling of the plane, until the whole interior was covered in a gorgeous wash of luminous color.

Then Rita set a little cup of orange juice with a tinfoil cover into the spot, and I shook myself back to reality.

"You got everything you need, sugar?" she asked.

I nodded yes and smiled my thanks. "Holler if you think of anything," Rita said, and I said I would.

Then I opened up my notebook, picked up my Blackwing, and began to draw.

## NOTE TO THE READER

About 16 million American adults live with depression—so lots of kids have a parent who suffers. If you recognized part of your own story in Olympia's, you're not alone.

Some other things to know:

Depression doesn't always mean going to bed. You might notice changes in appetite, a reduced energy level, sad mood, or not being interested in or enjoying activities as much over a few weeks or more.

Your parent's depression is not their fault; it is an illness. If they could snap out of it, they would.

Your parent's depression is not your fault, either. You can encourage and support them in getting help, but you can't make them better.

Sometimes the person suffering can't ask for the help they need. That's why it's important for you to tell another trusted adult in your life about what's going on. You could talk to an aunt or uncle, a teacher, a coach, a family friend, the parents of one of your friends, or someone from church or temple. It's okay to talk about it.

You can also call the Mental Health America Helpline 1-800-273-TALK or text MHA to 741741. People there will help you to make sure that your parent gets help, and that you get what you need, too.

Most importantly: depression is treatable. People do get better.

## ACKNOWLEDGMENTS

Olympia had some truly amazing champions. Among them: Susanna Einstein, dear friend and one of the best readers I know. My fantastic agent, Faye Bender at The Book Group: I knew from that very first letter that I'd be in good hands, but it wasn't until I saw you in action that I understood what that meant—thank you. And Kendra Levin, my brilliant editor at Viking, whose wisdom and faith and calm, quiet persistence helped me to make this a much, much better book.

I'm grateful to be inspired and nurtured by a community of tremendous writers, including John Greenberg, Robb Monn, and Joliange Wright. Bottomless thanks to Maria Baker, Ian Caskey, and Doris Vila Licht for their enthusiasm and insights, despite many drafts.

I'd like to thank my teachers at The Writers Studio: Lisa Bellamy, Lesley Dormen, Joel Hinman, and Cynthia Weiner.

I'm also grateful to Ellen Barz, Keiko Niccolini, Polly Shindler, Laura Siegel, Susannah Taylor, and Tracey Walters, as well to my family—Mimi, Bill, and Aaron Crowell; Traci Saxon; my dad, Robert Tucker, and my sister, Sarah. And to everyone at Buttermilk Channel and French Louie, especially my friends Jennifer Joan Nelson and Ellen Simpson.

Love and thanks to Doug Crowell, Olympia's first and most ferocious champion, and mine too; I'm lucky, lucky, lucky. And kisses to Lily, grey-eyed like the goddess and favorite of all my children—except for Foxy, who is the best.

# QUESTIONS FOR DISCUSSION

1. Ollie doesn't ask for help, even when the situation with her mom is really serious. Why doesn't she? Do you think she should have? Would *you* have? Have you ever waited too long to ask for help?

2. Street art—like graffiti, or the Wake Up Artist's posters—was an important way (and sometimes the *only* way) for artists outside of the mainstream to show their work. Many people consider it to be vandalism, however. What do you think?

3. Apollo mixes pigments into paint for his art, even though he could just buy tubes at Pearl Paint. Why do you think he prefers to make his paint? Is there anything you like to make from scratch, even though you can buy a similar product from a store?

4. Olympia tells Apollo she "can't stop wondering if it's possible to make something beautiful out of something awful." Apollo responds, "A lot of people would say that's exactly what art is." Do you agree? Can you give some examples from the book of people turning difficult feelings into art? Do you know of other works of art—paintings, sculptures, or poems, for instance— that came from "something awful"?

5. *All the Greys on Greene Street* is a mystery, of sorts—Ollie needs to figure out where her dad is, and she wants to know who Apollo is in love with. But she's also frustrated by the mysteries she finds in books. Have you ever tried to solve a mystery in your own life? Were you successful? Was it satisfying, or frustrating?

**6.** On their walk, the Wake Up Artist asks Ollie why she makes art, and Ollie says, "It's how I think." What do you think she means by that? Is there an activity in your life that helps you in a similar way?

**7.** On the Island, Ollie and Alex play a version of The Game, which they made up together in the playground by the Met when they were younger. Did you and your friends or siblings ever make up your own games? What were they? Do you still remember the rules?

**8.** The chapter called "Climb" is in present tense, as opposed to the rest of the book, which is set in the past. Keeping your tenses the same is a big writing rule—why do you think the author broke it and wrote that chapter in present tense? Can you think of other examples of an author or an artist intentionally breaking a rule in order to achieve an effect?

**9.** Ollie's dad steals the Head and returns it to the church it was stolen from in France. A lot of pieces of art in the great museums of the world were stolen from their country of origin. What do you think museums should do with those pieces?

**10.** For most of the book, Ollie is Miz Monochrome; she doesn't want to paint her diorama, and prefers to draw with her Blackwing pencil. By the end of the book, though, she's starting to use color. What else has changed for Ollie by the time the book ends? What do you predict will happen over the summer, and when she gets back from France?